Dancing Toward the
Edge of Forever

Book 2

Article 94

Paul Snider

Published by Jemenon, Inc.
Naperville, IL 60564
© 2019 Paul Snider
All rights reserved.

For permissions, or to order additional copies of this book, contact: JemenonMedia@gmail.com

Cover image used with permission from
the private collection of James T. Broumley
Author Photo © 2017 Jonah Levy

ISBN: 978-0-9634327-6-6

First Printing, 2019

Dedication

For the soldiers.

Section 894: The Uniform Code of Military Justice:

ARTICLE 94. MUTINY OR SEDITION

(a) Any person subject to this chapter who–

(1) with intent to usurp or override lawful military authority, refuses, in concert with any other person, to obey orders or otherwise do his duty or creates any violence or disturbance is guilty of mutiny;

(2) with intent to cause the overthrow or destruction of lawful civil authority, creates, in concert with any other person, revolt, violence, or disturbance against that authority is guilty of sedition;

(3) fails to do his utmost to prevent and suppress a mutiny or sedition being committed in his presence, or fails to take all reasonable means to inform his superior commissioned officer or commanding officer of a mutiny or sedition which he knows or has reason to believe is taking place, is guilty of a failure to suppress or report a mutiny or sedition.

(b) A person who is found guilty of attempted mutiny, mutiny, sedition, or failure to suppress or report a mutiny or sedition shall be punished by death or such other punishment as a court-martial may direct.

Chapter 1

Some come into the world with an inborn destiny, some unwavering singularity of purpose that dominates every moment of their waking existence. These are the fortunate few. For the overwhelming majority who inhabit the tribe of man, destiny has to hunt all over for us, clutching with ragged arms as we spin in the whirlwinds of time or bob to and fro in the rivers and seas of turbulent confusion. It seems to take forever to know what we want to do with our lives or where we really want to go.

Andrew Cameron belonged to the second group, innocently eluding the grasp of those ragged arms. Whatever great purpose slumbered in his genes—if there was such a thing at all—had so far made no vivid pronouncements to his evolving mind. For many years he had held a vague vision of himself trying to do something to change the world. How, he did not know. He remembered what Socrates once said, "Let him that would move the world first move himself." But how? Socrates didn't say. Or maybe he did.

Sometimes he hummed the lines from an old song.

"Don't know where I'm going but I'm on my way,

Won't get there tomorrow, but I plan to stay."

He liked to hum. Something about the definite indefiniteness of the old song appealed to him. He could easily see the humorous angle in life events, including his own. Time and again he found he had a gift for the appropriate quip or situation-relaxing remark, and he tried to remember to apply his sense of humor also to himself.

But for all of this he was still inwardly driven, in motion without clear direction, searching for a roadmap or guiding star.

He thought if he could gain enough emotional or spiritual altitude, the emerging patterns of his life would become more visible. But he had not the mental reach to rise that high. He could faintly sense the quiver of the compass needle within. He could feel its trembling as it struggled against an uncharacteristic period of doubt and indecision. He did not know the swing of the needle would finally aim for the geographic center of infinity. He did not know that on the way, he had a gun-on-hip rendezvous with destiny on the summit of Outpost Harry. It would be a strange and twisted journey from here to there.

*

Laura Boutin ("Boo-TAN" she would insist) came back into his life as a major surprise. It had been five years since he had seen her last. He assumed she was out of his life forever. He had almost quit thinking about her.

It was on a splendid moonlit evening in October, 1948. Andrew had taken residence in Cooly House in the East Quad on the University of Michigan campus, enrolled as a student in the school of architecture. Brundi Nasudovitch, long his closest friend, was his roommate. Brundi wanted to be a lawyer. Both of them frequently studied at the law library across the street. It seemed to be the most beautiful place on campus to read and think. With its granite and limestone solidity, cork floors and

2.

stained glass, it had the feeling of a cathedral. The Reading Room was so quiet, with 60-foot vaulted ceilings, sometimes if you listened carefully you could hear the hushed whispers of the Gods. The atmosphere was one of total elegance, and its quietness brought back for Andrew memories of the stillness of the Bush on the Cameron farm.

What attracted their attention on this warm October evening was an event outside the Cooly House windows. They went out to see. A number of male students, standing in circle, were about to conduct a fertilization ceremony. They had invited the girls from Stockwell dorm to participate. The crowd was already large and noisy when Andrew and Brundi joined in. Stockwell girls were asked to replace the men in the circle, which they did.

One of the male students, Sam Guderian, in a white hooded robe, had secured and decorated a very shaggy coconut. Eyes, nose, a floor mop for hair. This was now named Ishtar, goddess of fertility. Guderian had named himself Master of Fertilization. Guderian would move in a crouch from girl to girl, chanting some unintelligible mumbo jumbo, and where he stopped, move the coconut near the region of her groin, then touching. The girl was now declared fertilized. Each time to a big hooray.

As Andrew watched the ceremony unfold, he did not take immediate note of those in attendance. Not until the ceremony was interrupted. Mrs. Hall, the white-haired and rather formal House Mother for Cooly dorm, had come out to see what was happening. Guderian did not see her because the hood of the robe blocked his view. Then, there she was, directly in front of him as he moved the coconut toward the region of her groin, chanting

3.

his mysterious words. He looked up. Stopped. Straightened up. Dropped his hood. Almost saluted.

"My god," he said with some alarm. "I came within a hair's breadth of fertilizing the house mother."

In the ensuing disassembly of the crowd, Andrew saw her right away. He had not been among the circle of volunteers. As he came near, he heard her say to her companion "Charlene, I think they should just grow up."

Andrew gently took her arm, and with a serious face he said, "I think you were planning to suffocate me, Miss Boutin."

She whirled quickly, looked at him with startled eyes, but instant recognition.

"And did I succeed?" she said immediately.

"Time will tell," he smiled.

Five years had turned her from girl to woman, from pretty to beautiful. The same smooth, creamy white skin. The unusually large lavender colored eyes—those <u>knowing</u> eyes. The same raven black almost blue hair, now in a long ponytail. The same aliveness in her expressive face, responding to every nuance. The easy smile was now momentarily arrested as she contemplated him.

"While you're thinking about whether you survived suffocation, you will introduce us to our friend." Her bossy manner had not changed. Her French accent was still pleasing to the ear. Five more years in the country had made it less noticeable.

They made the four-way introductions. Charlene seemed intrigued with Brundi's name.

"Nasudovitch," she repeated slowly. "Curious name."

Andrew loved her whispering voice. It was very sexy.

Charlene Davenport was Laura's roommate and closest friend. She has straight straw-colored hair she wore in bangs, an oval face and soft brown eyes that had a curious twinkle as though she had just got away with something and was pleased about it. Like Laura, she was deeply Catholic.

"Don't pay any attention to Andrew's voice," Laura said to her. "He will try to seduce you with it."

Charlene winked at Andrew. "I think I am more interested in the other one," she said.

Andrew thought it curious that she winked at him while expressing interest in Brundi.

"I like women who know what they want," Brundi said, ignoring the contradiction. "Not so fast," Charlene said. "It's a long way to first base. And first, you have to get a hit."

The four walked all the way across to the far side of campus to Stockwell, two by two.

"I was startled to see you," Andrew said to Laura. "I didn't know what had happened to you."

"If you picked up a pencil and wrote three words, you would have found out," she smiled with a pout.

"What three words?" he asked with some apprehension, remembering Eileen.

"Dear Laura—the first two words don't count. Dear Laura, how are you? You dummy. The last two words don't count."

"Which one of us is the dummy?" he asked.

"Definitely not me," she said.

"So much of life seems to hang on three words," he mused aloud. And it's not even the same three words."

"You seem to be having a conversation with yourself," she said.

"Sorry, I was thinking… I noticed you told Brundi your name is Laura. Do you still have those intense feelings about your name?"

"Oh that!" she laughed. "That was just a little childhood affectation. I got over it."

"But I see a lingering sense of formality in you. And your accent still has a touch of elegance and refinement. Actually, it's quite pleasing. Gives you a coloring of royalty, or something."

"Or something," she laughed again.

"Nevertheless, I really enjoyed the vigorous way you went about the attempted suffocation in Dearborn … you had a determined strength."

"I tried. There's too much life in you."

"You once told me not to start something I wasn't prepared to finish. Well, the same goes for you. You haven't finished me off yet."

"I wouldn't know where to begin with you, or whether to begin. You never wrote. I cried waiting for your letters. Forget I said that."

He stopped, hugged her in a warm embrace. "I didn't know," he said. "If I had only known."

"Well, now you know. What are you going to do about it?" she challenged.

"Are you seeing anyone?"

"I left my old boyfriends in Vermont." She looked with deep interest directly into his eyes. In the mellow moonlight, it was almost as if there was a backlit quality to them. "And you?" she asked.

"I had a serious relationship, but it's over."

"So you are capable of a serious relationship." They both laughed.

"How's your mother? Is her book done? What's your father doing? Have they got back together? Have you been back to France? I have a thousand questions."

"I will say this. Maybe this is a risky thing to say. Maybe I shouldn't say it. I'm going to say it—why do I have this incessant need to confess? I tried to shake you out of my mind. I couldn't shake you all the way. There's something about you that left me with a feeling of ambiguity. I don't like ambiguity. So there's part of me that's ready to climb all over you and beat you up. How dare you make me feel ambiguity?" But she said this with a gentle, easy smile. There was no bite in her words. Only a reflective search for understanding.

"Whatever we had together seemed so real, so utterly real," he said in recollection.

"Maybe you were just a great big huge mistake," she said, still smiling, still bundling the adjectives, watching carefully for his expression.

He deflected her oblique inquiry. "I remember you would not leave me when I was injured. That meant a lot to me,"

"Oh, I forgot. How are your eyes?"

"I can see perfectly how beautiful you've become. You're

20-20 beautiful."

She looked at him for several moments, as if trying to gauge his sincerity. "You're not so bad yourself. Did you always have those big shoulders, or did I fail to notice?"

"These are the shoulders that carried you to victory three times in the Rouge Pools."

"I remember that," she smiled. "You were a good mount. I was ready to keep you in my stable."

The line the conversation was taking brought back into his immediate mind the recollection of great warmth pouring into the back of his neck as she had held him tight between her velvet smooth thighs. The thought of it aroused him so much he turned sideways to talk to her. "We should do it again sometime," he said.

"Kid stuff. I don't do that anymore. I definitely don't do kid stuff anymore."

"Can I see you again? I want to find out what you do now, now that you've outgrown childish things. Besides, I have a thousand questions. Beginning with, How are you?"

Now she laughed. "How could I say no to such a prize horse? Are you retired from racing and out to stud now? Do you still play guitar? Don't answer my stud question. Just tell me one thing—have you found religion? You had no religion to speak of five years ago. Are you any smarter now?"

He paused, remembering the depth of her faith. "All I can tell you is I know there is a God somewhere, but I'm not sure he likes me very much. I'm not even sure he particularly cares about us as individuals."

"We'll have to work on that," she said.

"I'm more restless than I was."

"So am I," she said. "But I think maybe we're not restless about the same things."

It was almost curfew time at Stockwell. Laura looked at Brundi and Charlene nearby. "I can tell by the way they're standing and talking they like each other. Instant attraction. Maybe you should bring Brundi when you come."

He smiled. "Are you afraid to be with me alone?"

"I'm not sure of my feelings. I hate it when things are in a flux. I want to see you. I don't want to see you. I'm attracted to you. I'm afraid you'll hurt me again. Oh, Andrew, help me decide."

He took her in his arms, kissed her gently on the forehead. "You will see me again," he said softly. "You want to see me again. You can't wait to see me again. And my heart will ache with loneliness until I can see you again, get to know you in all your faults and glory. I really like you. I am very much attracted to you."

"Still the seducer," she mumbled softly.

*

Now that she was back in his mind, Andrew couldn't stop thinking about her. Brundi was in the same state about Charlene. "I really like her. I never met anyone like her. She wants to be a teacher, like Laura. Andrew, I think she may be the one. I haven't got to first base yet, but I've got my eye on the ball. I think I'm ready to hit a line drive into the bleachers."

"Laura and I seem to feel the same way about each other.

9.

Some coincidence. You and me. Laura and Charlene. I don't know where it will go yet."

School was already becoming a disappointment to Andrew. He studied diligently, worked many hours as a busboy, and spent all the time he could with Laura. He learned he had an excellent mind for the engineering aspects of architecture, and that he was a fastidious draftsman, but he couldn't draw worth a damn. He liked the prospect of beauty he might bring into the field, but he did not have the creative power to show what was in his mind. Schelling had once written that "architecture is frozen music." But try as he might, his renderings did not look like "music."

His professor was accomplished in architectural renditions, an Italian still struggling with the English language. One morning as Andrew worked diligently in charcoal, trying to sketch a still-life display, he noticed Professor Valiano standing behind him. Valiano stood there for several minutes, then shook his head. "Meesiter Cameron," he said, "It looka like a da mess a garbage." And walked away.

Andrew also discovered the awful complexities and mysteries of local zoning laws. They were so many, so varied, so touched with politics. There was no uniform standard for the housing industry. A house fully suitable in one location would not be suitable 100 feet away if it crossed a political zoning boundary.

He had chosen the field of architecture for a simple but ignorant reason. A house was too costly a purchase. Too many people could not afford to buy a home until they had worked for years, even as home prices were rising along with their savings.

It was taking families too long to get a start. He thought he had found a way to help them.

He thought he could manufacture the basic structural elements of houses in a Henry Ford-type assembly line. He had made some bold and simple designs, beautiful in his imagination. He would construct floors, walls, roofs, out of ultra-light materials using basically a honeycomb "sandwich" structure, and design elements to provide strength. He would attach a skyhook and fly the modules to people, using large helicopters. They would be positioned on lots already set up with foundation, plumbing, electricity, heating and sewage connections. Windows and all else needed for completion would be trucked in. He spent months working out the technical problems, logistics. He calculated he could cut the total cost of an average home in half. He would set up geographically dispersed factories.

But the more he learned, the more he came to realize it was only a dream. An impossible dream. He thought maybe he could start small, with simple structures in more remote areas. He thought and thought, and finally concluded he was not a naturally born architect. He was dreaming in the sky.

Where do old dreams go to die? Do they wander like tired elephants down into some mysterious valley where their bones can never be found? Do they dissolve like vapors into the dry air of new realities? Do they wonder what gave them birth?

All Andrew knew was that the dream had died.

*

What he knew he was, was a born explorer. He had begun to explore the whole of the U. of M. campus soon after his arrival.

And when he had learned what he could about what was on top of the grounds, be began explorations of the subterranean tunnels and chambers that stretched beneath the entire campus. He found the hidden entrances.

Heating and plumbing pipes and ducts, and electrical wiring cables stretched into every building. Long, long corridors of cement, with periodic switches that would turn on an array of lights ahead. Off some of the corridors lay hidden rooms—some apartment size—lighted, heated and empty. There were also pumping stations. But there were dangers, too.

Once, in one of his first explorations, walking along a tunnel in total darkness not having found a light switch, he discovered one of the dangers. He suddenly stepped into black, empty space. But as he fell, he instinctively reached out his right hand and found a grip on a pipe railing he had not even known was there. He pulled himself up onto an adjoining platform, carefully worked his way along a wall to find a light switch, then went back to see what had awaited him below.

The passage along which he had been walking was only the short side of a longer passage. It ended suddenly, with no barrier. About six feet below were the protrusions of pumping equipment that stuck up like blunted spears. He might have been impaled, or at a minimum, may have sacrificed his chances to father children. He was grateful for his instinct and for the quick strength of his sudden grip.

The other danger was expulsion. The rule was that anyone unauthorized, caught in the tunnels, would be expelled. But this did not really bother him. He was careful, sure he would not be caught. His curiosity drove him past the warning signs.

Of all the curiosities in the tunnels, what intrigued him most was an abandoned subterranean room he found under the original old red brick English building. It was actually somewhat difficult to find. The old doorway was now hidden closely behind large heating ducts. But once inside, he found a switch. The room was lighted, warm, and the harbor of several leftover things—an old sofa, a table, a few chairs, and a bookcase still containing a number of volumes dated from the 1890's. No rats or vermin. Only a little dust. Apparently, when the English building was reconstructed, this room was abandoned and a new basement room built over it, with no connection. He almost felt as if he had discovered a lost treasure.

He took Brundi into the tunnels with him. Brundi was intrigued that they could go all the way to Stockwell underground. But Brundi was more nervous than Andrew about the threat of expulsion and did not go with him again.

*

Andrew and Laura had resumed their relationship with a quick gradualness, first over coffee, then over lunch, then over simple dinners and long walks or, on rainy days, in long conversations wherever they could find quiet, rather secluded space. Sometimes just walking in the rain together. Andrew learned Laura's mother had found a teaching position, had finished her book, was looking for an agent or publisher, and as far as Laura could discern had remained utterly chaste since her separation.

"There's something wrong with this picture," Andrew said.

"If they can't be divorced, they shouldn't be in a sexual prison for the rest of their lives."

"I'm not sure my father is," she said sadly. "I hear rumors he's back in France making up for lost time. There's a shortage of men over there."

"There should be a way…"

"Women can go without sex. They're better at it than men. They definitely are."

"I know at least one woman who would hit that assumption like a freight train."

"I could go through my whole life without sex if I had to," she said. "I could be a nun."

"Laura," he smiled, "there is so much beauty in the way you kiss, there would be a passion clawing inside you for release. You could never be a nun."

"I definitely could be a nun."

"Maybe a highly frustrated nun."

She slapped him gently. "Don't make me feel ambiguous about that."

Andrew and Laura had broken through the barriers of old memories and had now become very close, kissing whenever they could, touching each other every chance, hugging and stroking. Laura had lost none of the fire of her earlier youth. Her kisses were passionate and engulfing, teasing. It seemed she would let him do almost anything with her, except "it." And Andrew was pleasantly surprised that she let him proceed quite far with his explorations. So that she would have to gasp for breath before making him stop. He had not felt this close to anyone since Deannie. But "it" was a huge barrier, and a complex one, filled with contradictions.

Once she confessed a very vivid dream. "If I don't have sexual relations before I'm 20, I will go crazy. I wake up with that ringing in my mind. Stupid, isn't it?"

"Sounds quite logical to me," he joked.

"But it would still be a sin."

"An illogical sin," he said.

As they became closer and closer, Andrew became ever more curious about what, years earlier, had seemed to be the fire within her. He longed to bask in its sweet flame. He <u>did</u> want to seduce her. And if he were to judge by the strength of her kisses, and the license of his, it seemed she wanted it to happen.

One evening as they embraced, she whispered, "There's an old saying in France. A man falls in love with his eyes, and a woman with her ears. A woman likes what she hears. What do you think of that?"

"I think you are falling-in-love-with beautiful. The rest I'll tell you three days from now."

"What will happen then?"

"Come with me, then. You'll see. I'm going to take you to a place you've never been."

*

Before their excursion, he had invested in a bottle of French wine, and two wine glasses. He had taken them beforehand with a pillow and blanket to the abandoned room under the English building. He had turned over the old cushions and blanketed the long couch.

15.

It was a cold and rainy afternoon in mid-December when they slipped in together. A snapping, grizzly rain that made the warmth of the tunnels all the more welcome.

"I'll take you to a place no one knows about. The only risk will be getting in and getting out," he told her.

"I'm excited," she said.

He led her carefully down the dark corridors and into the old abandoned room. He switched on the single bulb in the ceiling. She went immediately to the old bookcase and thumbed through several volumes. "This is amazing. I think one or two of these may be classics."

The room was nice and warm. He held her for a while in his arms as they kissed tenderly, then led her to the old couch. He opened the wine and poured two glasses.

"I didn't even ask if you drink," he said.

"No, I don't, but I'm willing to share the experience with you. I want to share everything with you... What should we toast?" she asked. And while he was thinking about it, she continued, "I know. Let's toast the end of the war. I know it's been three years, almost four. But I never did *that*... I'm a great big huge patriot. Ever since I saw Miss Liberty, the spirit of France."

They toasted the end of the Second World War, and the spirit of America.

"And may there never be another war," he said, and kissed her to seal the toast.

"I hate it when they number the wars. Makes it seem like a logical progression. Something with no end in sight."

She spoke in a wondering voice. "This whole thing—the

tunnels, this old abandoned room, the aroma of the wine, so subtle in its flavor, you and me sitting here, far from the world— it reminds me of the story of Phantom of the Opera. What are your intentions, sir? Are you a phantom or are you for real?"

"You forgot the passion. You forgot to say I have a passionate interest in you. My passion is real."

"Do you?" she asked, sipping the wine, watching his expression."

"It's more than passion, Laura"—now he found the words— I think I'm falling in love with you."

She put down her glass, kissed him hard, hard, all the while talking into his mouth with a new excitement. "I'm so glad you said that. I <u>know</u> I'm falling in love with you. Definitely."

"But you didn't want to be the first one to say it."

"I've almost said it three times already, but I held back. I wanted to hear it from you first. I wanted to know your feelings are definite."

They proceeded slowly, sipping, kissing, caressing, touching more and more daringly. He knew she was with him in spirit. And she did not resist as he removed every article of her clothing, then his own. She only asked at one point, "Are you sure we're safe? This is <u>so</u> risky. We'll be expelled for sure if anyone catches us." He assured her no one ever came here, especially on an evening such as this. They listened for a few moments. All was quiet in the darkened tunnels beyond the door.

"I feel sinful, but I'm confused about it."

"Your skin is like velvet," he whispered.

She felt the muscles of his arms and chest. "You're like

17.

steel," she whispered back. "All over."

"Whatever you're doing…" she breathed, "it's all connected to the same place."

He removed a condom from his pants pocket on the floor, stripped its wrapping, and began to put it on. She reached down to stop him. It was the first time she had touched him there. Her touch was electrifying.

"Your hand is so beautiful, so personal," he said.

She squeezed him hard, removed the condom. "I don't want you to use that. One mortal sin is enough."

"It's for your protection."

"It's like taking a bath with your socks on… I don't want to spoil my first experience."

"You're sure?" he asked.

"It will be fine," she said. "You picked the right time."

"It's like Russian roulette," he said.

'I know my body. I definitely know my own body. Besides, using a condom is a sin."

"I love you, Laura," he whispered.

"I love you, my dear Andrew," she whispered back.

Then she paused. "Tell me this is not a great big huge mistake."

"This is not a great big huge mistake," he whispered with a kiss.

She was reluctant to let go her grip on him, but she finally did, and swept her arms around him.

The experience was beyond what he had imagined in his daydreams. She <u>did</u> have a special fire within which engulfed him, a tender flame that licked at all his thousand sensory nerve endings. This had been the source of that burning warmth against his neck years ago. For reasons mysterious to him, this part of her body was like a small furnace, so sweetly unbearable he almost withdrew. What a remarkable physiology, he thought.

He could see the rapture lines forming across her face. Her beautiful lavender eyes—those <u>knowing</u> eyes, now more knowing than ever—registered every nuance of feeling with animated expressions of delight.

"I can't describe how beautiful you look, and how good you make me feel."

And finally she gasped hoarsely, choking back her voice, as she released in unison with him to the heavens.

And when he caught his breath again, he kissed her rapturous, swollen lips. "Wow! What a lover you are!"

"Takes one to know one," she whispered hoarsely.

And for a while they lay whispering and stroking, she running fingers through his hair and along his cheeks, he stroking the full length of her neck and back and tender buttocks with both hands.

"Wow," she said. "You're my first."

"I'm deeply honored," he whispered.

"You've taught me things I didn't know about myself."

"You're a fabulous lover," he said.

"I didn't expect to go off like a fourth of July rocket. Maybe it was the risk of being caught."

"How could you have known?"

"Or, maybe it was you. Maybe you've spoiled me for life."

"I think it's the other way around. I think you've ruined me for life. What can ever equal this?"

"Do you think anyone has ever loved this much before?" she asked.

"How could they?"

"Now I'm feeling lazy… I think the excitement of the situation affected me, put a rocket under me."

"You don't know what your normal responses are yet. Maybe this was your normal response. In this case, you are God's gift to your lover, namely me."

"If that's what it takes to bring you to God, I'll work on that with you," she smiled sweetly.

Then she turned thoughtful, and for a time was silent. "What are you thinking?" he asked.

"I won't tell you. I shouldn't tell you. I have to tell you." She looked at him with great seriousness.

"If you really want to know, I was thinking Oh, my God! I wasn't thinking. I let my heart carry away my brain. Sex is meant to be endured, not enjoyed… But I enjoyed it so much. Have I sinned again? Don't answer… Who are you to answer?"

Andrew never went into the tunnels again.

*

After the first time, the relationship deepened further for them both and, quite to his surprise, Laura became very possessive. In a way he liked it. There was a feeling of security in her possessiveness. But in another way, it was slightly alarming.

"You're mine, you animal. 100% mine," she would say with a smile.

"So <u>this</u> is the way you planned to suffocate me," he would joke, "by possessing me to death."

"Don't you like it?" she would tease.

"I like everything about you, everything."

"I want you to feel possessive, too. I want you to feel the same way about me as I feel about you."

"Laura, it's not in my nature. I can't even conceive of wanting to <u>possess</u> someone. I have such a profound belief in free will. I want only what you bring to me from the freedom of your heart, not something I own. Not something that's already mine."

"I'm not sure I understand you sometimes."

"The thrill of being with you, especially when you give your whole self to me, has a wonderful tenderness when it's a gift of will."

"Don't you understand how much a woman needs to be <u>needed</u>?"

"I can need you without possessing you."

"No, you can't. You definitely can't."

"Sometimes you baffle me," he said.

"Touché."

Now that she felt he was hers, she began in earnest to bring him within the folds of her religion, to "Christianize" him. She seemed to need him to share her beliefs as a way of coming closer to oneness in their relationship, but Andrew resisted with a quiet, steady strength.

He brought a copy of <u>The Prophet</u>, and read to her the words of Kahlil Gibran, speaking of marriage.

"You are born together, and together you shall be forever.

You shall be together when the white wings of death scatter your days.

Ay, you shall be together even in the silent memory of God.

But let there be spaces in your togetherness, And let the winds of the heavens dance between you.

Love one another, but make not a bond of love; Let it rather be a moving sea between the shores of your souls.

Fill each other's cup but drink not from one cup.

Give one another of your bread, but eat not from the same loaf.

Sing and dance together and be joyous, but let each one of you be alone.

Even as the strings of a lute are alone though they quiver with the same music.

Give your hearts, but not into each other's keeping. For only the hand of Life can contain your hearts.

And stand together yet not too near together; For the pillars of the temple stand apart,

And the oak tree and the cypress grow not in each other's shadow."

"I need to be possessed," she said firmly, with a kiss, "by love possessed."

"I want my love for you to be free, soaring on the winds of freedom, never possessive," he answered.

"Andrew, sometimes I think you just don't understand women."

"Does anyone?" he joked.

"I'm not trying to change you," she said.

"Yes, you are," he said. "I know you don't mean to but if I gave into your wishes, I think I would feel a bit suffocated."

"I feel the same way about my religion. I want to be possessed in the same way as my religion possesses me."

"I think you're just trying to feel secure."

She kissed him gently, as though a child about to be disciplined. "Andrew, my love, how could true religion make you feel anything but secure?"

He thought for a while before answering, and when he did, the words came out slowly, haltingly, as though he were discovering what he thought even as he spoke the words. "What is religion... I think religion is everything... Every atom, every breath, every curved calf and white thigh... I think religion is the holiness of the swamp, the chirp of the sparrow, the clinking of two dry martini glasses over moonlit bars... Religion is man and his children, man and his wife, the whole thing... Every pebble dark and silent in frozen mountain streams. Every desert sunset witnessed by no man... It is all, me and you, talking now, whatever we should say. This is religion. Because religion is all that moves us forward toward a mystical and mysterious God and all that exists to make that journey possible. Religion is a journey..."

"Darling," she interrupted. "That's not religion. That's pantheism."

"That's where I am at the moment."

"I'm going to buy you a ticket to a better place."

"You're trying to make me a Christian."

"No, I'm not. I'm trying to bring you to God."

"But you think there is only one way to God. You are so sure of yourself… You're not content with my restless confusion. You want me to have the same kind of certainty you have. I feel the pressure of your need."

"I'm certain because I'm right. I want you to worship God with me. I want us to worship God together."

"But your way of worship is only through the church."

"That's the only way there is… If only I could make you understand."

"First of all, I suppose there is a God, somewhere. But I think He's too busy running the universe to have any time to care for us."

"You know the opposite is true."

"No, I don't know… But second, assuming there is a God, assuming there is a contactable God, there must a million pathways… I can't believe the only pathway is through the Pope. God would be more creative than that, and more fair."

"We were made to worship God."

"I think if there is a God, He's got better things to do than create us only for his vanity."

"Andrew, I am absolutely right about God. How can I reach you?"

"I don't know what would convince me anymore… If only I could see a little proof."

"Proof is for dummies," she said with a quick shake of her head. "That's why there is faith. Faith makes sure we think about things, explore the mysteries."

"But if I understand your faith, once you become a believer, all exploring stops."

"What's wrong with that?" she smiled.

"God must love dummies," he joked.

"I'll bring you around," she said. "I'm not done with you yet. You're a hard nut to crack."

In the beginning, he would join her in going to mass, and sometimes just to be near her as she prayed. He found her to be especially beautiful, almost radiant, when she emerged from prayer. In the cadence of their evolving new relationship, he tried again and again to join with her in the spirit of her communion, but he could make no headway against the cacophony of thoughts that leaped and played around in his mind when he tried to be still. Maybe I'm just not cut out for prayer, he thought.

And then he began to explore other churches. He wanted to explore all faith approaches. Laura would never go with him, insisting it was a mortal sin to go to other churches or worse, to synagogues and temples.

"You have to explore to learn," he said.

"I already know what I need to know," sue said.

"I will join with you from time to time, but I have to explore. That's the way I am."

*

25.

But she didn't bring him around. Even in the deepest arousals of love, when she told him the closeness of their physical union was verging on the spiritual, he could not bring himself to see the world her way. He tried. He tried to abandon all preconceptions, to picture reality through the innocent beauty of her faith. But his sense of logic always overpowered the attempted vision. He did truly love her and wanted to do things that would bring them closer, but it could not be. He had to see reality through the unfettered vision of his own independent mind.

"It hurts me to see you wandering around in a wasteland," she said one night as they joined together in their love in the room of an absent friend.

"In every chamber of my heart I want to be one with you," but I don't think we'll ever be able to work through our religious differences," he told her.

"We don't have religious differences," she said. "I'm religious and you're different."

"Laura ..." he began to say.

She put a finger to his lips. "Quit talking. Just hold me. Just love me. And for a little while we won't think of anything else."

"When I'm with you in this way, nothing else exists. Nothing in the world. There is only you." And then he let his mind fully focus on that utterly warm sensual beauty of her inner being. What an engineering masterpiece.

She kissed him with deep passion and enfolded her legs tightly around him. She kept her eyes open almost until the end, registering every nuance of sensation. And when they were through again, and again she lay on top of him as he caressed her, he felt the warmth of her tears running silently across his chest.

"Did I hurt you?" he whispered hoarsely. "If I did, I'm truly sorry."

"You didn't hurt my body," she said. "Your bigness did not hurt... I feel wonderful in my body. As though I had not a care in the world. Like a gardener had just tended the plants."

"But I feel your tears."

"My tears are because I love you and you are drifting away and you are too much of a dummy to see the lifeline in front of your eyes."

He was silent for a few moments. "Some of your religion is okay." Now she was silent, too, and in thoughtful words she responded. "You can't pick and choose. You're not in a cafeteria. You have to take the whole thing."

He held her very close and caressed her for a long time and neither of them talked. And he thought to himself, if only their spiritual union could be as close and satisfying as their physical union. He could not think of a way to build a bridge. Some architect! He chided himself.

*

In the meantime, Brundi and Charlene were developing what appeared to be a permanent closeness. Charlene's Catholic faith had only shallow roots, but she was firm and positive in her views. Brundi didn't mind. He seemed to follow her lead in matters of religion. "Women are smarter than men about these things," he told Andrew. "They have more intuition."

"But what if she insists you raise your children Catholic?" Andrew asked. "Assuming you get that far."

Brundi smiled. "I've already hit that line drive into the bleachers. It's even better than I thought it would be. I think Charlene is the one for me."

"Catholic children and all?"

"Well, at least they'll have a strong foundation."

Andrew decided to say nothing more. Brundi was intelligent, a man of free will, utterly sincere. He would make his own choices.

On occasion, when work and study schedules allowed, the four of them would gather for an evening of music and discussion. Andrew played guitar, but neither he nor any of the three others had much of a singing voice. So they tended to play and sing with all four voices together, or just listen to the pleasant vibrations of the strings. There was warmth and laughter and a sense of comradeship among them. For Andrew it was like the most enjoyable times of his high school days. For a while he experienced happiness.

It was during one of these evenings when Andrew, thinking out loud, confessed his secret ambition to be a writer. "I haven't made up my mind yet. It would require a whole different kind of education…"

"Most writers starve," Charlene laughed.

"So do a lot of architects," Andrew joined her in the humor.

Laura was silent.

Brundi turned to a serious question. "How would you have to change your education? Why couldn't you be an architect and be a writer on the side?"

"Haven't thought it through yet," Andrew said. "The thing

is, I don't really think I'm cut out for architecture. I'm looking for a career that will occupy my whole existence."

Laura punched him. "You mean the rest of your existence after taking care of the needs of a dutiful wife and children." She formed her lips into a pretend pout.

He kissed her pouting lips. "As Brundi has sometimes said, women are smarter about some things than men."

"And don't you forget it," Laura punched him again.

"Punch him one for me, too," Charlene said.

"How am I going to bring home the bacon when I'm all beat up?" he laughed.

"Seriously," Laura said, "are you really thinking about changing your major?"

"Even more than that, if I really want to become a writer, I have to learn the right words. Words can help change the world. The right words. I think I may have to experience every human experience… I mean every human experience that has meaning and value. I would have to understand the human condition."

*

The little fracture lines that had begun early to appear in their relationship ever slowly widened, but both of them, still smitten with the early wonders of love, looked past the deepening rifts. The relationship as a whole seemed solid. They liked each other, felt an emotional closeness, and had found a wonderful physical chemistry with each other. He told her every time that she was a fabulous lover, and meant it. She told him every time she did not know how she had ever lived without him and seemed to imply she meant this to be a permanent condition. They were happy together and could not wait to be in each other's presence.

During Christmas holidays they went to their separate family relationships. He thought of driving to Vermont to see her, but the roads were heavy with snow, and his tires were almost bald. He hadn't promised. It would have been a surprise. Instead, he thought maybe be would drive her home in the spring, when classes ended.

But as the freshness of spring penetrated his soul, it seemed to catalyze his restlessness, poke at his wanderlust, and on an afternoon amid the flowering buds of April he decided he needed to get away for the summer, travel to someplace where the people were different, begin to learn and understand how some other small fraction of humanity lives, how they think, how they speak, how they eat, how they relax, how they relate to someone unlike themselves. He also wondered how they made love, what the women would be like in bed. But he washed that thought out of his mind. He was committed to Laura and would not violate the commitment. This had to be part of the bedrock of his sense of integrity.

He wondered about New Orleans and Paris and Rio and Heidelberg. He pictured Gaugin's Tahiti and Jack London's Alaska. He wondered about the entire Asian race. He longed for the world and wanted to roam it. Watching the buds of spring unfold, he was not so much thinking as forming pictures in his mind. Where to go first? Assessing his meager financial condition, he decided on Mexico.

He calculated that if he scrimped, he could spend two months traveling before working on O.H. Frisbe's trucks again at the end of summer to get some startup money to augment the scholarships for his second year. He told Laura of his plans right away.

"I thought you were going to work all summer," she said.

"Next summer. I'll do that, summer of '50. How would you like to come with me now? We can backpack, travel light."

"Where would we go?"

"I'm thinking Mexico. I've heard you can live real cheap down there."

"Too may bandits."

"I'll be with you all the time."

She thought for a moment. "No, you go by yourself. Get this restlessness out of your system. I want you entirely focused when I reclaim you. I want your full uninterrupted heart."

"And you...?"

"I'm going to work in Vermont all summer."

"I'll come get you when you're done. We can drive back to Ann Arbor together."

"Promise?" she smiled.

"I promise."

"Hope to die?"

"I'm not superstitious. But you know I'll keep my word."

"You are reliable."

That was the plan.

The night before he drove away, they made love with each other one last time, in a sleeping bag in the arboretum, so they could see the stars. It was a warm and dry and pleasant night in early June.

"Will you think of me when you're gone?" she whispered.

"Every moment. Even after all these months, you still fill all my idle thoughts. And even when my mind is concentrating on something else, you are there in the background, waiting for my thoughts to come back to you, like a beautiful presence. I can't help thinking about you."

"But out of sight out of mind?"

"All I will have to do is see a butterfly, or a sunset, or an evening star, or a violet... Everything that has a spark of beauty will bring you rushing into my mind. We will be close. You will not fade from me. You will be with me on this whole journey."

"For me, too," she whispered. "I'll hold you in my heart like a hungry tigress."

Chapter 2

Andrew worked for a week in Detroit, moving furniture on O.H. Frisbe's trucks, to get some extra cash for the trip. Joe and Jessica were both a bit puzzled by his decision.

"What do you want to go to Mexico for?" Jessica asked. "We got Mexicans right here."

"I can't afford to go to Europe. I have to go someplace cheap, and foreign."

"What about Montreal?" Joe asked.

"It's a little bit foreign, but not cheap."

"Well, you can put your car beside the garage."

"First, I want to visit my grandfather's grave, and to see my grandmother."

*

He drove to Lucknow, to stand before Kenneth's grave, pondering the significance of Kenneth's life, and his own. The warm weather had continued, and the aromas of spring blew like fresh memories on the breeze that folded across the high ground of the Lucknow cemetery. Remembering Kenneth's life, and his simple, unconditional love, brought poignant reflections into his thoughts. Kenneth was born and lived and died, but his life had made the world a richer place. His life <u>meant</u> something.

Andrew spent an hour at the gravesite, stirring memories, trying to learn from them. He knew Kenneth was not here, but the grave was a way of trying to touch the sleepy borders of immortality. Kenneth could not be lost to the universe. What he stood for—what he fashioned out of the experience of his stout and wonderful heart—was an undying commitment to truth, a reverence for beauty a passion for goodness. This could not be lost. Otherwise life would have no meaning. Kenneth had gone somewhere—it had to be <u>more</u> than sitting on a cloud playing a harp—and carried with him all that was truly valuable. Not knowing what else to do, Andrew kissed the small gravestone before he drove away.

He drove along the Cameron Sideroad to look at the old farm and see the trees in bloom, but he did not go into the lane. He spent a few minutes, idling on the side of the road, looking for changes. It still looked pretty much the same. No one around, quiet.

Then he drove by the Riddle farm, half expecting Eileen would rush down the lane in bare feet to greet him. But all was quiet there too. He wondered again what had happened to her, where she had gone.

*

Andrew spent the next day visiting with Clara in Belgrave, then stayed the night, before he drove back to Detroit. Clara's older brother had arranged for her to buy a small home in town just a few doors from his own place. He told Andrew that while Clara was quite self-sufficient, she needed "some looking after." It was an enjoyable visit, but not with the same emotional bond that Andrew had always felt with Kenneth.

Nevertheless, he left with a quiet tingling in his heart. He was grateful for her life, and what she had taught him. She was the salt of the earth, a quiet pillar supporting the foundations of stability. Clara had been a steady, tireless worker. She never complained. She was never cross. The world was a better place for the life she lived.

Clara had spent a lot of time telling him about his father. He found the information interesting, but it was almost an abstraction. Donald Cameron had perished when Andrew was still very young, and memories of him had grown dim.

Back in Detroit, Andrew quickly arranged to take a brand new DeSoto, from the factory as a drive away car, to deliver to a new car dealer in Corpus Christie on the Mexican border. DeSoto would pay for boarding and all gasoline charges. Andrew's job was to get it there without dent or scratch. He drove straight through, 32 hours nonstop, pausing only for gas, a restroom or a hamburger.

Laura's call to Joe and Jessica came the morning after Andrew had left Detroit. They did not know where he was, only that he was headed south toward Mexico.

"It's urgent that I talk to him!" Laura said.

"I wish I could help you, honey," Jessica said. "But we don't expect to hear from him for two months."

Laura's first letter arrived three days later.

*

On the open-air bus on the way down to Mexico City, sometimes through dry stream beds, Andrew found he had acquired an inadvertent companion, being that they were the only two gringos in the group.

35.

Slade was a non-stop talker. He took a seat next to Andrew. Lean, angular, with straight black hair and darkly handsome, he told Andrew right away to call him Slade the Blade. "I'm a crazy mixture and it shows," he said with beaming pride.

Slade was about Andrew's height, perhaps five years older, had a broken front tooth, and a habit of constantly touching you when he talked. He had a passionate interest in his own interests. Slade also carried a long, spring-loaded stiletto which he enjoyed playing with, sometimes almost obsessively propelling the sharp thin dagger forward and pulling it back inside its shaft again and again.

"I feel naked without my shiv," he said, "balls flapping in the air."

Slade had dark eyes, almost a mask of darkness in the area around the eyes, but there seemed to be an even deeper darkness within. The first time Andrew looked into those eyes, he decided he could not trust him. Slade had the eyes of a killer. But he also had a way of becoming, seemingly at will, a smooth talker, even an interested listener, adding a mellowing sparkle to his look. He did not ask Andrew anything about himself, and Andrew volunteered very little information.

He did not want to hook up with Slade, but Slade seemed to have attached himself. At every stop in the desert for tortas, while all the locals were crowded around the little restaurant hut, Slade would preoccupy Andrew with his talk. It was a bit annoying because Andrew had come here to learn and understand. He tolerated Slade as best he could, thinking once they got to Mexico City they would go their separate ways.

Andrew found it fascinating that from time to time the bus would pull up to a mud brick hut in the middle of nowhere, and suddenly there would be food and dozens of people. He could see no other dwellings in sight. It seemed people just appeared. Magic. Alive. Happy. A bus stop exit to happy nowhere.

"I'm a 32nd degree Mason," Slade told Andrew. "See my Mason ring? When I get in trouble, I just flash it. Boom! I'm out. You oughtta join the Masons."

"How often do you get in trouble?"

"Plenty. The heat's on me right now. I'm from New York, Long Island actually. Rego Park actually if you want to know. Well, here I am, minding my own business, practicing with my .45 out along the railroad tracks. Boom! The gun exploded in my hand. A bullet exploded. Gave me some burns. Had to go to the Emergency Room. The cops came and I flashed my ring, but they're Micks. They want nothing do to with Masons. So they start questioning me about some holdups—small stuff—dry cleaners, grocery stores, you know what I'm saying, small stuff. No banks. Nothing big. But they wanted me to come back for more questions. Waste of time."

"Did you do the holdups?"

"You bet your sweet shit I did. I needed some cash."

"Did you hurt anybody, kill anybody?"

"Didn't have to. Everybody was nice and cooperative. I like cooperative people. You know what I'm saying?"

"What are you planning to do?"

"Just bum around for a while. Get me some fresh cunt. Take it easy while the cash lasts."

"You said sometime back that you're married."

"Sure. But my wife, Elaine, is very tolerant. I like tolerant people, if you get my drift."

"With you gone, how does she support herself?"

"She moved in with my mother. She's not too happy about it, but as I said she's tolerant."

"Are you still carrying the .45?"

"No, the cops took it, but I stole another one. Getting it past the border was a cinch."

"Slade, I'm not going to travel with you."

"You're not traveling with me. We just happen to be going to the same place at the same time."

"Just keep your distance." All the remaining seats on the old bus were filled. But this conversation seemed only to whet Slade's appetite to draw Andrew into the world of his fantasies. He especially liked hypothetical situations and escape scenarios. He would sketch a verbal portrait of a scene in which (1) you had committed a terrible crime, or (2) people were after you and wanted to kill you, or (3) you had to disappear, assume a new identity, to carry out some super-secret assignment. Things like that. In all of them you were on the run. The world was against you.

"Where would you go?" Slade would pester. "What would you do first? You see where I'm headed?"

"No. But you're on this bus, the only gringo around, except for me. Are you trying to disappear?" Andrew questioned.

"Only for a little while. I gotta lay low. Nobody would ever figure I'd go to Mexico. They would peg me for Holland, or Italy.

I'm a Dutchman, half Italian. I got relatives in both places."

"So where do you go next?"

"Gotta stay in motion. Think about it. Put yourself in my place. What would you do? Change your identity? Get fake papers? A hundred bucks in New York—get you anywhere. Just pull off a few jobs and boom! You're out. That's the beauty of it. Nobody knows…"

But by now Andrew had fallen half asleep, his senses cocked for any unusual movement from Slade. The 32-hour drive had tired him and he needed some catching up. But Slade went on and on with his scenarios, ignoring Andrew's closed eyes. Every scenario was a different way of escaping, getting money through armed robbery, finding some exciting temporary freedom, eluding his constant pursuers. Running, always running. Always away. Never toward.

When the bus finally arrived in the center of Mexico City, this great city at 8,000 feet altitude—someone told him the whole city was sitting inside the giant rim of an ancient volcano—Andrew made a number of inquiries to try to find a place to live. Very few people spoke English, so it took some time. And when at last he found a most articulate English speaker, actually an Englishman, he listened carefully to his guidance.

"The place you want to go is the French Quarter. Go see Mama Goose. She'll have a place for you."

And as Andrew wrote down the address, he noticed Slade hovering nearby, listening carefully.

He found the place. It was more of a neighborhood than a "Quarter." Mama Goose was a sturdy, big boned aging French woman with straight gray hair. She had been an ambulance driver during the First World War. "The great war," she called it in her broken English. "I drove with Hemingway." She owned a large villa and rented a number of apartments to travelers and tourists. For 10 U.S. dollars a week she gave Andrew a clean, furnished apartment with separate bedroom, tiled floors, and a large living room. He shut the door—there were no locks—lay down on the bed and slept for 12 hours.

He found it was a casual place, spotlessly clean but open to wandering tenants. They seemed to feel free to enter each other's apartments at will. At first, Andrew was not happy with this situation, but he quickly adjusted and found the free-flowing neighbors a source of continuing interests. Several other people in the Villa intrigued his curiosity.

He found the first, sitting on the side of his bed when he woke up—Honey Suckl.

"You sleep like an old dog," she said.

"Who are you…?' he asked, still sleepy.

"Call me Honey, honey."

"Did Mama Goose put you up in this room?"

"No. My place is across the courtyard. Me and Johnny. I just came by to see our new neighbor."

"Hi, neighbor," he yawned.

"I'm blind," she said sleepily. "Is it day or night?"

Andrew looked at her carefully. Since he always slept naked, he wrapped the sheet around his waist before he rose from the bed to sit beside her. If she were blind, where was her cane? How did she find her way alone to his room? He looked into her eyes— "Checking me out?" she asked. They were large, watery, pale blue. She had an expansive head of dishwater blonde hair, now rumpled and in some disarray. He could not guess her age. She seemed prematurely old, maybe in her late thirties. He could see that she may have once been pretty, but as she had aged too quickly her features had begun to lose precise distinction. They were now loose and puffy.

"I'm Andrew," he said, shaking her hand, surprised she knew just where to put it. He looked into her eyes again. She seemed to be seeing him.

"My last name is Suckl," she said. Parents named me Honey. Thought it was cute. Took my maiden name again when I got divorced... I get a nice alimony check every month. Keeps me in tequila, cigaros, and you-know-what."

"Does your husband know you're here?"

"Don't give a fuck. He's too busy raising the kids."

"You have kids?"

"Three. All under 10."

"How could you leave them?" he asked, startled.

She looked at him as though he had asked a stupid question. He saw tears beginning to form along the lids of her eyes. "Let me paint a picture for you, honey. Here I am in the middle of New Jersey, kids climbing all over me night and day. Laundry, cooking, apron, groceries... I was the typical suburban housewife. I'll throw some more paint on the canvas. Dull husband, accountant, never any fun. Not sure why I even married him—oh, yeah, I know. Got me away from my parents. Out from under. Then I went straight under, if you know what I mean."

She smiled, pleased with her joke.

"I still don't understand."

"Here I am, washing dishes, scrubbing butts, looking out the window at this picture-perfect yard. And I got to thinking. 'Honey,' I said to myself, I said, 'this is the way you're gonna spend the next 20 years.' It felt like prison. I had to break out."

"So you came here?" He saw the tears were for herself.

"Not right away. I just up and left the whole kit and caboodle. Picked up and left. I was <u>not</u> gonna spend the best years of my life as a manicured suburban New Jersey housewife."

Shades of Zeedie crossed his mind. "That's quite a story," he said quietly.

She went on without noticing his remark. "But I stuck that creep right where it hurts. Ka'ching! Ka'ching!!" She made expressions with two fingers of each hand, as though punching a cash register. "Got me some nice alimony. Amazing what a good lawyer can do for you, especially when you tickle his balls."

"So what have you been doing since?"

"Just live each moment as it comes. I make up the rules as I go along…Say, have you got any tequila in here? I'm already blind, but I could use some more."

"No tequila. I don't drink much."

"Well, ain't you the fancy one? Drinking makes me sober. Helps me see reality. That's what I do. I fuck reality every day. Reality is a hard fuck. That's what reality means. And that's what living is all about. Learning to do things for me, that make sense for me…And having fun."

She stood, a little woozy, so Andrew helped steady her.

"Where's your toilet? I gotta pee. Bad."

Andrew showed her the door and quickly hopped into his trousers. She did not close the door. Just let it all out. She was like a horse. She was still pulling her panties up when she came out.

"If I can't get a drink here, you're no fun," she said.

Andrew took her arm to steady her. "I'll walk you back to your place.

"Don't need any help. Just need a drink."

"But you said you're blind."

"Blind <u>drunk</u>!" she explained, as though talking to a stupid person. "Once you stay here for a while, you'll come around. We have good parties here." And she left with uncertain steps.

Andrew began to explore the local neighborhoods and shop for food. He found the earthy aroma of the beef ("bif") much more pungent in comparison to what he had been used to. He bought meat and vegetables and fruit just as he would have back in Detroit. One of the customs he found fascinating was the use of Chicklets as local currency for the smallest amounts. The Chicklets would pass back and forth freely as "ponies," then go into someone's mouth to suck and chew.

In the mornings he noticed trucks lined along the street delivering five-gallon jugs of water to residents. He wondered why. In Detroit nobody drank water out of big jugs. He assumed it was only an affectation of local culture. In the meantime he was learning Mexican Spanish rapidly, by necessity. He enjoyed the exercise of these new muscles in his brain. Every phrase he learned gave him a tiny new insight into the culture, into the minds of the people. He was now fully rested, eating regularly for an incredibly few pesos, and thinking about what to do next.

Ralph Buckits snapped him quickly out of his new complacency. It happened on the first Saturday after he had arrived. Honey and Johnny were having a party in her apartment. It was casual, open house, people wandering in and out of each other's apartments. Even Slade was there. He had taken an apartment but steered clear of Andrew. Andrew learned that Slade told everyone his name was Zorro.

Honey's current lover introduced himself as Johnny Maloney, but Andrew sensed right away that was not his real name. Johnny was a disheveled, bisexual, unshaven, seldom-published poet who, like Honey had prematurely aged. He seemed, behind the wrinkles, to be a little older than Honey, maybe in his forties. He was tall and wafer thin, had gray washed-out eyes, and stringy dark hair in need of a good haircut. He lived on the support of Honey's alimony checks. Andrew asked him if he had published any of his work, but Johnny was vague in his answer. Johnny seemed to have an unusual pride in his self-identification as an intellectual. Unlike Tom Wharton, as Andrew remembered, Johnny would never recite offerings from his poetry.

Honey offered tequila to Andrew, which he sipped very slowly. One drink would last the evening. Honey had cleaned up, hair now in place, fresh makeup, and cologne. She was almost pretty. She asked Andrew what his shoe size was. He thought it a strange question. "I always check out shoe sizes," she said. He thought she might be hovering on the edge of madness. But he told her, and she smiled.

Cookie the Bookie was another long-time resident. Cookie was a short androgynous hazel-eyed male with straight thin blonde hair he combed in a bang over his right ear under which hung a large earring. Whatever betting needed to be done, Cookie could make the connection. He was also on the run. He had had a thriving business on Miami Beach until the "misunderstanding" with Aldo and some of Aldo's friends, at Al's Bar on Collins and Fifth Avenue.

Chuck the Washroom Menace—his own description of himself—was also there, "traveling through." He said his claim to fame was that he left lewd signs and/or graffiti in almost every washroom he ever entered. For him it was a passion. "You know, when you see that stuff in the washrooms, and you always wondered who put it there, who was the artist? Well, it was Chuck. Meet myself, Chuck, the Washroom Menace."

"Do you really take pride in that?" Andrew asked.

"You gotta take pride in something. This is what I do."

Carlita Menendez was one of the more interesting people at the party, in large part because she was so different from most of the rest of the crowd. Carlita was Mama Goose's niece, living here while she completed her education. As cynical and rumpled as most of the others appeared, Carlita was the opposite—young and fresh, still in her teen-age years, with a most compelling sense of innocence. She had deep, brown, shy but trusting eyes, very pleasant features, long hair which she wore in an attractive bun, and a slender figure. She drank no alcohol but sipped from a green bottle of Coca-Cola she had brought from her room. Andrew could see that Slade spotted her immediately, as prey.

Ralph Buckits seemed to be fairly normal, a jovial and slightly rounded expatriate from Kentucky. He had prematurely thinning reddish hair and intelligent eyes. Already a college graduate, he had fallen in love with Mexico, its people, and its culture. After much interaction with government officials, he had at last gained permission to become the only American Disc Jockey in Mexico City. He called himself Arble the Marble, "Just rolling around." He worked six days a week and rented an apartment in the large Villa. If he was in flight, no one knew it.

Andrew smiled quizzically as he watched Slade introduce himself around as Zorro. "I don't know if that's my first name or last name," Slade would say. "My parents were killed when I was four. They never had time to tell me."

"What's your birth certificate say?" Honey asked.

"I never saw a birth certificate. It was destroyed in a fire. I don't even know where I was born."

"You're kind of like a man without a country," Johnny said.

"How did you happen to come here?" Ralph asked.

"I'm a writer" Slade continued to weave the lie. "I write for The Saturday Evening Post. But not under my own name. I've published two articles already. I'm working on a book now."

"What's it about?" Carlita asked, innocently nibbling at the bait.

Slade had found an audience. "Actually, I'm trying to reconstruct it. It's a fantastically beautiful book, all about a young girl in Mexico. But a woman I was seeing at the time read it one night and became very jealous of my heroine. So jealous in fact, she burned the manuscript. My only copy..." He fixed his most pleasant smile on Carlita. "My heroine was a lot like you."

"What was her name?" Carlita asked.

"I can't tell you her name until it's all back in my head. I'm afraid if I say the name, I'll lose it."

"Not like Rumpelstiltskin," Johnny jested.

Slade ignored the jest. "I need to be hypnotized so I can recall the whole thing. I can't start over. I need to find someone who can hypnotize me, reach into my soul, pull it back out."

Slade was smooth, Andrew thought, as he noted Carlita's compassionate interest in the story. He could see that Slade's words were touching some deep reservoir of her sensitivity, something ancient and mystical. He knew he had to warn her about Slade. He had to somehow break into her unawareness, help her understand that beneath Slade's (Zorro's) surface charm lay the heart of a rotten scoundrel. When Slade took a bathroom break, Andrew tried his best.

"Don't go near Zorro," he said. "His name isn't really Zorro. It's something but it's not Zorro. He just made up that name."

"Do you know him?"

"I rode down here with him on a bus."

"But his story is so moving. He makes you want to help him."

"Don't go near him. Don't be alone with him. He's dangerous."

"Are you sure?"

"I'd bet my life on it."

Just then Slade reappeared. "You talking about me?" he asked them both, flashing his most cordial smile.

"Yes," Carlita said innocently.

"What did he say?" Slade asked.

Carlita hesitated, but in her innocence could not think of a lie or subterfuge. "He said you're dangerous."

Slade laughed and put on his most charming smile. "I'm a pussycat," he said. "You could hypnotize me and I would be in your power. He's the dangerous one."

Carlita excused herself to join a discussion now underway nearby. Slade's killer eyes bore into Andrew with vengeful intensity.

The nearby discussion, which Andrew also joined, was about a movie, The Red Shoes. Several had seen it and come away with different interpretations.

"The story is about a ballerina who has to make a fascinating choice—whether to climb the heights of joy, ever with the risk of failure, or to live as a contented clod," Johnny said.

'I disagree," Honey said. "She had to choose between living for a little while—while she was still young—at the highest peaks of existence, or choose a humdrum life of safety and boredom."

"You're both wrong," Ralph said. "Her choice was whether to give up everything—the love of her life, marriage, children, everything—in sacrifice for her art."

"But you forgot to mention her boss. Waiting in the wings to possess her as soon as she gave up everything for art," Honey argued. "He was an extremely selfish man."

"Her boss was consumed with extreme selfishness and control, disguised as a quest for perfection in art," she added.

"I haven't seen the movie, but for me the choice would be

simple," Carlita said. "Love comes first. Over everything. Family and children, over everything."

"I feel the same way," Andrew said. "You can live a normal life without being a clod. There is the possibility of beauty even in simple things. There can be a search for truth even in the darkest alleyways."

Carlita put her hand on his arm, warmly in agreement. It reminded him of the way Mienda used to do it.

The discussion went on well into the night, with no consensus. Andrew decided he would see the movie as soon as possible. But the tenor of the discussion drifted into the ruts each one (except Carlita) had carved into their lives. There were no high moments in their lives. Andrew could see this clearly. Only a steady narrowing of their lives and possibilities, even a strong aroma of selfishness. Carlita was the bright spot that redeemed them all. She stood for hope, for growth and progression, for the possibility of a peak experience. But she had gone to bed. She wanted to be up for an early Mass.

Later in the discussion, Andrew went into Honey's kitchen to get a glass of water. He thought nothing of it, placing the glass under the faucet and filling it. He had raised it halfway to his lips when a startling cry arrested his movement.

"St-o-o-p-p-p!" It was Ralph Buckits, shouting from the living room, now rushing to his side. "What are you doing?"

"Getting a glass of water," Andrew said.

"Nobody drinks water out of a tap here. Even the locals. You can get sick real bad. Dysentery, typhoid... the tap water supply can have some bad stuff in it. It's only for taking a bath or washing dishes."

"I've been drinking out of the tap for more than a week."

"No touristas? No problems?"

"Not a one."

"You're either lucky, have iron bowels, or have an over-worked guardian angel. All the gringos get Montezuma's revenge."

"I didn't know there was a problem. Is that why I see all the trucks delivering jugs of water?"

"You got it," Ralph said.

"Thanks. I'll be more careful."

"You're lucky you're still alive. One more thing. Wash your vegetables. Peel your fruit."

"Thanks," Andrew said. So far he hadn't.

The party had begun to dissipate. As Andrew left, he noticed Slade sequestered with Honey in a corner of the room, sharing a bottle of tequila. From Slade's body language, Andrew could see he was still on the hunt. The night was not yet over. Slade would take what he could get.

The eruption came a week later. Slade had brought two cold, open bottles of Coca-Cola, in the pleasant pale green bottles, and offered one to Carlita. He said he needed her help to sort something out. She reminded him so much of the heroine of his story, she was the only one who could help him. He had a writer's block. She let him trustingly into her room and accepted the cold drink. It took very little time for the drug to do its gruesome work. She was not even aware she as passing out.

For him she was only a momentary satisfaction, a "fresh piece of cunt." For her, he was the destroyer of her innocence, the deep betrayer of all she held precious, the vultured memory sucking at her future happiness.

Mama Goose arrived too late, walking into the room to visit with her niece, just as Slade finished his grizzly act. Carlita was still passed out, naked on the bed. Slade was hurrying desperately into his clothing as Mama Goose attacked him. But he held her off with his .45 as he made a hasty exist. And as Mama Goose checked Carlita's condition, covered her, and swiftly called the police, Slade quickly gathered his few belongings and made a hasty exit from the building. By the time police arrived, Slade had vanished into the city streets.

Andrew heard the commotion and came to help if he could. Carlita was now awake, weeping, devastated. Mama Goose was preparing her for the hospital. There was nothing Andrew could do. But he could not shake out of his mind the image of her destroyed innocence. He recalled something Slade had said in his rambling conversation on the bus. "Sure they'll find out I'm a piece of shit. But by the time they find out, I'll be long gone."

*

On the bus down to Acapulco, Andrew had much time alone to reflect. What am I doing here? he thought. Among so many selfish people? Meeting mostly gringos like myself. Selfishness seems so confining. The takers never have enough room. They always want more. When you see it in a man-woman relationship, it's deadly.

I am surrounded by a colorful culture, but because of language limitations, I am unable to fully experience it in the short time I have. Why am I spending time doing this?

He had thought of Laura over and over again since he had left, wondering how she was, assuming she was enjoying a summer of work in Vermont. He began to visualize the permanence of their relationship. What beautiful lavender eyes he would wake up to every morning, what sweetness in her kisses, what fire in her passion. They would have to find a way to work through their religious differences. But so far, there could be no field of compromise from either side.

As the narrow highway wound southwest through the mountains, along one hairpin turn after another, Andrew saw the sites where cars and buses had plunged off the no-guardrail highway from time to time. There were quite a few such places, each marked with a collection of small white crosses. At every scary turn, Andrew wondered if his destiny was to become a little white cross in these remote Mexican mountains.

There were many English speakers in Acapulco and Andrew had no trouble finding suggestions where to stay, and associated directions. At Hungry Herman's, an American restaurant along Acapulco Bay, he found the information that appealed to him most.

"Don't stay here in the big bay. Too crowded. Too many tourists. Too much noise. Just walk along this road, up over the mountain, and on the other side it's like a whole different world. The Morning Beach at Caleta. You want a cheap place to stay? Go to Quinta Mitchell. It's not directly on the beach. There's a Jeep trail. That's why it's cheap. But it overlooks the beach."

Andrew followed their advice and presently located Quinta

Mitchell. The owner, Señor Montuvedias, was a cheerful, portly fellow who had once moved to Chicago, spent 20 years there as a short order cook, then came back to Acapulco to buy the small hotel. Despite 20 years living in a large American city, Montuvedias had acquired only a limited command of English. He knew enough to get by, which was all he needed. He seemed to have no concept of "J." He referred to himself as "My person."

Someone had just moved out of one of the best rooms in the Quinta, with a private bath, on the second floor (top floor) with a balcony, looking directly over the Morning Beach and the Pacific stretching endlessly beyond. Since the hillside descended steeply to the beach, nothing obstructed a most spectacular view. The price of 10 dollars a week also included cooking privileges in the kitchen. Montuvedias told him he would teach him how to make refried beans—pintos, onion, salt, maybe a little lard—cook and mash.

Like Mexico City, there were no locks on the doors, and since Andrew now had one of the three best balconies in the Quinta, occasional individuals would feel free to come through his room and sit to enjoy the view. Every day at about two o'clock in the afternoon it would rain for 10 minutes, then stop. And every sunset, framed within the ever-changing billowing white clouds over the Pacific, was a new exercise in the beauty and endless articulation of the colors of creation.

Tequila was cheap, and Andrew purchased a bottle so he could have a drink while watching the view. Because he was not used to the effects of alcohol, it took very little to put his mind into a reflective, sentimental and nostalgic mood.

He tried to think of <u>significance</u>. He thought he should try to write a book. Or poetry. He thought of Laura again and again. Sometimes he thought of Zeedie. But on his balcony, the most he could write was two pages of uncertain prose. No poetry was rising in his soul.

Of the several people who, in his first few days, had come through his room to join him on the balcony, the most interesting was Blossom. She liked to watch the sunsets but had a room with her mother on the cheaper side facing the road. Blossom was 20, rather tall, slender, half Hawaiian, half Japanese, and had a pleasant Asian beauty. She had black hair down to her waist, which reminded him of Laura.

She said she was marooned here with her mother, waiting for her father to finish a sea voyage and come back for them. She had a casual sense of friendliness about her that made her easy to be with and to talk to. She also had intriguing dark eyes. Andrew found it hard to read their expressions. She had a way of flashing changes of mood or tone instantly from one expression to another. One second her eyes would be saying "Come here and possess me, you fool," and the next second her expression would be saying "Touch me and I'll cut your balls off." She was like a walking kaleidoscope and Andrew found her interesting. She told him right away he fascinated her. "You're not like the other men here." She also told him how lonely she was.

She did not attach herself to him in the way Slade had done, but she seemed somehow to be nearby whenever he went to the store, or the beach. She especially liked the beach and was a strong swimmer. She also wore a small two-piece bathing suit that brought envious looks from women and long stares from men. The little natural ripples of muscle along her long flat stomach were most attractive. She usually accompanied Andrew when he went to the beach, especially when they swam at night. Andrew would swim in the morning, then again after dark. Blossom said she was afraid of the jungle and wanted his company, particularly at night.

The Jeep trail, perhaps 500 feet in length, was so named because even a Jeep would have trouble negotiating it. It was not so much a road as a pathway down a steep hill, with closely entwined jungle growth more than the length of a body. The trail was deeply rutted from rivers of rain. At night it had a black and spooky feeling. But once the trail ended at the beach, there was all the night life of the cantinas. Lights, laughter, love in secluded places, free flowing cerveza and tequila… a party atmosphere.

By his second week in the Quinta, Blossom was becoming a regular visitor to his balcony and a regular swimming companion. They sipped tequila together and watched the magnificent sunsets unfold across the Pacific. He put his pen aside and decided just to enjoy the experience.

"This is so different from anything I've ever known, in some ways it seems like Paradise," Andrew confided.

"Why don't you stay here?" Blossom asked. "Why go back to Detroit, to those terrible winters?"

"This is not reality," he said. "I don't know what reality is, but I know this ain't it. Mexico City ain't it. Acapulco ain't it."

"What are you looking for?" she asked, sipping tequila on the balcony.

"In some ways, this is what I'm looking for. I can picture myself at the end of my life just relaxing on a beach like this, with warmth and sunshine and endless beauty."

"You don't have to wait for the end of your life. You could do it now."

"Be a beachcomber?' He mused. "It wouldn't take much to live… No. The thought was passing through my mind. But I've shaken it out. Permanently."

"Why?" she asked with genuine puzzlement in her eyes.

"A lot of things. First, I'm committed to a girl in school. We love each other. We'll probably get married and fight a lot about religion."

"You're planning to get married so you can fight?"

"No, but I think the fight about religion will be part of the total package."

"You said 'a lot of things.' What else?" She laid her hand along his arm in a friendly way, a show of interest.

"I want to get married, have children. I don't know how to raise children yet, but I know a lot of ways <u>not</u> to raise them."

"I want to get married too," she said wistfully. "I love children."

"But even more than that," Andrew continued. "There's something fundamentally wrong with living your life as a beachcomber."

"Like what?"

"Like, you're not making any contribution to the world at all. You're not doing your share. You're not rising to the potentials of your creation. You're taking leisure you haven't earned… If you look at a man spending a lot of time on the beach, you might be looking at someone who has spent a lifetime doing something useful and productive. You might be looking at someone who's <u>earned</u> his leisure... Or, you might be looking at a bum. You're looking at the same activity, but each perspective gives it a totally different set of meanings and values."

She raised his hand to her lips, kissed it.

"I love it when you talk like a philosopher."

During his third week at the Quinta, several incidents in a row, each from the natural world, left vivid impressions on his mind, all dealing with the reality experienced by creatures attempting to survive in the only way they knew how.

Sitting on his balcony one morning, sipping coffee, a large moth fluttered casually in the gentle air only a few feet in front of him. He watched it idly for a moment before its extinction. Suddenly, from out of nowhere, a large hornet drove into the belly of the moth, held on with its front legs, and slammed its stinger several times into the gray fluttery belly. It happened swiftly but seemed in distinct slow motion. The action was so close in front of him, he could see every detail clearly. The vividness came from the way the hornet would plunge the stinger, then arch back in a sleek black pulsing motion, withdrawing the stinger while still holding on, then plunge the stinger in again with great determined strength. Three times, before the moth fell with the hornet still grappling it to the jungle floor below.

Walking down the Jeep trail one morning for an early swim, he encountered a snake that had captured a small frog. The frog was almost wholly within the snake's digestive system. All that protruded from the snake's mouth were the small front legs and head. The little front legs were fully extended and open, wiggling furiously in the attempt to escape. It seemed there was almost a forlorn expression in the frog's dying eyes. Andrew gave thought to rescuing the frog if he could but decided to do nothing. Most of the frog had already been consumed. He didn't think there was enough left of it to save. He walked on. This is the way of nature, he thought.

The third event occurred during a walk across the small mountain, down toward Acapulco Bay. In an open field beside the road he saw the dwindling remains of a large black dog. A collection of vultures stood nearby, each taking turns at the remaining flesh. The entire skin was intact, but the vultures had ripped a passage through the rectum and, in turn, would thrust their long necks and beaks into the passage and emerge wet and glistening with a chunk of meat. They were almost up to the shoulders area when Andrew came by. He watched in fascination for several minutes, then walked on.

Early mornings were especially filled with images when he walked over the mountain into town. The dog and the vultures were the grittiest. Many of the others were rather sad, as though empty of meaning—a scrap of newspaper blowing along the beach off the bay, a lone seagull swooping down to scoop some little fragment of meat left from the night before, a mop pail propped against the doorway of the empty Riptide Bar, Hungry Herman's closed until noon.

You could almost sense a haunting mood lingering among the dark shadows of some of the streets and alleyways. It was the early morning hour when no drifters roam, the bright sunlight having beaten them back inside like vampires into their coffins from a bloodless night. The whole week seemed heavy with symbols and forebodings. The images of nature that he saw would take a permanent place in his memory.

And to add to the forebodings, Blossom came to his balcony one morning to offer coffee and to continue their conversations. "Some new guy just moved in," she said, "next door to me and my mother. It's hard to avoid him. He talks to me as though he had a claim on me. My mother told him to leave us alone. I told him too. He said his name is Ringo. I'm afraid of him. Will you protect me?"

"I'll do what I can whenever I'm around. But if you're worried, maybe you should have the police talk to him. If they tell him to leave you alone, he probably will."

"You don't mind if I hang out with you?"

"No, I enjoy your company. But I'm leaving for Detroit next week. You're going to need a more permanent arrangement. Talk to Señor Montuvedias."

Two nights before he left, he encountered a pack of wild dogs roaming a stretch of the Acapulco seaside jungle. It was a dark and cloudless sky with a brilliant full moon, a little later than usual for his nocturnal swim. Blossom had joined him, holding his left arm for balance as they descended the steep trail just as they had done in nights before.

Suddenly, about 50 feet below them, four wild dogs rushed out of the jungle growth and onto the trail, not barking, making no noise at all. They took position in a phalanx across the path, blocking it except for enough space on one side for someone to get past them. Andrew assumed they would not be bothersome if he and Blossom made no threatening moves. But their lack of barking registered a warning to him. Always in the past, he had simply walked past unfriendly dogs or, with Guardo, fended them off if they attacked. He knew turning back was not an option. Blossom's long fingers clutched his arm with such strength it was almost painful. All was dark except for the brilliance of the moonlight on the trail, and its glistening reflection off the dark black skintight smooth hair of the dogs.

Blossom was on his left. Carefully negotiating the slippery ruts, he walked slowly toward the dogs, keeping her out of their range. The small opening was to the left of where the dogs silently stood. The dogs made no sound at all. No wagging tail among them. As he came even with their lineup, and without a single bark or growl or gesture of hostility, all four dogs suddenly attacked in one motion.

He spun into them so quickly Blossom lost her grip on his arm, but he instantly shielded her. One dog lunged for his throat, a second for his right arm, the third and fourth for his legs. Not a bark or growl, only lunging teeth. Their attack aroused in him an instant, profound response of anger. It was so unfair! He and Blossom had been minding their own business. There was no provocation. The action of the dogs was extremely unfair, he thought.

And out of the powerful depths of his anger and rage, he instantly tore into the dogs with a disposition to destroy them. Out of the corner of his eye he saw Blossom had fallen, but the focus of the attack was entirely on him. He whirled and punched one dog with such impact the dog was down. Almost in a single swoop he threw the other three off him. At the end of this encounter, which was over in seconds, they were now in reversed positions on the trail. All four dogs were now lined up on the sloping ruts above himself and Blossom. Still without bark or growl, one dog somewhat shaken. They stood there, as though in military formation, poised for the second attack.

Andrew took a long single step toward them—a swordsman's step. Because of the steepness of the slope, all four dogs were at just about the level of his head, perhaps 10 feet away. Still with consuming rage, now with the ancient Cameron fierceness fully aroused within him, he leaned forward and extended his right arm. He motioned with his hand.

"Come on," was all he said, just above a hoarse whisper. He was determined to tear them limb from limb with his bare hands. And somehow the dogs understood him. They paused, broke rank, and ran back into the jungle.

"Are you okay?" he immediately asked Blossom.

She rose, held him very tightly to her for a few moments. "Just bruised from where I fell, she said. "You're bleeding."

Andrew noticed for the first time the dogs had drawn blood. He had prevented their seizure of his neck, but his right arm and left leg were bleeding form their bites. He did not know that wild animal bites often carry rabies. He thought of the bites as no more than temporary wounds he would clean in the salty waters of the Pacific. The thought of seeing a doctor never entered his mind.

"Better not swim out," Blossom warned. "The sharks bite harder than the dogs. The blood will draw them."

"I'm ready to bite a shark myself," he laughed. "They better watch out."

"You're very tough," Blossom said with a big smile.

"I'm not tough, just determined. And a little cussed."

They swam, but only in the shallow waters of the bay. They did not go out far. And when they finished, Blossom told him she was nervous about going back up the trial. "It will be okay," he reassured her. "Those dogs are long gone. They won't hang around."

"Can I hold your arm real tight?"

"Tight as you want."

And when they ascended the trail without further incident, Blossom did not want to release his arm.

"I'm still shook up a little bit. I don't want to go back into my room just yet. Can we sit on your balcony for a while, look at the stars? Maybe a small drink would calm me down."

"Let's change clothes first," Andrew said. Which they did. When Blossom returned, Andrew got out his bottle of tequila. "That's about all there is, enough for a couple of small drinks. I'm leaving first thing day after tomorrow. I won't buy more."

"I'll keep you supplied for as long as you can stay," she smiled.

"Make me a kept man?" he joked.

They sat on the balcony for some time without talking. Even with the passing moon, the stars over the Pacific hung with silent glory and grandeur. "I never get tired of looking at the stars," he said, now feeling the mellowing influence of the tequila.

Blossom moved her chair so she could look directly at him, not at the stars. Her kaleidoscopic eyes had settled into patterns of warmness and deeper interest. Finally, she spoke, laying her long fingers across his hand. "All my life I've been looking for a man like you."

"You won't have any trouble. There are plenty of guys like me around. And with your beauty and your figure and your personality, they'll be standing in line wanting to be near you."

"Do you want to be near me?"

"I already am. In a very short time I think we've become good friends."

"I mean really near me?"

"I'm not exactly following you."

"Do I have to draw you a picture?" she smiled.

"As I said," he said, "you are very beautiful. You have a stunning figure. Every man in the world would want you."

"Do you want me?"

Now he understood. "Blossom, I've told you. I'm committed to someone."

"She's not here, is she?"

"No."

"Well, I'm here, and I want you to come inside."

"Can't do that…"

Now Blossom's eyes changed expression. In almost an angry tone, mingled with hurt, she said "What are you, some kind of queer? Some idealistic nutcase?"

"I want your friendship, nothing more."

"Aren't you tempted?"

"I'm always tempted, but I can't step over the line."

"Your loss," she said, rising. The thought of Cynthia flashed through his mind.

"Do you ever swim naked?" she asked, with a suddenly changed expression.

"I love to swim naked."

"So do I," she smiled. "There's a secluded cove just beyond the cantinas…"

"Maybe another time," he smiled.

Just as he walked in from the balcony with her, while they were still in his bedroom, Slade burst through the unlocked door.

"Ringo!" she said with alarm.

"I thought I'd find you here," Slade said. "But I didn't know it would be with this shit." He had been drinking heavily.

Blossom took Andrew's arm again, holding herself near him.

"If you give it to this shit, you can give it to me," he said, pulling his .45 out of the back of his belt and pointing it at the two of them.

"Thought I was done with wild dogs for the night," Andrew said. "Are you trying to follow me?"

"Ringo's the one I told you about," Blossom said to Andrew.

"His name's not Ringo. It's Slade the Blade," Andrew said. "Or something."

"Sweetheart, I'm gonna take you right here, while Andrew watches. Normally, I don't like sloppy seconds, but I'll make an exception in your case. I want him to see how a real pro does it."

Blossom moved behind Andrew. "Help me," she said

weakly.

Andrew lunged for Slade, grabbing his right wrist while still in midair. Slade got off a shot that Andrew deflected into the wall, before wrestling the gun out of Slade's hand. He felt the pressure of the air shock as the bullet whizzed by his ear. But Slade had pulled the spring-loaded stiletto out of his pocket in the tussle and snapped it into position. He was holding the stiletto above Andrew's heart when, in a great burst of energy, Andrew threw him off and against the wall. Furniture was being broken and mangled all around them. Andrew punched Slade so hard in the middle of his chest the air rushed out of him and he dropped the stiletto. Andrew quickly retrieved both instruments of destruction and handed them to Blossom.

Blossom was still holding herself together behind an overturned chair. Slade was bleeding from the mouth, angry. Andrew came toward him, remembering Carlita. He had an urge to kill him, to remove his presence from the earth. He could think of him as nothing but scum, of no value to civilization. He thought of Carlita's innocence, her trusting eyes, the depth of betrayal she must have felt.

But in the seconds as he moved toward Slade with a passion to destroy him, a sudden arresting thought flashed into his mind with vivid intensity. I am not "Slade's judge." I am not his executioner. If there is a God at all, this has to be up to God to decide, not me. And so, in an almost instantaneous change, Andrew redefined his mission. He would capture Slade, turn him over to the police, let the law do its work. And so he took Slade, still struggling, and held him tightly in his grip. Just then the police arrived, along with Señor Montuvedias, Blossom's mother, and all the other tenants awakened by the shot and crashing noises.

It was fortunate that Blossom was there. She was a frightened, reliable witness. She told the police what had happened. They arrested Slade and took his weapons. They asked Andrew a few questions. He told them about Carlita and Mama Goose.

"You sonofabitch," Slade said to Andrew as the police were leading him away. "Because of you I almost lost Carlita. You're always interfering with my life. Because of you I had to make another plan. You're responsible for what happened to Carlita, not me."

*

Hitchhiking back from the Mexican border, the most interesting ride he had was with a drunken southerner who spoke with a casual drawl. What made the ride really memorable was the way he drove. He was driving with one of his buddies, and both were drunk almost beyond recognition. The driver said his name was Waldo.

"I'm drunk and happy and I f-e-e-e-l good."

Waldo sat sideways in the driver's seat, his right leg propped against the back of the seat, his right arm hung over the back, clutching a pint of bourbon. With his left hand he was holding the steering wheel. His left foot was angled down and on the gas pedal. His head was turned away from the road so often, Andrew was certain they would crash. Waldo kept offering Andrew a drink, but Andrew declined. If this were to be his night to die, at least he would die sober.

What added to the sharpness of the memory was that this ride was all through a mountainous area, and the roads were full of curves and steep hillsides. "I know these roads like the back of my hand," Waldo reassured Andrew. "Just stay with me, buddy. Know what I mean?"

But Andrew wondered how Waldo would ever apply the brake if the situation arose. It was a lucky night. Somehow Andrew emerged from the ride alive and vowed to be more careful next time in choosing with whom he would ride.

Chapter 3

Back in Detroit, two letters awaited him. Both from Laura. The first was dated the day after he had left.

Dearest Andrew,

I tried to call you when I found out, but you were gone. Vanished! I desperately need to see you! I need to hear from you as soon as you get this letter. I don't wait well!

Andrew, darling, I'm pregnant. I'm due in early March. I don't know what to do! I need you with me. I was foolishly so fixed on you I forgot to listen to my own body. For a while my whole world was you, and now I'm paying the price. Time is marching on! Don't abandon me! We need to make decisions together. Now! Please, please, please call me immediately!

I love you,

Laura

The return address was her dorm, Stockwell, in Ann Arbor.

Andrew called the dorm immediately, before he read the second letter. But he quickly realized she was no longer there. The letter was dated early June. This was now mid-August. He read the second letter, dated mid-July, from Vermont.

Andrew,

I can't describe the horrible sin I've committed. I went against Mother. I went against you (I think). I went against God! Please forgive me.

I had an abortion. It changed everything between us. Just like snapping our fingers. We can't go on together. You can't know how much I needed you. I can't live like that. Don't you know most relationships die of neglect. Anais Nin once wrote "Love never dies of a natural death." Well, mister poet, take that! You left me alone! You abandoned me! I didn't want to fall in love with you—I definitely did not. Why did you make me fall in love with you? I thought you were the one. I really did. But you're not. You weren't there for me when I really needed you. Maybe you were only my practice lover! So there!

You told me you want to understand the full range of human experience. Well, you should have been smart enough to start with me! I can't begin to tell you what I've been through. And you, nowhere in sight. I guess it's over between us. We can't turn back the clock. Maybe someday we can be friends again. I'm not sure.

Laura

(Burn this letter)

On reading the second letter, he called Laura at her mother's home in Vermont. "She doesn't want to see you," her mother said. Andrew then took a bath, changed clothes, and drove straight through to Vermont. He arrived tired and anxious, in late afternoon the next day, with a powerful need to see Laura. He knocked on the door of her mother's house.

"I told you, she doesn't want to see you," her mother said in the doorway. But Laura appeared behind her. "I'll see him," she said.

Inside Andrew reached out to take her in his arms, but she drew away and offered him a seat.

"I've transferred to Dartmouth in New Hampshire," she said.

"So we will no longer have to live in the same world."

"Can we talk about it?" he asked.

"What's done is done. Talking won't change that."

"If you had called, I would have come to you immediately. I would have abandoned my travel plans."

"You dummy, I did call."

"Laura, I've come here to ask you to marry me." He could see the rush of emotion in Laura's face, in the way she repositioned her body. But she said nothing for several moments. "Did you hear me?" he asked. Still she did not say anything.

"It's too late," she said finally.

"Laura, if I had known… I would have asked you two months ago. You <u>know</u> me. You should have known I would be at your side the moment I found out. You should have known I would never leave you," he said.

"How can anyone really know something that deep and personal about anyone? I needed something definite. That's what love is," she said.

"I came to marry you, to start our lives together," he said.

"Don't cheapen me. Don't think of me as someone who gets married just because she's pregnant."

"I say this, ask you this, to honor our relationship, to honor your virtue, to honor the love we have for each other…"

"Had," she corrected.

"Laura, you're my woman."

"I'm <u>not</u> your woman!"

"Is this your final answer?"

She was silent for a while as emotion built up in her. Her face became pale. Her lips quivered with anger. And when she spoke, the passion rushed out. "My whole life with you has been one sin piled on top of another! Sin upon sin! Where would it end? Where would it go? It would only get worse..." She paused, gathering renewed strength. "With God as my witness, you're gonna burn! You're gonna fry! Oh, I wish you won't, but you will! I asked the Holy Mother—woman to woman—if I should burn with you. She said No! No way. You should burn alone! How I will miss you."

"At least we didn't use condoms," he tried to joke.

"Sin is not charming! Don't try to charm me with your humor! We are definitely done with!"

There was no hug goodbye. Her emotions were still too raw.

He did not hear from her again until the following spring.

*

Andrew entered sophomore year dispirited and confused, still somewhat shaken by his experience with Laura. He was at low ebb. He had switched from Architecture to Journalism, but he wondered if there was much strength in his second choice. His meager output in Mexico—two pages out of all those sunny afternoons—led him to question his career decision. A real journalist would have produced something. A real writer would have soaked up the colorful atmosphere and found a story worth telling. The thought that echoed through Andrew's mind was haunting. What he had experienced in Mexico was not reality. It was anti-reality.

He brought images of Laura back into his mind. He thought again and again of Laura's savage words. Was his whole life anti-reality? "You're gonna burn! You're gonna fry!" she had said. What value had he brought into the world? What value lay potentially within his slumbering sprit?

How do you find your way in the world? How do you begin the search for the meaning of life? Not in Mexico. As Laura would have said, Mexico was a great big huge mistake.

He worked part-time moving furniture, both for a local Ann Arbor trucker (Carpenter's) and, on weekends, for O.H. Frisbe in Detroit. The heavy lifting, the sweat and exertion, not only kept his waistline thin and muscles trim, it was almost like a salve to his wounded spirit. As much as he tried, he could not go for any period of time without thinking of Laura. He would have married her, focused his life, become father to a beloved child, now disappeared, lost forever in the universe; a child who never was. He would have applied himself with new industry to complete his education, helping Laura to complete hers, and they would have set out in the world together with great ideas to do something worthwhile. Of course, there would have been the battle over religion, and how to raise the child. And as he tried to come to grips with this, rationalize it as much as possible, he knew in his heart of hearts he could never give in. Nor could she. Both were too strong willed.

Andrew spent time with Brundi and Charlene whenever possible. He enjoyed their company on many pleasant evenings. Although Brundi was still his roommate, whenever Charlene was with them, the couple acted like freshly married, comfortable and secure in their love. They were planning to marry as soon as they graduated. Charlene now planned to become a nurse and help get Brundi through Law School. Andrew never mentioned Laura to Charlene, never asked about her. Charlene was mum about Laura.

Sometimes, engaged in conversation, the three of them would walk all the way to Stockwell without thinking of time or distance. Andrew enjoyed seeing the girls from the dormitory, coming down from their rooms, all dressed in bright sweaters and dark skirts, signing out as they left for the football game or with their men, to other pleasures. They all seemed so wholesome, so reminiscent of his days and evenings with Laura.

He was cheered one bleak day in December to find a letter from Cynthia. He knew immediately who it was from. Cynthia had a bold and distinctive handwriting.

Kemo Sabe, Darling

Here I am again! I keep coming back like a song. Where has the last year gone? Radcliffe isn't sure <u>what</u> to do with me, but I'm hanging on for dear life—their rules are so <u>yesterday</u>! Well, on my way to another year. Of all the flux in my life, somehow you keep coming back into my mind as a constant presence. Like an old pair of comfortable shoes. Dear Andrew, I do miss you. You don't know how I worry about you. You must take care of yourself... I realize how hard it must be for you to write to me, but that's okay because we two are not bound by words... Time is meaningless to us. I'm just getting into a crazy jumble. There is so much I want to tell you but there is no beginning... One thing I must tell you, on some nights I'll look up at the moon and think of you so strongly that I know you, too, are thinking of me...

Until Death—

Your Unexpected Lover

P.S. How would you like to spend Christmas Eve with me, and

New Year's too? My parents will be in Europe. It would just be the two of us, reminiscing about old times.

He wrote her back.

Dear Cynthia. Your letter warmed my heart, lifted my spirits. Just at the right time. How did you know? It was so good to hear from you. Christmas Eve with you would be wonderful. New Years, too. It will quicken my aging pulse to see you again. Let me know when you're back in town.

My warmest thoughts,

Andrew (aka) comfortable old shoe

Cynthia wrote back immediately.

Lover,

Just to hear from you in writing yet, sent me halfway to heaven. Can't wait to see you, to hear your voice again. I'll call you as soon as I come in.

Coming home with expectations.

*

Cynthia Downing did everything her own way, and with characteristic style—bold elegance. She was what some would call <u>a presence</u>. She had great fashion sense and wore a new hairdo that framed her face like a composition in mysterious beauty. And she had adopted new makeup colorations that heightened her dramatic appearance. Andrew's first impression on seeing her was that, while she had always been beautiful, now she was movie-star stunning. She did in fact quicken his pulse.

She had a friend, traveling to Chicago, drop her off in Ann Arbor after she found Andrew's dorm. "I couldn't wait to see you," she said as she kissed him warmly and hugged him like a long-lost friend. "Tomorrow would be too long."

Andrew had packed a few things for the week, and Charlene came over to see Brundi. Andrew introduced Cynthia. He could see an immediate feline reaction in Charlene. "No grass grows under your feet," Charlene said to Andrew with a throaty whisper. He decided to move the conversation into different avenues, some neutral ground.

"What was that all about?" Cynthia asked him when they were alone.

"She's best friend to a girl I had a very serious relationship with. But it's been over for months. I've moved on."

"You're always having serious relationships," Cynthia laughed, kissing him gently. "You could learn a thing or two from me. I'm the master of having serious relationships that never get too serious."

It was snowing heavily when they got into Andrew's old car. It was late on a Saturday afternoon. And no sooner had they got onto the old Bomber Road (so named because the expressway had been built from Detroit to a huge bomber plant [Willow Run] during the Second World War), than the windshield wipers quit, dead in the midst of what had become a blinding snowstorm. There were no service stations in the area, so Andrew decided to power his wiper by hand.

With the driver's window open, and hugging the steering wheel, he reached around the corner of the windshield and began to move the wiper arm manually to keep one side of the windshield clear. "I'm not the nervous type, but I think you're making me nervous," Cynthia yelled with some concern.

"Don't worry. I rode through some Tennessee mountains hitchhiking, with a driver who was doing worse than this."

"If we get killed, will you promise to hold onto me til we get wherever we're going?"

"We won't get killed."

"You're always so sure of yourself... That really juices me," her voice still raised against the outside noise.

And so he drove about 20 miles with his left arm stretched to its limit making the wiper work.

"I can't see a thing," Cynthia said in a dramatic pitch at one point. The wiper on her side didn't work at all. The snow caked heavily over the entire windshield in front of her. "It's worse when you can't see. It's like driving in a coffin."

"Well," Andrew joked. "You can't say I'm not exciting."

"You're too exciting," she yelled with a worried laugh.

But they arrived without mishap. Andrew dropped her off at her parents' home along the Detroit River in Grosse Isle, then went on to the Southwest side of Detroit to see Joe and Jessica on West Fort Street. Even though he had worn gloves, his left hand and wrist were half frozen when he arrived. Jessica gave him a bowl of chicken soup. For a while before he ate it, he held his hand and wrist over the warmth of the gentle steam, until he felt his blood warmed up again.

*

Making love with Cynthia was an original experience of fresh discovery. There was something easy and relaxed, comfortable between them, a deep kinship touched by intertwining streams of life experiences—a sense of peace and security. He told her about it, and she told him she felt the same thing. "Identical," she said. "Spooky."

There was none of the previous sexual tension of their relationship, as though it had never existed. From the time Andrew came to her door, bearing a gift on Christmas Eve, they moved along in the process of discovery in an almost casual progression.

"Aphrodite is the goddess of sex" Cynthia said. "I want to explore all the chambers of her boudoir."

"I'm a born explorer."

"I like a lot of foreplay," she said.

"So do I," he said.

"I could do the whole thing on foreplay."

"I came with expectations too," he laughed.

In kissing, Cynthia had a way of moving her lips so that a maximum amount of the most tender and sensitive flesh came in contact with his lips. She reminded him of Laura. He tried to mirror what she had done, and after a few tries was able to do it.

"Bravo," she whispered. "You're the first man in my life who's ever really kissed back."

"I'm learning at your feet."

"We'll get there, too, after a while. You can work your way down, inch by inch."

"You first," he whispered.

"You've been like a rock ever since we started. I better take care of that right away," she said.

Cynthia was so skilled she could have given lessons to Miss Whittle. And she wanted it all. She liked the taste of it, she said. "Good to the last drop."

They rested for a while and let the aroma of expensive brandy linger in their mouths. Andrew continued the long foreplay.

"My turn," he said.

"Christmas is for giving," she said.

"Giving and receiving."

"Which do you like best?" she asked.

"I think if I had to choose, I would choose giving."

"I like it both ways. Giving and receiving. Back and front. Up and down. Top and bottom. Do you think I'm bisexual?"

"You're so much woman it wouldn't occur to me that you could share yourself with anyone but a man."

"Well, I haven't yet. But the thought intrigues me. Women know things about love no man could ever know."

"Do you really think you could do it?"

"Would you think less of me?"

He held her tightly as he whispered. "I have such a deep and permanent connection with you, nothing you could ever do would make me feel less about you. I place no conditions on you, and never will."

"Would you be willing to explore with me?"

"Right now, all I want to explore is you. There are depths within you that are still mysterious."

"I'm going to keep my offer on the table," she smiled.

And for a long time they explored each other with lips and

throbbing fingers, saying no words, almost in a time cocoon. And when Andrew reached for a condom, she brushed it aside. "I wouldn't dream of letting <u>any</u> barrier come between us. I want to feel your raw, naked power."

But Andrew hesitated, remembering Laura. "Are you sure? Really sure?"

"Trust me," she said.

Andrew proceeded. He liked her description of "raw, naked power."

"You're unusually small," he said.

"You're not claustrophobic, are you?" she laughed.

"I'm not afraid of tight places," he laughed

"I told you a long time ago, but you were too much of an idiot to listen—I was blessed with nature's gift."

"Getting to know you in this way, adds a whole new dimension to our relationship," he said.

"A very large dimension," she laughed.

But, for all of her experience, and the sensuousness of her nature, Cynthia was unable to reach a glorious climax, except after prolonged ministrations. As highly fluid as she had been in the beginning, she was now on the verge of losing all lubricative assistance.

"Should we add some saliva?" he whispered.

"No, not yet. Later, yes. Right now, just be patient with me. When it gets a little dry and sore the pain makes me high." She was whispering in his ear, all the while increasing the rhythm of her breathing. "I love your firmness," she whispered. "I love to feel you hurting me like this."

But she seemed to move <u>into</u> the pain, even embrace it. She began to move vigorously. Now her eyes were alive, wide open, with strained delight, and by the increasing rhythm of her breathing, Andrew knew she was almost ready. She pushed her lips hard and open against his mouth, shoving her tongue so deeply into him, the length of it surprised him. She was breathing in blurted gasps thought her nose. She suddenly stiffened, with every muscle in her body clenched as she whipped the shy beast out of its cage. And it came out with a lunging roar, first into his mouth, then with terrible shouts against his neck, mixed cries of anguished-near pain and extreme pleasure. She made so much noise Andrew thought the neighbors would come over to investigate.

And in her awesome, threshing conclusion, she held him more tightly than he had ever been held before and bit his neck so hard it drew blood.

"You give me everything I need," she gasped. "I knew you would be a wonderful lover."

Andrew was still coming down from the experience, gathering his breath. He felt the blood seeping slowly from his neck wound, and in a little while as he lifted himself over to her side, several drops of blood fell onto her lips. She licked the blood with considerable satisfaction, then moved her lips against his neck to suck the wound.

"I'm sorry, my darling, ever so sorry," she whispered. "I didn't mean to bite so hard."

"It's okay," he whispered.

"I love to suck your blood. It's my nature. I love to mingle it with my spit and heal you," she spoke quietly as she sucked and sucked gently at the open wound. "You don't mind me drinking your blood, do you darling? It tastes so warm and salty sweet. Your blood on my lips juices me all over again. I think I'm part vampire."

"Whatever pleases you," he said, holding her close, running his fingers through her beautiful hair.

"When I put my spit into the wound it will heal you," she said.

The thought of it brought brief images of Skootchie-Skootchie into Andrew's mind. "Spit heals," he said.

"Suck and heal. That's me," she said.

Her lips were warm and sensuous against his neck. And as the bleeding stopped, he joked. "I thought vampires were from Transylvania."

"They have a few cousins in Hungary. I came from a long line of bloodsuckers."

"That's a gruesome image."

"Then just think of me as one who heals using fluids from her body."

Now they lay side by side, Andrew holding her, caressing her, she caressing him. She wrapped herself over him. She reached down to stroke him. "Did I hurt you? Did my dryness make you sore, too?"

"I should ask you the same question. I was afraid I was hurting you."

"It was a delicious pain," she said. "I don't know why I'm so slow."

"You are an amazing woman."

"It takes an amazing man to bring out the amazing woman. You are caressing a V.S.L."

"What's a V.S.L.?"

"A very satisfied lover. It doesn't get any better than this."

And that was only the beginning. During Christmas week, right into the New Year, they met like this and explored their passions in the most pleasurable way with each other.

At one point Cynthia hinted again that she had a girlfriend who might be interested in joining them. But Andrew demurred. "She's your type," Cynthia purred. "She's leggy, like me."

"I'll wait til you catch a small one," he joked.

"If you're serious, I also have a friend who's not even five feet. She's slender, terrific boobs, juicy nipples, beautiful eyes, and I think she wants to experiment with a threesome. She calls herself Lucky Linda. She says if you make it with her, she will bring you three years of luck."

"I'm not superstitious."

"She is so tiny, she's probably got a pussy tight as mine."

"I was just joking," he repeated. "You're tiny enough."

"I'll keep the offer on the table," she smiled.

On New Year's Eve, which they decided to celebrate alone, they built a fire in the fireplace, and sipped champagne as they felt the warming flames. Andrew held her close as the clock came upon midnight. "I feel I can do anything I want with you" he said.

The pleasant chime of the clock struck the new year as they kissed with deep passion. She spoke first.

"Andrew, we are <u>so</u> close. I feel the need to tell you everything, hold nothing back. This way I feel even closer to you. I'll tell you what's on my mind." She paused and held her gaze steadily into the depths of his eyes. "I'm wholly, entirely, absolutely yours, to do with whatever you want... I've never met a man like you. Don't you think we should get married? We are <u>so</u> much in tune."

"One step at a time," he smiled, returning her gaze.

She caressed him to a new state of arousal. "Andrew, two weeks ago I was halfway to heaven. Now I'm almost there. Won't you carry me over the threshold? Marry me and you'll never be hungry, or bored." She continued her caress.

"I care for you very deeply," he said. "I'm more comfortable with you—emotionally comfortable—than with almost anyone I can remember. When we make love, time disappears. There is only you. I can't think of you without wanting to hold you in my arms. I enjoy our relationship more than I can tell you. You are unique and precious. I can even tell you... I love you."

He hadn't planned to go that far. It just slipped out through the bubbles of champagne.

She stopped her caress, brought both hands up to hold his face. "I've waited forever to hear you say that. And when you say those words, with the richness of your voice, I get thrills all over. Up and down my spine. My nipples rise up to see what's happening. I get all juicy. Andrew, my darling, I love you too, with all my heart."

And for a while they held each other without speaking, and Andrew noticed there were tears along her cheeks. She did not sob, and let the gentle salty waters flow in running drops.

"What's to become of us?" she whispered.

"Only God knows," he whispered back.

"You once saved my life. Remember? In Indian tradition, that makes you responsible for me. Darling, I think you and God better get together and talk things out."

*

Back in school, now in January 1950, he resumed his old energies. His time with Cynthia had snapped him out of a quiet state of depression and loss of focus. He did care for her very deeply and was entirely comfortable with her, as she was with him. But he felt a bit uneasy about having uttered those three words to her. He had meant it when he said it, but what he thought he meant, and what she thought he meant would be somewhat different, and he knew it. He was doubtful he would be able to satisfy her expectations.

He wasn't sure where things would go with her. If they married, her father's wealth would be confining and limiting. There might be fewer options. He could foresee an early clash of wills with Cynthia's father, one that would be harmful to the marital relationship. Cynthia's father needed to control and Andrew would never submit to such control. It was as simple as that.

Cynthia wrote him right away in January.

Dear Love of my Life,

I'm writing this on the train. I want to hurry up and finish so I can think of you the rest of the way home. Darling, you may not know this, but you have a way with women. I feel so good about myself, about life, even about our prospects. In some subtle way you changed me. I'm a better woman than I was a month ago. And I bet you are totally unaware of this power you have. I bask in it and want more and more. What a lover you are—

Until Death and Resurrection,

Cynthia.

(PS - I know you almost never write letters, so I will understand—I think—if I don't hear from you. But you'd better write.)

Andrew wrote back. He wanted her to know she had helped him too. He wanted to harmonize his thoughts with hers. He was inherently much more reserved than she—just as passionate, but more quiet and controlled in expression—and he wanted to match her tone, to continue the sense of attunement they had found together.

Cynthia,

I miss you already, think of you all the time. You changed me too, snapped me out of the doldrums. For a while I felt like the Flying Dutchman, sailing over lost and forgotten seas, never to touch land. But you, in the sweet sincerity of your love, brought me to a landing place. I was at home with you and that's more of a compliment than I can ever explain. I miss every part of you, every part, your whole entire being. You are such an unusual woman. I soak with mellow spirit in the luxurious warmth of your love. And you know I return this to you in kind.

What a giant step we've taken.

Until whenever—

*

Andrew found he had a knack for journalism, and there were fundamental principles that would help him in his writing—

provided he held them in a loose rein. It would be easy to slip into stylistic ruts, without being aware of it. He liked his professors and instructors and enjoyed the assignments. But there was something missing for him. He began to feel a sense of impatience, a regathering of the old Cameron restlessness. He wanted to explore, see the world, learn firsthand about other peoples. If Mexico was non-reality, where next? He read a lot in his spare time to find clues that would lead him where he sensed he wanted to go. And at least, after much consideration he got it in his head he wanted to go to Australia. The thought would roll around in his mind for months, gathering strength. The thing about Australia was that it was on the other side of the world.

And this was his state of mind as winter ventured into spring, when three letters came, two from Laura, one more from Cynthia. Laura's first letter, in April, was brief, confessional.

Dear Andrew,

I hope you are okay. Charlene tells me you are doing fine. By now I'm sure you have forgotten me. But there's something inside of me I've got to say...

Forget I said what I said. Forget I blamed you for my own unruly heart. When I said I loved you I meant every word, but you know as well as I it could never be between us. It was wonderful while it lasted but we had to wake up to reality. What I lost we lost together, and that will always be a bond between us. Dear Andrew, what I really want to say is, I'm asking your forgiveness. Forgive me for telling you those horrid things in Vermont. I'm sorry I said you're going to burn. I was so upset when I said that. Only God knows what will happen to you, I don't... I want us to stay friends. You're really a first rate guy except in places where you're stupid.   Forget I said that.   I definitely want to be your friend for a long time.

Sincerely,

He wrote back:

Dear Laura,

Your letter aroused my heart.   I guess we've both become more mellow now.   What's gone is gone and we can never bring it back.   As you said, and I agree, it was wonderful while it lasted. There will always be a place in my heart for you.   There was a special bond between us that can never be entirely broken.   You ask for my forgiveness.   Of course you have it.   You didn't need to ask, it was there all along.   Slumbering in the chambers of our lost love.   Laura, we will always be friends.   Time and circumstance can never diminish the affection I still feel for you.

With fragrant memories,

Cynthia's letter came in May.

Andrew Darling—

It's a lovely night, full of the smells of spring.   A bit of rainy mist covers the grass and trees.   I've been walking for over an hour in the streets without any reason, just to walk and try to think, but as always, it's useless.   Maybe I shouldn't be writing this way, but the words just fall into that melancholy pattern without stumbling around in my head waiting for a smoother ride.   Maybe I shouldn't be writing to you at all about this.   At least not just yet.

Oh hell!   I wanted to write and now I can imagine what this letter sounds like.   Maybe if I were drunk I'd get out a masterpiece, but I'm too sober to write anything worthwhile.   I thought the night might improve my styling.   I even tried writing in the rain but it was washable ink and my words were lost as soon as I wrote them. Do you think there's a philosophical principle buried in this?

Dearest Andrew, to begin with, today has been about the most miserable of all days that I have lived. This morning I awoke early only to behold a glorious sight in my face—an abscess. It's been coming on since Monday morning. I think it's due to an emotional upset... I don't know whether or not you'd care to know, but nevertheless I'm going to tell you. My roommate, Ginger, doesn't even know. You see, I've met this fellow here who is really a Wheel. And, well, I guess I've been swept off my feet. At any rate, he and I went to his cottage last Sunday afternoon about five. I guess you know what followed...

Dear Andrew, I don't ask you to forgive—I don't even expect you to. I feel as if I don't get out of this place soon, I'm going to go insane... Lord, I'm way off the tangent.

What I've been trying to tell you is that my mouth is so large it looks like a kangaroo pouch. I can drink a glass of milk at three inches.

Today I was supposed to go to an all day picnic with the Delta Tau Deltas, but the farthest I ever got was to the hospital. I had my lip lanced and a shot of penicillin. Then I wended my footsteps homeward amidst a burst of uncontrollable tears—And I'll be damned if I didn't meet 20 people I knew on this first Memorial Day weekend. As a matter of fact, Ginger and I are the only ones on the floor staying this weekend. It's almost frightening it's so quiet...

At present I'm feeling a wee bit melancholy and just sitting and gazing at the sidewalk outside this window where I imagine you would walk if you came to see me.

Just now you feel so close I believe I can reach out and touch you.

Andrew, I miss you terribly.

(PS As the song says, I'm always true to you darling in my fashion.)

Andrew was both concerned and relieved. Concerned because her normally buoyant personality was showing clear signs of anxiety, self-consciousness, and depression. He remembered what she had written in January, how she said he left her feeling so good about herself. He thought if he were to go see her, spend some time with her, he could pull her back to shore. He called her right away, was able to reach the sorority. But Ginger said she was out with her new crush. "She's fine now. She looks good. She bounced back. She's in love…"

Even before the phone call, Andrew was relieved because Cynthia was now moving on de-escalating the growing bond of forming love between them. He was relieved because he would no longer have to fulfill a set of expectations that had grown beyond his ability to master. He felt an unexpected release, a new sense of freedom. The prospect of marriage was now just an old memory.

*

Laura's final letter came a few days later.

Dear Andrew,

Can I call you friend again? You said it would be all right. I just have to tell you my news. I've met the most wonderful guy. He's everything I always dreamed of. And he's <u>Catholic</u>, so no fights! I always felt so bad when we were fighting about religion. You, I'm sure, can appreciate better than anyone else what a relief that is for me.

Nicky speaks French fluently. This is another connection I guess I was always seeking, but I had put it out of my mind. Love is a whole different experience when you do it in French. There are subtleties the English language has never mastered.

Oh, and I should tell you, Nicky knows the name of every insect, every flower, every bird. It's like traveling with an instant encyclopedia.

I also want you to know—and this is very important—I told Nicky everything. I <u>had</u> to tell him. Confession is in my soul. I just <u>hate</u> this need to confess. But he was wonderful about my sins. He's a relaxed Catholic.

I guess that's all for now. I am definitely infatuated with Nicky. He's in ROTC at Dartmouth. He will graduate a year ahead of me, in 1951. I don't know what his military obligations are exactly, but we plan to be married after I graduate.

It's <u>so</u> good to know that we have remained friends, that there are no leftover hard feelings,

Affectionately,

The combination of the two letters, one on the heels of the other, somehow catalyzed Andrew's restlessness into a full-scale decision. He would drop out of school and travel the world, working and earning his way, learning all he could about other people, trying to become a writer. Beginning with Australia. He wrote Laura a brief note wishing her and Nicky every happiness in the world and told her he was moving to Australia. He had made inquiries with the Australian Consulate and found that Australia would welcome him. Their motto was Populate or Die! Australia would pay for two-thirds of his passage and guarantee him a job if he agreed to remain in the country for two years.

Chapter 4

A strange mixture of melancholy and excitement came over him and lasted for weeks. Laura was now gone—definitely. Cynthia was now off to new adventures and affairs. Joe and Jessica, patient rocks of common sense and stability, would hold the fort at home.

As he began to make arrangements for his journey, he thought he should try to see Zeedie one last time. She had never called or written. Maybe, he thought, he had inherited his reluctance to write from her. Joe said she was still at Sarah's. Andrew called and Zeedie told him she would be home Saturday afternoon.

Driving across town to see her, his heart mingled with heaviness, anxiety, and anticipation, he wondered what he should say to her, other than his travel plans. As in times before, he dressed in slacks and tie and jacket. He didn't know why he felt the need to do it—Detroit was a blue jeans town—but for a long time he had felt a sense of formality in their relationship, a feeling of apartness and estrangement that came over him like a deep loneliness when he allowed himself to think about it. It seemed the estrangement could not be altered. But he had long since mastered the technique of quickly shucking it off. He would not succumb to such feelings. They could drown him. He would stay in the sunshine, stay in the light.

Zeedie seemed to share the sense of formality. She was

dressed to go out, she explained. She was now working steadily as a taxi dancer at Tree's Studio. Long gone were her days as a welder, and the steady pay and benefits. The men returning from the war had taken back their jobs. Lovers had come and gone, with promises and hope, but all had abandoned her after a time.

"I'm beginning to feel nervous about my age," she told Andrew.

He looked at her more closely. She still had a rather dramatic hint of wildness in her persona. She had maintained a svelteness in her figure. But he could see that she was now wearing a little too much makeup and had begun to dye her hair to an even blacker shade. He also saw that little wrinkle lines were growing a bit more noticeable in her face, especially around the eyes and mouth and along the lines of her neck. But she was still an attractive woman.

"I need to be attractive to hook the man," she said. "I've got a lot of steady customers."

"You look fine," Andrew said.

"Well, how've you been?"

"I've been in school. I'm going to Australia."

"Why so far?"

"That's part of the reason. It's so far."

"One of my customers wants to marry me and move to Canada."

"Why don't you?"

"Canada is dumb."

He wasn't sure what to say next. He had no script or agenda, and he felt the conversation was a little strained, like discussing the weather when issues of life and death are swirling all around. "In school, the day before I left, I had an experience that really moved me… I met a Chinese student who was just graduating. By now he's on his way back to China… I met him on the stairs. He was just standing there alone, and he was weeping. I thought he was hurt, or some hard blow had struck his life. I went up to him, put my hand on his shoulder. 'Why the tears?' I asked… he was slow to answer. Then he finally said, 'I'm ashamed to go home.' I asked him, 'Why? You've just graduated at the top of your class.' And he said, 'In America I have lost my manners…In China, if I were to meet my mother on the stairs I would pause and bow respectfully until she passed…I have forgotten, in the rush of America, how to do that…I am afraid my mother will regard me as an uncouth barbarian.' "

"Why doesn't he just learn to walk slower?" Zeedie asked. Andrew made no answer for a while. Then he tried to change the mood with a joking comment. "Can you imagine me pausing and bowing to you if I met you on the stairs?"

"Sure I can imagine that," Zeedie said in serious response. "I'm your mother. Mothers are supposed to get some respect."

Andrew had not come here planning to say this, but the words burst out of his heart. "…Every time you showed some tenderness toward me, my heart would leap with hope."

Zeedie put her hand on his arm in a gesture of affection. "My sweet, dear boy. That's what I would expect."

Chapter 5

Earlier this year (1950), Dean Acheson, Secretary of State, had given a speech in which he said that South Korea was outside the United States' area of interest.

*

On June 25, North Korea invaded South Korea. Separated by the 38th parallel, arbitrarily decided by the victors at the end of WWII, what followed immediately was a UN Security Council declaration that North Korea was an aggressor. (Russia was absent from the Council meeting). President Truman immediately led the formation of a coalition of UN member nations to launch a "Police Action"—he would not call it a war— to stop the aggression. He would never call it a war.

Andrew responded immediately to the war news. He had been listening to The Warsaw Concerto when he heard it, and his heart was already quickened. He abandoned travel plans. His only thought was to go to war, to do his part. Even as he formed the words in his mind, realizing as they lined themselves up across his brain, they sounded corny. Nevertheless, this was his sincere thought:

If my country is at war, then I am at war. I'm young and strong. I should be right in the thick of it.

With the themes of the Warsaw Concerto still echoing in his mind, he thought for a moment he understood the deep yearning of the human race. He understood once again at a deeper level—life has enduring significance. It was almost as if World War II had not fully ended. There was this one last great battle to be fought. Truman, who was otherwise courageous, did not seem to have the courage to call it a war. In 1950, fresh on the heels of WWII, "war" was a deadly political word.

Andrew chose the infantry because it had been described as the Queen of Battle. He chose it because Ernie Pyle's columns from the front lines and particularly his book, <u>Brave Men</u>, reverberated in his soul. He chose it because Bill Mauldin's wartime cartoons about Willy and Joe in foxholes, and particularly his book, <u>Up Front</u>, portrayed a steady strength and nobility of spirit among the infantrymen that reached deeply into the ancient Cameron roots of his imagination. He felt a keen sense of identification and wanted to be one of them. To share the load, to share the foxholes, the dangers, the hard burdens of battle. To help his country.

The fact that it would be a difficult, wrenching, grueling way to live only whetted his appetite. He had no desire to kill. Killing did not enter his mind. Somehow, the picture of mortal combat played across the fields of his thought only in terms of great hardships and heroic struggle and dignity. The idea of pulling a deadly trigger, or plunging a bayonet into someone's chest, never became part of the mental imagery that struck his mind. In his otherwise logical thought processes, he never connected his desire to fight all the way through to its logical conclusion.

He thought it would be romantic to parachute into battle, so he enlisted in the Airborne, but not before making an important clarification.

"I want to go to Korea," he told the recruiter.

"Oh, don't you worry. We'll get you there fast enough," the recruiter smiled.

"Is that a promise?" Andrew asked seriously.

"That's a promise," the recruiter said seriously.

"You're sure I can get into combat—"

"Guaranteed! Sign here."

"Even if I'm in the Airborne?"

"The Airborne will get there ahead of everyone else," the recruiter chuckled.

There was one early struggle he had not anticipated. After the initial testing he was taken aside to talk about becoming an officer.

"You scored at the top on every test," he was told. "You would be a great candidate for OCS [Officer Candidate School]."

"I don't want to be an officer. I want to be a plain, foot-slogging infantryman."

"You're crazy. You would make a great officer."

He thought again of the images still fresh in his mind from Ernie Pyle and Bill Mauldin. It seemed to him if he became an officer he would skip over the essential heart and guts of ground warfare. Officers could never know the entire range of hardships and deprivation endured by the men they commanded.

"My mind's made up. I'm joining the army, not a club."

"What if we give you some specialized training for a job in intelligence?"

"That's rear echelon. I want to fight."

"You'll change your mind. The test scores will still be in your file."

"I won't change my mind. I'm joining Ernie Pyle's army, Bill Mauldin's army."

He had a similar conversation months later. The army assigned him to take a Leader's Course after basic training, both in Fort Knox, Kentucky, home of the 3rd Armored Division. Following his performance there, and more testing, he was pressed once more to sign up for OCS. And once again he said no with the same firmness. He could not imagine how an officer would ever know the full depth of the experience a foot soldier would come to know. Andrew wanted the whole thing, undiluted.

*

On August 23, 1950, General MacArthur declared: "The boys will be home by Christmas."

In September 1950, George C. Marshall, Secretary of Defense, sent a cable to MacArthur: "We want you to feel unhampered tactically and strategically to proceed north of the 38th Parallel."

By November 1950, the Chinese felt sufficiently threatened to join the battle. An overwhelming number of Chinese soldiers drove the UN forces almost back to Pusan, where the UN forces held on with tenacious strength. In October two out of three Americans supported MacArthur's plan, and wanted to capture all of Korea. [By January 1951, two out of three Americans were in favor of getting totally out of Korea.]

*

Andrew began to smoke. It seemed a natural part of his new

life. He also thought it would make him look tougher. He remembered the scene in the movie <u>Wake Island</u>, where John Garfield pulled an air-cooled 30-caliber machine gun out of its tripod, held it against his hip, and with cigarette dangling from the corner of his mouth, started shooting down attacking Japanese fighter planes. The cigarette added to the authenticity of the image. Andrew thought he would try cigarettes for a while, then quit. He could quit anytime he wanted, he thought. He started with Camels, switched to Lucky Strikes, then back to Camels. Camels punched up the lungs with a greater intensity.

Army life was built to accommodate smokers. During the hard training and field exercise and road marches, whenever there was a ten-minute break, the noncom in charge would invariably say, "smoke'em if you got'em." Protocol demanded that cigarettes be "field stripped" before throwing away the butt, slicing with a fingernail the white tissue that held the tobacco over the ground. [This was long before filter tip cigarettes became common, except for an off-beat brand or two which no one smoked.] Even in the latrines there were reminders. One sign said: Please don't throw cigarette butts in the urinals. It makes them soggy and hard to light.

Police call every morning would ensure every stray butt and scrap of paper was retrieved from the grass fields, and sandy lots and streets surrounding the barracks. The noncom in charge of the cleanup detail would invariably send forth the same charge. "Let's get this field cleaned up. All I want to see are assholes and elbows." But one of the more colorful noncoms prefaced it a little differently: "Let's get all this <u>derbis</u> [sic] cleaned up."

The training program was moderately difficult, but Andrew was already in good physical condition. Road marches with full pack up Agony Hill and Misery Hill tested muscles he had not previously exercised in this way. But the hardest part was the army's insistence on total submission to given orders. Even though he had volunteered it was very, very difficult for him to make the adjustment. He did it but was beginning to learn to curse under his breath. In no time at all, he seemed to be cursing all the time, sometimes out loud.

He enjoyed the barnyard humor of his new acquaintances, especially those from the rural South.

"Tommy told me you wasn't fit to slop with the hogs, but I stuck up for you. I said you was."

He learned that shooting is not simply a matter of aiming and pulling the trigger. You also had to estimate wind velocity and force of gravity. If you zero-in your rifle at a hundred yards and are shooting at something at a greater distance, the bullet may drop as much as several feet below where you're aiming. Even a slight breeze can shave the bullet sideways by a foot or two. They were not using telescope sights, and the old-timers taught how to use "Kentucky windage." You wet the end of your thumb with spit hold it into the air, twist it until you feel the bite of wind, and from the complex interaction of moving air calculate direction and velocity of wind, then aim and adjust accordingly.

But the old-timers said more. "You have to squeeze the trigger. Don't jerk it off. Like little cow tits."

For all his trying, Andrew could never get it 100% right. He was very close, but not 100%. He qualified as Sharpshooter, his score a single point below Expert Rifleman. He wished he could do it over because he felt he had the feel of it now: the spit, the calculus, the cow tits, everything. But there were no second chances.

He didn't ask to go to Leader's Course, but the army assigned him there. He had heard there were airborne soldiers already in Korea. He wanted to get through jump school quickly and ship out. The Leaders' Course assignment would be another delay. But there was no way he could refuse the assignment. During the final month of Leaders' Course Andrew was made field first sergeant, on temporary status, and for the time being would remain in the company. It was on-the-job training with the task of breaking in some new recruits. He tried to teach them everything he had been taught. There was one stock reason for everything: It's going to save your life in combat.

This thing works like this and you better remember it because it's gonna save your life in combat. This maneuver goes like this and you better remember it because it's gonna save your life someday. First-aid is rendered this way. Rifles are assembled and disassembled this way—you do not call them guns—and you better learn how to do it in the dark. You fire them like this. You hold your arm like this. You clean them like this. This is a mortar. It works like this. This is a machine gun... and so forth.

You try your best to teach them to make their paycheck last through an entire month. Many of them would run out of money by week three and fall victim to the camp predators, led by the smooth-talking and crafty Slick (the only name anyone knew). Slick or his cohorts would lend "five for seven-and-a-half." Five dollars for seven-fifty a week later, at payday. But Andrew never knew if anyone had taken his advice.

You teach them when and how to salute. Day and night, you teach. You teach them dismounted drill, tell them it is important, how it teaches you to obey commands quickly, instinctively, that it is the quickest, most efficient way of moving large bodies of men from place to place in an orderly fashion. You teach them how to shoot, and about the little cow tits.

"Was you in combat, Sarge?"

"No."

"Then how do you know what you's saying is true?"

"I know," you answer, pretending to be all-knowing, pretending to be a tough old soldier. Wondering: How does anyone know anything? People teach you, but the teaching may range all the way from perfect knowledge to the twisted and ridiculous, depending on the teacher. Then there are the things you read, but you have to be careful there, too. Strange things often appear in print.

Then there is your own experience and how deeply you comprehend the meaning of your experience. That, at least, is one secure foundation. But how do you know when you are being led toward the true, the beautiful, the good? Is there some inner voice that whispers: This is the way? How do you struggle through the confusion? How do you know what you know?

Cleanliness, strangely, is the easiest and yet the hardest thing to teach. You can make them clean up, but you cannot make them want to if they have never had a lifetime of wanting to. Nothing is so clean as a military post on Saturday morning before inspection. You cannot command the gods to stop the dust from falling or dirt and mud from splashing, or soldiers from throwing lit cigarette butts around. So everything is picked up or cleaned or oiled or painted, and if it is not, as the old saying goes, salute it.

You lead them into muck and snow and show them how to set up in bivouac so the rain will not wash in and drown them in the night. You march them endlessly, up and down Misery Hill and Agony Hill, hoisting the same field pack they carry, running back and forth alongside them as they slog yelling "close it up!" the responsibility of leadership overcoming the first half of your own fatigue.

"Close it up, dammit! Close it up! Hustle." Growl at them. "Hauugghhhut! Move!"

One incident in Leaders' Course unsettled him a bit, until he got it under control. After morning calisthenics he marched his platoon to the mess hall for chow. It was a biting cold Kentucky morning. The mess hall had not yet opened. He placed the group in line outside the door, then went inside briefly to find out how soon the doors would open.

In the minute he was gone, one of the recruits—a smiling, timid boy (Raymond)—had stripped naked and was standing in the cold air with nothing on but a smile. Andrew had never encountered this kind of behavior before. His mind raced through possible decisions about how to proceed. He wasn't sure what to do, only that he had to get the young recruit dressed immediately.

"Put on your clothes," Andrew told him.

The boy simply smiled.

"Put on your clothes…" But the boy would not respond, only smile.

What in the hell do I do now? Andrew thought. Then an idea struck him. "Pick up your sock…." He did. "Put it on your left foot." And the boy responded and did as he was told. By now the mess hall doors had opened, and all the recruits except the naked boy had rushed in. Andrew thought he had hit upon a solution. "Now pick up your other sock… Put it on your right foot." The boy complied. And in this way Andrew was able to get him fully dressed again, article by article. And when he was done, Andrew led him to the Orderly Room and called for a medic to take the boy for psychiatric evaluation, and probable discharge. The boy would not answer questions, only smile. Give them something to do, Andrew mused to himself, trying to assimilate the experience. The smallest thing they can do.

Before he graduated from the course, he was called aside. The weeks had passed quickly and winter was full on. The recruits were not yet fully trained, but Andrew's orders for jump school had arrived. On the evening prior to his departure the company commander (Locker) came into the barracks, to Andrew's room.

"Put on your jacket and come outside," the captain said.

They walked together to the Orderly Room and the captain motioned him to sit beside the big pot-bellied stove in the center of the room. He sorted through papers on his desk. There was a big square sandbox around the stove, about six inches high. It was a quiet winter evening, long, dark, and the faint orange glow from the iron sides of the stove gave Andrew a sense of peace that wrestled with his apprehension. Why was he here?

"Cigarette?" the captain offered, drawing up a chair.

Andrew accepted, still feeling uneasy.

The captain pulled off a broom-straw, which he ignited against the hot side of the stove, and lit the two cigarettes. "Tonight," he began, "I have one sergeant, two corporals, and four PFCs coming in on orders to the company."

Andrew nodded.

"We're getting an awful lot of men in, and we just aren't equipped to train them adequately… I've had a close eye on you, Cameron. You seem to be the man I want. Stay here. I can arrange it. I'll put the stripes on you very quickly."

In the most diplomatic way possible, Andrew declined. "I want to go to Korea, sir. That's why I enlisted."

"If you want rank, I can give you the rank right here."

"With all respect to you, sir, I'm looking for something else."

"What?"

"I'm not even sure only that I feel a very powerful drive to go there and do my share of the fighting."

"It's your war, Cameron," the captain said, disgruntled.

Andrew stood, saluted. "Thank you, sir."

*

Jump School in Fort Benning, Georgia, was the hardest test of physical endurance he had yet experienced. The winter weather offered some relief the old-timers said. "You oughtta see this place in July, your spit will boil before it ever hits the ground. You got it easy."

Nevertheless, even though he thought he was in good

condition. Jump School training demanded a whole new level of physical performance. "You got it easy," an old regular said. You oughtta see how the Rangers train. They jump them off the back of trucks at 30 miles an hour."

Andrew had never heard of the Rangers.

"There's a whole company of them in Korea now, the 9th Ranger Company, getting their asses kicked good."

"I want to join them," Andrew said.

"Too late," he was told. "Besides, you're not ready yet."

By the third morning of training it takes you and almost everybody else several minutes to rise off the cot and work the muscles grudgingly past the pain. You learn to run with a heavy backpack, until the brain is fogged with sweat and the legs feel like cast iron. All you can think of is don't wash out, no matter what. Take a salt tablet, curse through salty lips. Curse in cadence.

The corporal running beside you shouts to the platoon: "Count cadence…count!" He snaps his words. His lungs are kegged like whisky vats and he is breathing easily. You sing along, at 180 steps a minute. After the twelfth mile the fatigue is so deep the eyeballs ache in their sockets, the lungs are desperate. The second wind has given out. You hope for a third, but it doesn't come. Someone beside you mutters, barely audible: "Christ Jesus, keep me from washing out." You finish the run, after the fourteenth mile, but not the punishment. The corporal smiles with savage delight. He needs to display his displeasure about some unnamed thing. You know what's coming.

"Drop for 10! Down! Weak sonsabitches! All of you! Quit,

why donchya? You can quit right now! You don't have to take this shit! I don't want no quitters here! Go on back if you wanna quit! Nobody gives a damn, not a goddam, not for nothin'! Sign your name on the quit slip! However, if you can even spell the word, get out! We don't want anybody here that can even spell the word!"

The corporal thinks the 10 pushups are too sloppy. He orders 10 more, then 10 more. "You'll keep doin' it til you get it fuckin' right."

You attempt 10 perfect pushups; the backpack feels double its former heavy weight. Then 10 more. Perfection is the aim. You want the corporal to believe you are worthy to jump out of an airplane.

A strong remnant of the old army had remained in uniform, and those who had seen combat seemed especially toughened and strong. There had been some talk in the press of a "new army... the kind of army mothers can be proud to send their sons into." But the old regulars were suspicious. "New army" meant "soft army" to them, and they were not about to let it happen. They would entrench themselves against this new enemy—softness, indulgence, fuzzy lines of discipline. They would stick to the old-time training rules. Very physical. Fist-to-fist confrontations when necessary.

Many of the old-timers belonged to the first airborne division ever to be formed, and they liked to remind young soldiers that it was tougher then. Parachutes didn't open as easily then as they did now, sometimes not at all.

The hardcore corporals and sergeants who ran the training

program were united in one basic belief. There is only one way to condition a man to jump out of an airplane into the enemy's tonsils. First, kick in the spine. If he winces too hard, make mincemeat out of him, wash him out. And if he does not wince put him on his hands and toes all day in the "leaning rest position," with a heavy weight on his back. And if one button scrapes the ground, then hand him a Quit Slip and send him back to a straightleg unit where this kind of thing is permitted. Destroy the old body cell by cell. Rebuild the new body to the Army's liking, cell by cell.

And if he gets angry and spits in your eye, then wash him out for having no discipline. And if does not, then run him around the airfield for being stupid, being careful to carry the same load as he carries, so he will understand you are one tough sonofabitch.

And when he is beaten into all but a corporeal wreck, put him in the swinging harness and watch to see if he winces when the straps crush his testicles into a pulpy deformity. And if he still does not wince, teach him how to jump and how to land, and take him up on a plane and make him jump five times. And if he hesitates, wash him out. And if he makes it, give him a pair of shiny paratrooper wings and tell him without words he can lick any five men alive, singly or all at once.

In Fort Benning the body is torn down cell by cell, then rebuilt into a fighting machine. And in the same process the mind is torn down and rebuilt. As one rebuilds, so does the other. The mind becomes accustomed to obeying commands.

Jump School is a dangerous school, not because the danger

of jumping is relatively great—almost all the parachutes open now, and the rattletrap planes used for training usually land before their defects are discovered. The danger is that if you wash out, you become permanently impaired, psychologically damaged in some way, notwithstanding the power of rationalization. You are a long way from Sparta, so you sublimate your complaints in jokes and bravado. The only way to come to this place is to volunteer.

"Now," the corporal said after the 14 miles, after he had halted them and commanded them to rest in place. Only half the platoon that had begun this run was left. "Is there anybody here which did not volunteer? If there is anybody which did not volunteer, would he be kind enough to step forward?"

No one steps. "Okay. That's settled. You're all volunteers. Now..." his steely eyes survey the group. "Is there anybody here which would like to quit at this point?"

The quitters have quit. "Platoon!" he commands. "Ten-Hut!" He pauses, looks for some small sign of evil. Finds one. "That man in the second rank which wiped his tongue on his lips, drop for 10!" The second rank drops for 10 pushups. "That man which wiped his tongue on his lips," he repeats with a hint of menace, "drop for 10!" Everybody else drops for 10. If you are accused and do not drop, then it is 20, and 10 is better.

"You are all looking a little peaked." Then he shouts, "What's the matter, troopers? Does your pussy hurt?" He scowls in scorn, then continues. "Is there any man here which is not ready to run another 14 miles?" No answer from the ranks. Certainly you would run for another 14, should you be asked.

"Then I say you're all purty stupid, and if you're gonna be that stupid then I say drop for 10...20...30!" Second by split second, he jams up the numbers, but after these weeks of training everyone is accustomed to the fast count and are all down by 20.

Up again. Sweat still running down across the eyes, the brain shut down of all thoughts except to survive and make it through, watching the corporal walk like god among them. Although he was only 24, he had made one combat jump in the Pacific before the war ended and had jumped more than 200 times since. He created an image of one who would outrun them, outfight them, and out blaspheme them. And he hinted that if it came to bayonets and rifle butts, he would come up with the bloodiest buttplate. He walked that way among them. Like an Old Testament god with power to punish and eternally condemn, power to wash them into hell, power to deny them a chance to earn their wings.

He stopped in the third rank. "Soldier, how'd you like the 34-foot tower?"

"It was fun, sir."

"I ain't a sir. Drop for 10 for insulting a corporal."

And to another man, "Whaddya think of the 250-foot tower?"

"It was fun, corporal."

"Soldier, you ain't here to have fun. You're here to function! Drop for 10!"

So it went, the average number of pushups being done each day, each man measuring above 400, in addition to all the regular training, the instruction, the calisthenics, the running, the inspections, the discipline—taut as banded steel. The company had begun with 700, and 400 had washed out. They had not yet set foot in a plane.

"I'm gonna dismiss you for chow," the corporal said. "At ease!" The mess hall was two miles away. "And the last man which arrives I am personally going to kick the crap out of!" He stood back, drew in his big lungs. "Platoon! Ten-Hut!"

"Snap to!" he commanded. "Drop for 10!" he commanded.

He waited. And when they were up again—swiftly—he squinted at them. "Now, goddammit, this time when I call you to attention, I wanna hear them assholes sucking wind... Platoon! Ten-Hut! That's better." He paused. "Dismissed!"

No one came last. Everybody arrived at once, in a rushing throng, in the same yelling assemblage of bodies, so that perhaps one man's arm lagged an inch or two behind another man's foot. It was improbable, physically impossible. But it would be hard to pick out a last man. They were all there in the same place at the same time waiting noisily for chow. The corporal grinned.

Chapter 6

They would jump on Monday, Tuesday, twice on Wednesday, finish on Thursday; five in all. As the time approached, Andrew thought about it, tried to feel unafraid, but could not eliminate the undigested pit of fear in his stomach. He imagined the primary scenario, going down in a streamer, fighting to shake wind into it, fighting to get the reserve chute open in time. Or caught in the prop-blast and being rolled into your chute. It was unlikely to happen, but he was mentally prepared. The thought that propelled him forward was simple. Friday he would get his wings. Saturday morning inspection, Saturday night a lot of drinking. Sunday some rest. By Monday, he would be on the way to Korea. Or so he thought.

The schedule for the first jump was on a brilliant sunlit day, with only a small untroublesome unusually warm wind. The old C-46's, with doors on both sides, were lined up along the airstrip of the large field, their shadows already dark against the morning sun.

Everyone strapped on a parachute and an emergency chute. The parachutes were standard issue T-7 series designed to get you down as fast as possible without killing you. The instructors said the impact of landing was equivalent to jumping off a 15-foot wall. But everyone had been trained in how to cushion the jolt of landing. You made a PLF [parachute landing fall]. The PLF was developed to roll as much as possible into the shock, quickly absorbing the crushing strength of it over specific lines of impact along your body. That was the theory. In perfect conditions it worked.

The instructors pointed out that these would be easy jumps, from 1,000 feet. "In combat you'll be jumping with lots of extra gear and weapons and ammunition. Maybe more. You'll have to get down as fast as possible so you can't be machine gunned in the air. The planes will come in in stacked waves. The highest stack will be more than 1,000 feet, but when you get down to the lowest stack, you're maybe jumping from 500 feet. If you end up in the lowest stack, throw away your emergency chute. You won't have time to use it."

Andrew's harnesses were tight and he had to stoop a bit to accommodate their grip, carefully ensuring his testicles would not be obliterated. He shuffled into one of the planes with others in his group, watching their eyes for a sign of fear, watching for any trembling of the hands. They all joked with buoyant energy and bravado.

"I want your boots when you die" they said to one another.

"Fuck you, man, you'll need them 'cause you're gonna piss all over your own."

"You're gonna catch your lunch today."

"I got your lunch man—swingin'."

"Never saw a Tootsie Roll swing before."

"Do you know what old paratroopers dream about?"

"No, what?"

"Jumping into 10 acres of tits."

One of them broke into the old paratrooper song, to the tune of Onward Christian Soldiers.

> "He jumped into the propblast
> And through the wind he tore.
> His balls were under his legstraps,
> He ain't' gonna jump no more.
> Glory, glory what a helluva way to die,
> Glory, glory…"

With the C-46 engines running, and open doors and portholes, it was hard to hear anything less than a shout inside the plane. The little ball of fear inside his stomach had grown, like a dry sponge absorbing water. But he knew he did not show his fear, not did any of the others. They had come this far. They were in this place because they wanted to be. They were still yelling jokes and insults at each other, trying to be heard over the engine noise.

Sixteen men were aligned along each side of the plane, on bench seats. In the plane they were called sticks, 16 men to a stick. The Jumpmaster, taller than any of them, browner from sun and wind, yelling with a strong graveled voice, positioned himself between the doors, his hand on one of the two anchor line cables that ran the length of the interior. He wore only a free fall chute and looked out from time to time as the plane plunged through the morning air.

Andrew felt the rushing blast of wind through the open ports, grateful for it. The straps of his steel helmet were tight. The T-7 straps were tight, too tight to allow for any comfort. He checked his watch. Five minutes to go. He felt weak, as if any sudden movement would leave him too breathless to continue. He had to urinate. He had just done so half an hour ago, but the urge returned. Fear has a way of squeezing the bladder.

"Hey," someone was trying to shout over the noise, "if you get a streamer, try to land on your head, would you? I got my eye on your boots, and I don't want them full of shit." And those who hear it try to laugh, as though this were the only joke in the world and they had never heard it before. Except 50 times that morning.

"Talk to me through my tube!" someone shouts.

The Jumpmaster, scanning the terrain below, pulls his head in from the wind. "Get ready!" he blasts, louder than the engines. You grab your snap fastener and throw the static line over your arm, careful that it lies across rather than under the elbow so that it will not rip your arm off.

"Stand up and look up!" Now the little ball of fear becomes suddenly larger and attempts to consume the stomach. There is a feeling of some weakness in the legs. You wonder whether this was a good idea.

"Check your equipment!" You check the back of the man's chute in front of you. Someone checks yours behind you. You check your own equipment head to toe. You rattle the snap fastener against the anchor line cable. You adjust the straps around the testicles one more time. You bunch them out in front of the leg straps as much as possible.

"Sound off for equipment check!" The counting sequence comes down from the rear of the stick. The man behind you slaps your leg. He yells "Nine okay!" You yell "Eight okay!" as you slap the leg of the man in front of you. He yells "Seven okay!" as the count continues to the first man in the door.

"Is everybody happy?" the Jumpmaster shouts.

Everybody screams, "yeah, yeah, yeah!"

"Stand in the door!" the red light is still on. The sticks shuffle down tight toward the doors. The plane dips slightly, adjusting for the shifting weight. The motors roar harder as the plane struggles to find its rhythm again. The first man in the door pivots precisely. His hands, including the thumbs, are flattened straight along the outside surface of the plane. He looks straight ahead, crouches a little so he can leap with momentum.

The green light. "Go!"

For one second as you follow the quickly vanishing bodies into the vacant space in the door, you glimpse the green brown blob of earth below you. No thought is in your head except to go through that door. You pivot sharply at the door, grab the outer surface of the plane's skin, crouch swiftly and leap with all your might. The propblast from the propellers makes a gushing screaming cyclonic blast against your head.

You assume the position you have been taught to assume for all these weeks—head down low on your chest so the metal clips on the raisers won't tear the back of your skull off, elbows snug against the body, hands spread tight with the right heel of the palm resting in the handle of the reserve chute on your chest, feet and knees together, slightly bent.

The propblast catches the body like a mad tornado, hurtling it out, down. You glimpse the earth below. It is blurred for a moment, spinning slightly. And as you count: One thousand!

Two thousand! Three... The body snaps like the end of a whip. And the first sensation is one of quietness and well-being. Everything is still. Nothing roars. Nothing hurtles. The air around you appears strangely blue and thick, as you float through it at 20 feet per second. You wonder why you ever felt any fear in the plane. Hell, you could make 50 jumps a day. The stillness hums in quiet waves against your ears.

You reach up and grab the risers, look up and check the canopy for blown panels. You look around, slip to the left to clear somebody drifting in too close. A lot of soldiers, swinging like pendulums in the sky, blue and peaceful.

Treetop level. Assume landing position. Raise the eyes again, look straight ahead. Relax from the hips down, but keep the legs together, slightly bent at the knees, toes pointed downward. And in that rolling second when you make contact with the earth you do several things at once. Pull the risers down sharply so elbows are on the chest, arms protecting the face. Pivot instantly on the toes so that the calf hits the earth next, then thigh muscle, buttocks, and pushup muscle. Keep rolling on the back to absorb the shock. The swinging momentum of the chute may work to advantage or disadvantage in trying to absorb the landing shock over the greatest area of the body.

Now you get up swiftly and try to corral the chute like a runaway steer. Race along behind it as it picks up ground wind and tries to pull you. Get around in front. Collapse it. Flip the chest release, hit it. The harness falls away. Light a cigarette. For a moment or two watch the sky as others are jumping from later planes. Then, with bundled chute, run to the assembly area where trucks are parked and tell everybody you could make 50 jumps a day if it's this easy.

"I love to jump," Andrew said. "It's the second greatest physical thrill."

"What's the first?" someone asked.

Andrew smiled.

"The first time is easiest of all," an old regular said. "Because you don't know anything yet."

He never heard anybody yell "Geronimo" when they jumped, then or at any other time. That was movie fiction.

Tuesday, twice on Wednesday, Thursday, the same routine, with variations. There are blown panels, reserve chutes that won't open, men who hang on to their static lines as they leave the plane and have to be pulled desperately back in to go again, a few broken bones, a few men who freeze in the door and are not pushed out because it is only after you receive your wings such privileges are granted. Everything runs on schedule because the training school is well organized and intent upon its work. And almost all who may not jump have been weeded out in the network of that efficient screen long before they ever reached a plane.

Friday. Everybody lines up in company formation. There is a speech and wings are pinned. And for a little while afterward all the troopers glance down at them to see how they shine on their chests. Paratroop wings are commonly referred to among them, by oral tradition, as the "badge of honor."

Dawn, Monday morning. Orders are read, everyone is assigned to the Far East Command except Andrew and four others who are scheduled to join the 82nd Airborne.

Andrew swore under his breath, then aloud after the formation was dismissed. "I wanted to go," he said. "I thought I would just naturally go."

"I'll trade places with you," several said.

"I've got to get my orders changed. I want to go to Korea. That's why I enlisted."

"Nobody's gonna change your orders," they laughed.

"I'm gonna try."

But the company commander waved him off, as did Personnel. "Orders are orders," they said. "Your job is to obey them." Nothing would be done. "The army has its own logic," the CO explained.

It's going to be a lot tougher than I thought, Andrew cursed within himself.

Chapter 7

The 82nd Airborne Division, headquartered in Ft. Bragg, North Carolina, was being held in readiness for any outbreak of hostilities in Europe. It was usually referred to as "the famed 82nd Airborne," or "America's Guard of Honor." It had been designated as Eisenhower's Honor Guard while he maintained his presence as overall commander in Europe. It was regarded as an elite fighting unit. But none of this mattered to Andrew as he reported for duty.

He was assigned to a heavy weapons company, Company M ("Mighty Mike"), in the 504th infantry regiment. He would be an assistant gunner in a machine gun platoon.

Ace Benton, battle-hardened veteran of the Normandy invasion and beyond, served as first sergeant of M Company. His face was etched with lines of a strenuous life, but he was regarded as fair. He wore the presence of command easily. It showed in his lean and disciplined bearing and in his eyes. His eyes looked right into you.

One story about him had given him a legendary character. It was about a time when the company was performing a field exercise. They were all assembled in the shade of a grove of trees. Ace was teaching them. A bird in a nearby tree began to chatter so loudly, the noise interrupted Benton's lecture. He stopped, looked up at the bird with those penetrating eyes and the bird abruptly stopped its chatter and did not resume. The story circulated swiftly and became part of the Company M pride in the unit.

Almost everyone went by last name only, but Ace was usually referred to as Ace rather than Benton. Whenever he was off duty, he liked to chew tobacco. He would bite off a large plug of Red Man and hold it in the side of his cheek, from time to time leaving large, dark brown splotches of its juice in his spittoon or on the grass. It reminded Andrew of Zeedie.

Andrew went to Ace right away, to apply for transfer to Korea. He had heard about Ace's reputation for fairness.

"You can fill out the form," Ace told him, "but it won't get you anywhere. We got a manpower shortage."

"But they made a promise when I enlisted."

"Can't hold us responsible for somebody else's promise."

"But the recruiter was making a promise on your behalf."

"Wasn't on my behalf."

"I'm determined to go."

Ace surveyed him. "What for?" Ace was getting impatient. "The war is at a stalemate. Anything breaks in Europe you'll be on the plane. Hell, we get alerts regularly. Move out quickly with full equipment, ready to board, ready for action... Why do you want to go to Asia to fight gooks? French women are prettier, and the German women..."

Andrew's first application was returned within three weeks with a big red stamp: TRANSFER DISAPPROVED DUE TO CRITICAL SHORTAGE OF AIRBORNE PERSONNEL.

He immediately applied again.

*

The 82nd was what they had said it was, trim and disciplined, spit-shined. All troopers bloused their fatigues just above the ankle position, along the high jump boots that rose well into the calf muscle. A little more tightly crafted around the heels and ankles, the two versions of jump boots worn were Skymasters, with the more ordinary flatter toe, or Corcorans, with the exaggerated "Mickey Mouse" bulge over the toes. Both were permitted. Andrew preferred the Corcorans. They had a more dramatic appearance. Blousing was done either by rubber bands or condoms, holding the khaki fabric against the boot high enough to allow a neat, straight overhang folded down below. Spit-shining was an ongoing exercise, often well into the night, so boots would sparkle for inspection.

The men around him were tough and colorful, some of them borderline crazy. All were R.A. (regular army). None were U.S. (draftees). All thought they were pretty hard hombres. Most of them were. His immediate comrades reflected the overall mixture.

- Smitty (J.C. Smith, who was called either "Red" or "Smitty") was platoon sergeant for the machine guns. Smitty was a jovial redhead already half bald, who had a friendly, somewhat fleshy face and was a repository of folk wisdom. Smitty was from Tupelo, Mississippi, and talked about it as though the original Garden of Eden had been planted there. He had intelligent eyes and a pleasant manner. On encountering any form of near-altercation, his favorite saying was "Now what seems to be the principal maladjustment in this matter?" He was an expert gunner and a good tactician.

- <u>Jim Beemer</u> (Beemer). From a backwater town with a funny name in Alabama. Straight sandy hair and blue eyes. Tough and wiry. All muscle. Seemed to have a permanent sunburn.

  Beemer kept a small radio at his bunk which would awaken the sleeping squads with what he called shit-kickin' music. His favorite performers were Wayne Raney and Lonnie Glosson, announced with an annoying gusto. Jim could never say "this" without saying "here," as in "this here thing," or "this here music."

  Beemer was a storyteller, with many picturesque tales of farm life. The first day Andrew met him, Beemer told him the story of the bull humping a cow. "I noticed," Beemer said, "that every time the bull fucked the cow, there would be a hump that would rise up on the back of the cow...so the first time I fucked a girl I kept waiting for that hump to rise on her back. But it didn't and I felt like a total washout. So I tried again and again and I couldn't make it happen. I'm still struggling with what I did wrong. I keep fucking girls to find one who gets that hump up. This here little thing [pointing to his penis] is getting awfully worried. Maybe I should try it from the front next time."

  Beemer was a serious fundamentalist. He decided early on that Andrew was an infidel. He pronounced each syllable—in-fi-del. But Andrew never saw him reading a Bible.

- <u>Ed Lozado</u> (Big Ed). Straight from Chicago's West Side. A street fighter with fists six inches wide. Rather tall, slim and big boned, gawky in appearance, Ed had brownish hair and cloudy gray eyes that always seemed to be trying to disappear inside his brain. He had a big nose, busted several times and misshapen. Rumor was he had gangland connections, but he never spoke about it.

The first time Andrew talked with him was when the two happened to be sitting on adjacent toilet seats in the latrine—a row of open seats close together with no such thing as a privacy barrier between them. Ed sat down, and without interrupting what he had come here to do, said, "We have to fight."

"What the fuck for?" Andrew said. "You don't even know me."

"It's kind of a way of getting acquainted. You know, welcome to fist city."

"Okay. Name the time."

"I'm too tired right now" Big Ed said. "Maybe I'll have Conwell fight you. He handles my light work."

"I've met Conwell. Don't send a boy out to do a man's job."

"Okay. That's a deal," Big Ed said. They shook on it. But he never followed through. He instead became one of Andrew's new drinking buddies. They never fought. Big Ed was a gunner.

▪ Andy Kowalcik (Kowalcik). Brown hair already turning prematurely gray. Grew up in Boston. Deeply Catholic. He had unusual eyes—always serene, looking far off, as though interrupted from a dream he was trying to recapture. He wore a small cross. He did not seem to fit the cut of a paratrooper but he handled his duties well. His real world seemed to be inside of him. He didn't talk much, and if asked a question would frequently respond as though disturbed from some hidden train of thought.

Every now and then, right out of the blue, he would shout "shit, fuck, fire!" but would never explain what that configuration of words was supposed to mean. It was as though their utterance alone was purpose enough. It was hard to tell sometimes whether he was drawing a mysterious power from somewhere in the universe, or just plain stupid. Andrew was reserving judgment.

- Hidalgo Sanchez (Sanchez). Squad leader for Andrew's squad. On his second enlistment. Handsome features, clean cut, dark flashing eyes. Trim and very military. Sharp creases in his dress uniform. Boots spit shined to glistening splendor. Very quick mind, at ease with command. Sanchez grew up in New Mexico but liked North Carolina. He said he couldn't wait to make a jump in Europe. He had heard a lot about the women of France. One of his favorite phrases was "suck it in or I'll have you sucking dirt!"

- Wally J. Spitzel (Spitzel). Had a face that resembled Alfred E. Newman, the "What-me-worry" face of Mad Magazine, smile and all. Spitzel's face was bonier and he had all his teeth. His eyes had a half-delirious look as though frozen somewhere between delight and madness. He had grown up in Wisconsin. Trouble was everyone thought Spitzel was a nutcase.

All except the base "psychiatrist" who examined Spitzel after one of his misadventures. The "psychiatrist" was named private-first-class Wellman and had achieved his position on the strength of a single course in psychology he took during his only year in college. Spitzel had been sent for a possible Section 8 discharge because of mental instability. Wellman interviewed him and returned him to Mike Company with a note— "This man is as sane as I am."

Spitzel was an authentic paranoiac. He believed everyone was out to get him. Even walking to the mess hall for breakfast, if you came upon him and said, "Good Morning, Wally," he would tense up and ask, "What do you mean by that?"

But all his fears were mental. Spitzel had no physical fear anyone could discern. He was always trying to injure himself but could not succeed. On jumps he would shove a steel rod down his boot, hoping to break a leg and go to the hospital. When not jumping, drunk or sober, he would occasionally fling himself headfirst down a flight of stairs but could not even seem to bruise himself. He was like a rag doll. When not addressing stairwells, he would climb to the barracks roof and leap off, claiming he was practicing PLFs but never with resulting injury. Otherwise, he handled his machine gun assignment well. Like Andrew he was an assistant gunner.

- Lash LaRue (Leadpipe). His real name, except everyone called him Leadpipe. He was born and raised in Ohio, and was the shortest man in the platoon, barely above the minimum height necessary to qualify. Leadpipe had very dark curly hair, a choirboy face, and mischievous eyes. Strangely, he was rosy cheeked. He had won his nickname from repeated and dexterous use of a lead pipe against his opponents, large or small. He never went anywhere socially without one tucked in his boot.

Like Kowalcik, he was given to occasional outbursts that had no relationship to anything in the immediate surroundings. He would shout: "Details! Parts! Imitations!" but would never explain what he was trying to convey, except frustration. Alternatively, he would cry out "We'll all be dipped in shit!" but these outbursts were at least connected to real events.

- Tim Conwell (Conwell). A jokester. Conwell had a stiff reddish crew cut that looked like a rusty wire brush. He was among the shorter members of the squad. He had protruding front teeth. He laughed with sort of a rasp, and he laughed a lot. When he did so, his appearance would briefly turn him into something resembling a gopher. He could make a joke out of anything. New Jersey bred. He had something of a smart aleck attitude underneath the humor. His eyes always seemed as though looking for an opening to stick it to you. Conwell also did impressions. One of his favorites: "This is Robert St. John [a famous war correspondent], broadcasting from a haystack somewhere in North Korea…"

Two of his constant sayings were "talk to me through my tube," or "you're a good boy, Gonzalez [or whoever].

Trouble is, there ain't no demand for boys at the present moment."

Conwell had signed up for the airborne because he liked the uniform, especially the bloused trousers. He thought the uniform, embellished with paratrooper wings, was "a real cunt catcher." Next to Sanchez, Conwell was the most spit-shined man in the squad.

- Jack McNabb (McNabb). Had the kind of face that somewhat resembled Willy and Joe of WWII fame, with a few lines from Shakespeare, the kind of face you could talk to. There was a quiet dignity in his bearing that drew Andrew right away to form the beginnings of a friendship.

Up close McNabb was much more complex. Tough and cynical, he had intelligent dark eyes that were always questioning, always poised to ask, "Who's to say?" or "What does it all mean?" He squinted a lot, partly to let you know he really was ready to question everything. But he could not entirely conceal a faint lingering expression in his eyes of some remembered youthful pain. When he agreed with you his typical response was "Fuckin' A, man."

McNabb was taller than average and immensely strong, heavily built but not along the well-proportioned lines of a Charles Atlas. His uniform hung on him with an air of reckless fashion. His appearance could become easily rumpled. Except for his eyes, the most compelling feature on his face was a somewhat prominent hawk nose.

From early childhood he had had a special attraction to the woods and streams and hills of New Hampshire, where he had grown up. He spent almost all his free time in their domains. He liked the solitude. Winter, summer, it didn't matter. He especially liked the profound beauty of the autumn, and would spend uninterrupted weeks at a time feasting on all he saw, sleeping outdoors in what he wore,

Like Andrew, he had joined the paratroops with the intention of doing battle for his country. This was one of their earliest points of connection.

McNabb had a way of spacing out key words when he spoke that suggested he was aware, that he knew things most deep in life. If you looked through the defensive shield of cynicism he projected, you would see that at the center of his belief system were such things as courage and ideals. He always said the word as i-deeels, and would say it with a grin, as though there "weren't no such animal" any more. He spaced other words too. PAY-tree-oh-tism was one of his favorites. Words like "guts" he spoke as if he had bitten them out of granite with his own teeth.

He preferred cigars to cigarettes, and whenever not on duty, you would find an unlit half-cigar clinging to his teeth.

His father had been killed in a construction accident when Jack was 10. "My father used to tell me stories," he said. "The one I like best is the story of my roots. According to my father, I am a direct descendant of the most glorious of the McNabb Chiefs. He died in 1816. His name was Francis. My father says he was tall and very strong and full of piss and guts. He said he looked like a king, which he didn't mind. He said he was descended from a long line of ancient kings…

You could write a book about him. Maybe I will someday once I get through this shit and get some fighting done. Maybe I'm a king in disguise."

"An excellent disguise," Andrew would laugh.

Chapter 8

Andrew saw immediately that a line company is quite different from a training company; more sense of day-to-day order, more sense of permanence. Yet the amount of change that can exist within a permanent organization, without tempering its substance, is profound. In a line company the only thing that remains eternal is its name and history. When one man leaves and another takes his place it becomes a slightly different company. And as turnover continues, you actually belong to a succession of companies, each a bit different in morale, in *esprit de corps*, in attitude and essence.

In the short time in which Andrew had been a member of M Company, he could see changes already occurring, like standing on beach sand ripples trying to remain constant in the wash of waves. A new company commander had replaced the old. Several men had been temporarily assigned prior to jump school training. Two men had returned from Korea with purple hearts. And each change somewhat altered the fabric of the group, especially the presence of the new commander.

Captain Pickering, red haired and a little puffy in the face, bore every outward indication of masculinity but the way he looked as seen from behind when walking, was somehow a bit effeminate, something about the way he moved his hips. The many decorations he wore could not alter his posterior or his gait.

But the thing that brought him into a grievous relationship with his troops was his overbearing need to instill in them a greater sense of *esprit de corps*. The dissatisfactions were vague, the gripes were not specific, but there was an undertone of defiance in the attitudes of the troops. They would <u>not</u> muster enthusiasm and obsessive cooperation simply on command. It would have to be earned.

The two veterans of Korea added a subtle new flavor to the mix of changes. The aroma of combat was still fresh with them, more pungent because it was so recent. Even though most of the WWII veterans had experienced more combat than these two young men together, it was more like old history. The fact that the Korea vets bore themselves with a maturity beyond their years only added to the mystique. Andrew talked to both of them at length, over beers, trying to learn as much as he could, feeling an even greater sense of urgency to take his place in the fighting.

Pedro Alvarez, lean and handsome at 21, was the most communicative. He was quiet and moody but would loosen up after a few drinks. Peeling the label from a bottle of beer with his thumbnail, down along the cool sweat of the surface Alvarez turned to Andrew one night as though the thought had just struck him.

"Don't take the machine guns! They'll leave you, man... they'll leave you!"

*

A line company spends the majority of its time in the field, maintaining a sharp edge of readiness for action. For the airborne, the way to get to the field is quite often to jump into it.

131.

An assortment of old C-46's and C-47's was the preferred method of delivery. Andrew liked the C-47's, which had only one door instead of two, because the departure from the plane was smoother. But once landed, always with a mild euphoria, it seemed most of the time the shortest route to the point of attack was through the nearest swamp.

Out of continuing frustration with army rejections of his one-a-month transfer applications, Andrew threw himself into his daily duties with great earnestness. He learned the machine guns so well he could quickly disassemble and assemble them blindfolded. And he had become an expert marksman with the M-1 rifle. He kept his weapons clean, and personal belongings in order, his boots spit-shined.

In the ceaseless simulations of attacks during field exercises, he ran his gun with fury. Whether running the 53-pound tripod for the heavy water-cooled gun, or running the light air-cooled gun, he would sling it forward off his shoulder in a dead run as he approached the simulated enemy. Crouched low, in the method of his ancestors, running swiftly over sand or rocks or the dry prickly trunks of fallen pines, or through the black mud of Carolina swamps, as the weapon left his shoulder his hand would guide it down, clutching it, so that man and gun hit the ground in the same instant, then instantly position for action in whatever direction the invisible aggressor lurked.

He would fire the gun carefully on the range, scoring well, and would fire pistol or carbine or M-1 rifle with great accuracy. During attacks with live ammunition, it pleased him to rake his tracers across a sloping hill or down a draw or spread across a meadow, trying to hit dry stuff where possible with the tracers, hoping to set fire to the woods so the army would transfer him as a nuisance.

But instead he was promoted to PFC and to gunner. He didn't care about the promotion but getting the job of gunner was a relief. Now he could lie behind the gun rather than have his ears six inches away from metal smashing upon bare metal 760 times a minute as the firing mechanism would withdraw, catch a new bullet, and scream forward with another explosion. Deafening, ear-splitting, uncushioned noise. Andrew worried whether he would have any hearing left when this was over. Lying behind the gun, with head an extra foot away from the explosions, this would be a tremendous step forward.

But it was not all agony. Mostly, it was hurry up and wait. And, too, that made life more bearable. After a 20-mile forced march with full combat gear, coming into the last weary mile to the base, there would sometimes be a band playing for their final steps, the music lifting the weariness almost like a compassionate hand. It would weave itself into the bloodstream with resurgent vitality, help you stand tall and proud, forget the aches and bruises.

Another aspect of this life that reached unexpectedly into Andrew's emotions was the ceremony of retreat. The retreat formation is consistently regarded with special seriousness among the men. That mournful bugle strikes them all with its solemnity. Even at the command of 'at ease' there is little movement among the ranks.

The regimental commander turns to his regiment.

"Regi-meeehhhnnnt!" he commands.

"Bat-tal-lioohnn!" the battalion commanders command.

"Com-pan-yyy!" the company commanders command.

"Pla-toon!" the platoon leaders command.

It's all done very fast, like a ricocheting echo.

"At-ten-shun!" the regimental commander commands.

As a man, all snap to attention. For a moment there is silence across the field. Every man stands rigid, looking straight ahead. The first note from the bugle cries in the evening sun.

"Pre-sent!" the regimental commander commands.

"Pre-sent!" his commanders command as one echo.

"Arms!" The regimental commander makes an about face and presents arms with his regiment toward the flag. Everyone assembled does the same. The flag is being lowered slowly, timed so it would be in the hands of its two receivers at the last note of the bugle.

The ceremony always inspired him to think for a little while of all who have died in service of country. He felt the emotion in his heart in the tear he held back in the corner of his eye. "What does it all mean?" as McNabb would say. Andrew felt proud to be part of something larger than himself, a part of an ancient tradition.

There is something about being in a vast formation which is centered momentarily on one large idea or one thing, that drew up his emotions in a way that made him feel no longer small and finite, his raw fingertips seeming to touch the edges of infinity. He felt an almost indescribable feeling of belonging.

The bugle stirs the imagination. As the mournful notes trip

slowly across the silent field, they begin to unlock memories. Remembering the time he had gone to bed early, the barracks dark and quiet, taps sounding far away across the post. He feels lonely and a sense of tragedy. The sad song of the bugle evokes images of winds, centuries old, blowing through the chimney of a deserted, destroyed house where children once played and whose laughter is still caught in the cracks of wind worn bricks. He tries to pull the image closer and it vanishes.

And for a moment he imagined himself an old soldier, fighting in some faraway war, having been there for years, not to return for a year or more. And he imagined himself one of the forgotten, while ordinary life goes on and people marry and have children and laugh together. What stories I will have when I return, if I do.

His bugled imagination stands him near the rim of a fresh and sunken shell crater, now filling with muddy water. He leans like an old man against his rifle, looks out upon fields of endless waste and destruction. And he sees a tank on its side, with one hand clutched stiff and rigid on the turret. And he thinks the morning sky will be sick with grayness and the earth will never heal again, its arteries slashed open, and all is still, even the remoteness of the universe.

And he tries to imagine whether God was on duty all this time, or if he had gone to take a nap. Could <u>anyone</u> not hear that still-faint moaning sound carried in the wind, and not know it is the voices of the children slain? Where was the God of love? Life is big enough to include both love and hate, but can it include indifference? Or is indifference the final reality of oblivion?

What if you just say love three times. Isn't it always just three words?

And then the glow of mysticism begins to vanish. The sun is turning dark orange as it fades against the bright flag. The flag is most of the way down and the somber notes pierce the consciousness. There is a momentary feeling of absoluteness, security, even warmth. The thought of ever having this same relationship with authority again in civilian life is inconceivable. And underneath it all, he feels a deep and lingering sense of unfulfillment as a soldier, that only assignment to combat could ever relieve.

The flag is down and folded. The moan of the bugle is silent, and at the chain of commands the component units are dismissed. And Captain Pickering leads the march back to the company area and while all are standing at attention proceeds, before release, to lecture for five minutes on *esprit de corps*.

*

For relief, on their meager pay—although everyone on jump status collected an extra $50 a month in hazardous duty pay— many of the troopers would go to the Combat Club housed in the lower half of a barracks next to Company M, where beer was cheap. And among the regulars at the club Andrew found a broader range of acquaintances, some of them sinister. Most of the talk was about war and courage and sex.

The sex stories all followed a similar pattern, almost as if everyone were reading from the same script. One could improvise the beginning and the middle, but the end is written. There are certain taboos. Love is taboo. Dignity of women is taboo (except for mothers, sisters, wives and sweethearts). But the story must end in the passionate blind urge and its momentary satisfaction, together with whatever strange and kinky new positions that were tried.

Discussion of combat also seemed to follow similar ritualistic patterns.

"Here is the situation," someone would invariably say, "You jump into a fuckin' rats nest, swarming with enemy. You're behind the lines. You can't take prisoners—you know we can't take prisoners—and they've got you surrounded. They outnumber you 10 to 1..."

"Quit the long-story bullshit. Come to the point..."

"The point is, you get the order to hold at all costs, what would you do?"

Most say they would go down fighting.

"How important is the position?" Andrew would ask.

"Doesn't matter. What matters is, you get an order to hold at all costs."

"No explanation?"

"The army doesn't give explanations."

There were six of them sitting at their usual round table in a booth in the club—Big Ed, Spitzel, Beemer, Leadpipe, McNabb and Andrew, all from machine guns. All were pondering the question on the table, waiting for Andrew to continue.

Andrew peeled the wet label form the cold beer bottle. "I think I would make a personal assessment of the situation," he said. "If the position didn't seem to have any importance, I would be inclined to get the hell out of there, go somewhere where the fighting could have some meaning."

"Leave us there to die?" McNabb asked.

"No," Andrew said quickly. "I would never leave you to die. I assume, if the situation were hopeless, we would fight our way out of it together. If the choice was to follow a chickenshit order and die or to get out of there I would only leave if we all went together. Why you die is important."

"And who you die with," McNabb said, "Fuckin' A, man, that's why we enlisted." And they all toasted each other.

In between rounds of beer they would stand up and take turns punching each other in the gut with determined energy. Their hardened guts could take the blows.

One Saturday night Andrew skipped the Combat Club and went into town with a new acquaintance, Ned Scupper, from Mortars. Scupper was a lean and grizzled veteran of the whole European campaign, from Africa to Normandy to Berlin. He was born grizzled, full of lines and wrinkles that never quite smoothed out, with hair to match. His hair never looked neat, even at inspection. But there was a soulful quality in him that drew Andrew. Now in his late 30's, "an old warrior," he said of himself. Originally from Toledo, he made the army his home and hoped to retire some day with rank.

Problem was, Scupper could never hold onto rank for very long. He would get drunk and forget to be back in time, or find himself in a fight with local civilians, or mouth off to an officer, or in some other way end up in court martial and have his rank reduced. Most recently he had been a sergeant first class, but now he was busted down to private. When not drinking, he was highly proficient with weaponry and methods of attack.

Scupper invited Andrew to join him in "some real drinking," one Saturday evening in June. Scupper did not like the local town of Fayetteville—too many bad memories. Nor did he like E-town—the locals had once sold him some bad white lightning. Instead, he got the two of them a jeep ride all the way around to the other side of the base, to the quiet and pleasant little town of Southern Pines which he preferred.

Drinking bourbon in a hotel bar, Scupper would caution Andrew, "Just stay with me now. Pace yourself. Don't leave me to die."

"We got all night. I want to hear your stories."

Halfway through their first drink another paratrooper walked in, surveyed the room and left, without acknowledging their presence. He was tall and well built, with an intense face, and in general, an ultra-macho demeanor.

"That's Sexy Phipps," Scupper said. "He comes here because they kicked him out of Fayetteville. He's cruising."

"What do you mean, cruising?"

"Looking for a cock to suck. Everybody knows he's queer. His favorite sport is to give blow jobs in the boiler room. But he's careful, hasn't been caught yet."

"But he looks so macho," Andrew said. "That's the contradiction," Scupper said. "You can't tell what's in the package til you look inside... He's tough all right, one of the meanest fighters I've ever seen. He's tough as they come as far as infantry goes. Problem is, he's all cream and sugar inside."

"Does that bother you?" Andrew asked.

"Don't bother me none. Unless he fucks up some young kid and gets him busted out of the army. That would bother me… As for Sexy, he doesn't have any friends, just acquaintances, and he'd be the first to tell you."

All through the night, until the bar closed, they continued to drink, Andrew pacing himself, as Scupper told story after story of combat in Europe and his experiences with European women.

"Beware of German girls," Scupper said.

"Why?"

"They'll suck your cock while they're sticking a knife up your asshole."

Before the town closed down for the remainder of the night, Scupper and Andrew went 50-50 on a fifth of I.W. Harper. And then they began the long hike back to the entry of the base, stopping every now and then for a swig of the bourbon, as dawn very gradually approached.

It was a magnificent morning, warm and gentle, the sounds of insects vanishing with the rising sun, a cloudless sky, an atmosphere of serenity and peace. Nearing the road to the front gate, Andrew and Scupper had just finished the bottle, sitting by the side of the road as it worked its way through all their sense of relaxation. Scupper turned the bottle upside down one more time, hoping to catch any remaining drops. Then he stood and Andrew stood with him. He was a little wavy, as was Andrew.

They were facing each other and Scupper put his hand on Andrew's shoulder. He paused for some time, trying to find the exact formation of words. The early rays of the sun, orange and dramatic against Scupper's dramatic face, only heightened

Andrew's expectation that this would be a significant moment. He thought Scupper was trying to find a way to convey the whole wisdom of the world in a single thought.

And after a prolonged pause, his hand still on Andrew's shoulder, Scupper finally spoke.

"Son, you just stick with I.W. Harper and you'll be all right."

*

All the while the war in Korea had begun to develop its own twist and turns. The North Koreans had originally pushed an outnumbered and ill-equipped U.S. and South Korean force all the way back to the Pusan Perimeter, barely holding on. Then General MacArthur made a bold strategic move that caught the North Koreans by surprise. He swung his forces around the bottom of the Korean peninsula and, moving up through the Yellow Sea, landed a fighting force at Inchon, behind the bulk of the North Koreans, cutting them off.

From the Inchon landing, the U.S. forces drove the North Koreans back up North and past the 38th parallel. MacArthur had the army and the marines continue the attack northward, almost to the Chinese border. Whereupon the Chinese reacted by coming across the border in great strength and, in the clutches of the deadly winter weather in the Northern mountains, drove the U.S. forces south again.

In the meantime, President Truman, on April 11, 1951, fired MacArthur as Commander in Chief of the Far East Command, for insubordination.

MacArthur later described his plan for ending the Korean War. He spoke to Bob Considine on January 26, 1954. Considine reported the conversation in his book, <u>Douglas MacArthur</u>, published in 1954.

MacArthur told Considine: "I could have won the war in Korea in a maximum of 10 days, once the campaign was underway... The enemy's air would first have been taken out. I would have dropped between 30 and 50 tactical atomic bombs on his air bases and other depots strung across that neck of Manchuria from just across the Yalu..."

The war now included the Chinese. The landscape of strategic choices took on an entirely different tone.

*

The fight with Jimsun happened this way. It was a hot July night (1951) at the Combat Club. Jimsun had crowded into their table, already half drunk and bragging.

"I spent more time behind bars than in front," he said. "Suck on that."

Andrew had seen Jimsun quite often. He was from the mortar platoon in the next barracks, and was part of the physical training, the jumps, the road marches, the field exercises common to them all. Andrew had never said more than a perfunctory hello to him. Jimsun had never even said that much to Andrew.

Jimsun was a "half-breed" Apache from Arizona. Heavy and muscular, he was about an inch or two shorter than Andrew. He had a face chipped out of stone, with high cheekbones, wide and blocky angular features. His face resembled a skull, particularly in contrasting light. His eyes were deep sunken and expressionless. Whatever mood he conveyed, even laughter, which he seldom allowed, his eyes held that same sad, brooding,

142.

almost vacant tone. He looked like Death had come to visit and sat down for a beer.

At night, when not in the field or preparing for inspection, Jimsun would drink himself into a stupor and often take his fists to his drinking buddies. By morning he would have no leftover memory of the fight. His face wore scars from many such encounters. He liked to brag about his scar tissue.

In the daytime, whenever on duty, Jimsun was kind to the point of self-denial. He would give away his last cigarette without a grudge. He would help anyone, whether to clean up a mortar or level the bubbles for firing.

The Combat Club was noisy and crowded as always. Andrew and the machine gunners sat in the big booth next to the juke box. It happened that Jimsun sat immediately next to Andrew.

"Yer a college kid, ain't ya?" Jimsun said.

"I guess you could say that. I didn't finish."

"I only went to six grade."

"How come?"

"I hadda go to jail."

"In sixth grade?" Andrew asked.

"Yeah, I been in jail most my life."

"That's tough."

"Naw, it ain't tough."

"How come?"

"Learn a lot in jail."

"Better to be free."

"Indian should be free," Jimsun agreed.

Jimsun had been drinking beer by the quart, and when he

finished, he played with the empty bottle, then explained, "Gotta get a refill, but I'm timing it for when I gotta piss." Then he continued.

"You ever been in jail?" he asked.

"No, not yet," Andrew said.

"Why donchya go?"

"What for?"

"Learn a lot."

"How long you been in mortars?"

"Three years. I'm gonna re-up next month."

"Gonna stay in the paratroops?"

"Gonna stay til they push me out the door."

"I guess you can learn a lot here, too."

"I go to jail here, too."

"You been in the stockade?" Andrew asked.

"Yeah, I been there three times already."

"What for?"

"Fightin'."

"I thought this outfit went in for that."

"Some guys don't like me, so I go to jail."

"Learning all the time," Andrew laughed.

"What are you laughing at? You think I'm funny?"

"I think you're half drunk."

"I put in three months on the road gang too."

"What for?"

"I pissed on the sheriff's lawn."

"Where? In Fayetteville?"

"Yeah. The sheriff came out, see what I'm doin' an' he got

mad at me so I hit 'im an' he sent me on the road gang."

"Too bad."

"The sheriff don' like Indians."

"Maybe not," Andrew said.

"I whoppum onna head—" and Jimsun swung his fist up from under the table, whopping Andrew on the head, a little too hard to be playful.

"Settle down," Andrew said.

"Don't tell me what to do. Just because yer a college kid you got no right to tell me what to do."

"I ain't the sheriff," Andrew said.

"You like Indians?"

"I'm part Indian myself, Cherokee."

"Part ain't good enough. Don't suck my ass." Then Jimsun became silent for a few moments, went for another beer and sat down again. He was beginning to show some self-pity. "I ain't no good," he said.

"I hear you're a good man on the mortar."

"I'm best man on mortar."

"Suits me," Andrew said.

"They oughtta make me PFC."

"Maybe they will."

"I'm a no good Indian. I'm bad Indian."

Andrew said nothing. He didn't like where this conversation was going.

"I say I'm no good Indian," Jimsun said challengingly. "What you say I am? You don' say nuthin'. You think I'm no good."

"What do you want from me? I'm not your psychiatrist."

Jimsun let a smile break his lips, but his eyes bore into Andrew like death rays. "You don' like Indians."

"I'm drinking with you, ain't I?"

"Don't matter."

"Then shut up and talk about something else."

"I spent more time in the propblast than you spent in the chow line," Jimsun said.

"You got an admirable record. So what?"

"Yer usin' big words."

"Go fuck yourself. Are these small enough?"

"You don't like me, do you?"

"I like you better when you shuttup and drink."

"You don' like Indians," Jimsun's face was half grin, half sneer.

Andrew got up from the booth to stretch his legs, get a fresh beer, and end Jimsun's obsessive train of thought. He stood at the juke box and put a nickel in. The music was soothing and he began to lose himself in its comforting waves. He was in that off-balance position when Jimsun caught him squarely against the side of his jaw. Jimsun had unusually small fists for so heavy a man. He hadn't put the force of his weight behind the punch, but it nevertheless sent Andrew skewing sideways against the corner booth where his buddies drank, spilling some beer.

"You don' like Indians!" Jimsun yelled.

"Hey, watch it!" the drinkers yelled. Big Ed sprang from the table, huge fists cocked. "One of you guys better pay for the beer you spilled or I'll take on both of yous."

Shouts rose all around them. "Duke it out!" And again, "Fall out on the green!" And again, "Let 'em go Big Ed, I'll buy you a beer. Let 'em fall outside." And the whole club then emptied onto the grass in front. "Dukin' party!" they yelled. Everyone brought a bottle.

They exchanged no words, surveying each other for only brief seconds. Andrew moved in close and caught Jimsun just below where his ribs separated, but the punch was a little off balance and Jimsun did not go down.

Jimsun grabbed Andrew around the waist in a bear grip, and Andrew saw immediately that Jimsun's strength was not in his fists, but in his grip. It was like the crushing plates of a vise. Locked in that grip, bending back farther and farther, Andrew smashed an elbow hard against Jimsun's head. Jimsun dropped him and Andrew hit the ground.

Andrew came up swinging hard, connecting against Jimsun's jaw, but Jimsun shook it off with a bloody sneer. They circled each other. Andrew wanted to avoid further clinches. Jimsun's strength was a grip of iron. Andrew swung again with a hard right to the heart. It seemed that Jimsun was all muscle. Andrew quickly followed with a left to the jaw, but Jimsun lunged forward and had him in that grip again, smashing his head hard under Andrew's chin. And as Andrew spun back, Jimsun fell on top of him, locking those powerful arms around his neck. And Andrew saw that Jimsun intended to suffocate him.

Andrew punched short and with all his strength into Jimsun's stomach, and as Jimsun expelled a rush of air from the blow, Andrew freed himself and jumped up, Jimsun following.

Andrew braced himself and landed a hard uppercut to Jimsun's chin, then a blow to Jimsun's nose. Blood was now flowing with some abandon. But Jimsun lunged into him again, as though he had forgotten he had fists, and Andrew was in his grip again, being lifted and crushed in the same movement.

Andrew had both arms free, but he could feel the pain from Jimsun's paralyzing grip. Jimsun was holding him off the ground. Andrew grabbed Jimsun around the neck with his left arm, and as he struggled through the pain, began to pound his right fist against the side of Jimsun's head. Six-inch punches with all the force he could put behind them, smashing against the skull like a trip hammer. It took a dozen blows to soften Jimsun's grip, but finally he fell, a bit stunned. And Andrew never lost the rhythm of his blows until Jimsun was halfway down and falling hard. Jimsun lay on the ground, Andrew standing above him, until Jimsun finally regained enough composure to rise slowly, glare at Andrew with those skull-like eyes, and stagger away to clean up the blood off his face and fatigues.

Andrew and all his assembled buddies and acquaintances went back inside the Combat Club for another beer.

"You're fast as a black alley cat," Beemer said.

"Shit, I wouldda taken him with one punch," Big Ed said.

"Better watch out for him now," Spitzel said.

"He's got a grip like a vise," Andrew said.

"I like the way you use your right," Big Ed said. "Pow! Pow! Pow! Like a piston." Big Ed slapped his huge fist against his palm several times.

"Okay, don't get carried away," Leadpipe said.

"I'll carry you away with one small fart," Big Ed said.

"Eat it raw," Leadpipe said.

"So you don't like Indians, eh? Fuckin' A, man," McNabb grinned.

'I don't like stupid drunks, whatever they call themselves," Andrew said.

And when they finally hauled themselves back to the barracks, Andrew did not notice the shadowy form of Jimsun lurking in the shadows of the structure.

Lights were out. On the stairs two ammo bearers sat, spit-shining their jump boots in the thin light of the single stairway bulb. The sound of many sleeping men was the only sound in the big squad room. At the far end the fire exit door was dimly illuminated by a small red bulb. Here and there like fireflies, small patches of orange lights would show where men sat alone, smoking on the edge of their bunks, quietly in the darkness. A slight smell of locker room sweat mingled with the stale aroma of the smoke.

"I'm going to the latrine," Andrew said to McNabb. He threw his fatigue jacket on his bunk as he passed. He was tired and wanted to sleep. He would wash the blood off tomorrow.

In the latrine, brightly lit, he leaned his forearm against the wall as he began to empty his bladder into the small bathtub basin of the urinal. No one else seemed to be in the latrine in this hour, at least that's what he thought. His mind was seeking quietude and he was not paying close attention to his surroundings. He did not see Jimsun hiding in a darkened corner over by the toilets.

Andrew was caught by surprise. From the state of descending

quietude he was suddenly shocked to wakefulness by Jimsun's fist smashing into his jaw. It was so unexpected, so sudden, he reeled with the punch, and as he did, some urine ran down his leg before he could cut it short. More than getting hit, that, particularly, made him angry.

"I tole yer I see yer later, college kid."

"You sonofabitch," Andrew said, feeling anger mount.

"You don' like Indians."

"You got a brain like a broken record. You're cracked."

"I'll fix your brain for good," Jimsun said.

"Twice you hit me when I wasn't looking."

"I hit you anytime. You don' like Indians."

"Jimsun, you cut me short in the middle. I'm gonna stomp you for that."

"Ain't no college kid stomped me lately."

"Jimsun I'll let you go first. Take your best shot."

Jimsun swung. A roundhouser. All arm and fist. No body, no weight. Andrew took it on the left side of his jaw. It jarred him a bit but he kept his feet positioned on the concrete floor. He smiled. "One more time," he urged breathing slowly.

Jimsun swung again and Andrew took the blow. "Okay, now I'm gonna stomp you."

For a moment there was a faint flicker of fear in Jimsun's eyes, but only a flicker. It was gone in a split second. Andrew smashed his right into Jimsun's solar plexus and kept smashing his right. He did not use his left except to keep Jimsun from clinching. Jimsun seemed weakened by the blows, now half doubled over, his stomach inaccessible. He was not trying to punch, only to grip. Then Andrew continued to land blow after blow against that hard skull—to the temple, the eyes, the jaw, the nose. And as Jimsun rose up with both arms wide, as though to capture Andrew like a steam shovel bucket, Andrew exploded a solid punch to Jimsun's mouth.

Now the blood was even worse than before. Now it was gushing. It spewed out of Jimsun's mouth and nose and from above his left eye, running in a bright, heavy stream down his face and into his fatigues. But he remained standing, swaying slightly, with more of a deathly countenance than Andrew had ever seen. Jimsun seemed impervious to pain.

"College kid, if that's all the better you can do, you ain't gonna stomp nobody."

And now Jimsun charged against him with a regenerated determination. "I get mad when I bleed," he shouted through the blood. And by now the noise of the scuffling brought the troopers out of their beds. They gathered around silent all of them naked or in their shorts.

Jimsun knew his strength was in his grip. He was able to lock both arms around Andrew's waist, tightening them fiercely. Andrew arched back, completely off balance. He could not punch effectively from this position, but he was able to smash his elbow across Jimsun's bleeding nose. Jimsun held on. Andrew felt the pain arch maddeningly through his spine and ribs. His spine seemed inches from snapping. With the edge of his doubled fist he was able to hit Jimsun solidly across the back of his neck. The blow seemed to land in a vulnerable spot. Jimsun dropped him pushing him back as Andrew hit the concrete floor with a thud. Jimsun followed swiftly, jumping on top of him. For struggling seconds they fought for balance and leverage and position on the floor. Andrew emerged with the telling hold. He grabbed Jimsun by both ears and slammed his head once against the floor.

"Don't kill 'im!" somebody shouted.

Andrew pulled Jimsun's head up from the concrete again, thinking about it. The urge was compellingly strong. There was now so much blood it was hard to get a grip. Still clutching the ears, poised for another blow, Andrew's whole being was consumed with anger. He wanted to smash Jimsun's head against the concrete floor until the brains fell out.

But somehow, through the rage he heard the soft whisper of a calm voice inside his brain. "You crazy sonofabitch what are you trying to do?" It did not say Thou Shalt Not Kill. It said <u>you crazy sonofabitch</u>!

He let go of Jimsun's head. The head fell back on the floor, the eyes rolling back for a moment as though they had lost muscular control. Andrew looked at him, worried he had gone too far. Then he saw Jimsun coming around and he was relieved. He got up, Jimsun still on the floor.

McNabb spoke first. "That's some number, man."

"He clobbered me, Jack. I was at the urinal and he hit me, cut me short. Some of it down my leg."

"You don't have to explain," McNabb said.

In the milling bodies starting to disassemble, Andrew did not notice Jimsun rising to his feet, grabbing a blue milk of magnesia bottle someone had left on a shelf, and smashing the bottle against the edge of the big iron washtub next to the washbowls. The sound of it quieted the latrine, except for one voice.

"None of that, Jimsun."

Sanchez tried to wrest the broken bottle, but Jimsun swung the jagged shards menacingly and Sanchez backed off for a moment, and Jimsun lunged toward Andrew once again.

"Do I have to kill you to stop you?" Andrew said, evading the fast sweep of the bottle. And as though talking to himself, he answered his own question. "If I kill you, you won't even know you're dead... But me, I'd just be one more stupid sonofabitch in jail."

Jimsun clutched the broken bottle as though it were a familiar object in his hand. Blood from his open wounds splattered down over the glass, oddly bright and beautiful against the pale blue color and the remnants of the white magnesia. Its jagged teeth swung forward like the head of a mad cobra. And as Jimsun came in for the savage blow, Andrew spun quickly and caught his jabbing arm. There was so much sweat and blood on it, he could not hold his grip. Jimsun tore free and jumped back.

As he rushed forward again, Andrew crashed his fist so hard into Jimsun's face he hoped he had not wrecked his knuckles. A wild cheer went up, but Jimsun came forward again as though in a robotic daze. He was wobbly, but still standing, bleeding hard.

Andrew felt the cold white enamel of the urinal in back of his legs. And as Jimsun lunged one more time, Andrew grabbed the cool water pipe that fed water to the urinal, and using it for leverage, and to support his weight, threw his feet into the air and shot his boots forward like an exploding spring squarely into

Jimsun's chest. Jimsun dropped with a tremendous expulsion of air, collapsed to the concrete. The fight was over.

"I'll put him to bed," Big Ed said. "He won't remember a thing in the morning. He never does."

"Thanks," Andrew said. "Now I can finish my piss."

Chapter 9

Andrew and Jack McNabb each wrote to their respective senators asking for intervention, requesting assignment to a combat unit in Korea. Andrew's senator, Vandenberg of Michigan, sent back a form letter, on official Senate stationery, saying the request had been turned over to the Secretary of the Army. The army then sent Andrew its own form letter, with the big red stamp— "for appropriate action." TRANSFER DISAPPROVED DUE TO CRITICAL SHORTAGE OF AIRBORNE PERSONNEL. McNabb experienced the same rejection process from the New Hampshire senatorial offices, and the same army stamp.

"Let's face it, man," he said to Andrew. "We're never gonna get there."

"I won't give up," Andrew said.

"I won't give up either, but we've got to be realistic."

"I'll make them release me. I'll fuck up so bad they'll be glad to see me go."

"How you gonna fuck up?"

"Not sure yet. Maybe I'll freeze on the maneuvers jump, if I have the guts."

"That's a hard number, man."

"I don't know if I can do it, Jack. Maybe I'll just become an 8-Ball."

"Is there still a war going on?" McNabb joked. "They got rid of MacArthur. Maybe they don't want to do any more fighting."

"As long as there's fighting left to do, I've got to get there."

"I'll be with you, man," McNabb agreed.

*

The war games maneuvers involved thousands of paratroops and would be witnessed by quite a few high-ranking military and politically interested civilian observers. Somewhere in South Carolina a Red Army "an enemy force," had been created and would have to be vanquished. There would be weeks in the field, attacks, forced marches, swamps to cross, dark pine logs rotting with green moss, armies of mosquitoes and snakes and ticks and chiggers and wet boots that would never seem to dry.

The regimental commander, a Colonel, seemed determined to make a good showing. He addressed the assembled units with a brief speech. He wanted to stir them into the proper frame of mind. "Men," he said, "we are going to get a good writeup for this. We will overwhelm the aggressor at every encounter. That's what the papers and the television newsreels will say about us. I'm only asking one thing—try and live up to it."

Andrew and McNabb would jump in the first wave, with the Pathfinders and several observers. Their machine guns would be crucial to taking the first objective—capture the airstrip at Camp McCall.

On the appointed morning they jumped into the eyes of the television and newsreel cameras and a cadre of journalists. They jumped very low, into a turbulent ground wind. A French major, one of the observers on the plane, hit the airstrip badly, breaking both legs. One trooper had a streamer, which he was able to shake out and pop open only second above the concrete runway.

Andrew encountered a difficulty of his own. In the plane he had briefly contemplated freezing, in hope this would get him transferred. But with the Pathfinders on board, whom he respected, and the French major, he put the thought out of his mind. It would be all too public. If he were going to freeze, he would do it more privately. In these moments he could not find the courage to freeze. All the man were hustling, both in deference to the Colonel and because it was their nature. He did not want to let them down. This was not the time.

Even though they were jumping low, everything seemed to be going right, at first. The chute had opened properly. He was swinging hard beneath it, with little time to maneuver before landing. And then it happened. The neurotic groundwind suddenly developed an almost cyclonic small pocket of whirlwind intensity (a microburst). It caught Andrew with his chute and weapon and the supplies he was carrying. Its sudden force was so strong it literally whipped him upside down in the air, even though he was falling twenty feet per second. In the last few seconds before he hit, although upside down, he saw that his chute was actually above him, expiring in slow motion like a punctured lung.

He landed hard, almost directly on his head. Only the pendulum swing of the wind in what was left of his canopy deflected the blow somewhat. But the impact threw his head out of alignment, so that it lay almost at a right angle to his neck, along his right shoulder. He could not straighten it up. He also felt as though his right eardrum was busted. It was not going to be a good day.

He tried to shake the dizziness and confusion out of his brain. He could not move his head from its position almost on his shoulder. There seemed to be a permanent stiffness. It was locked in place, and it hurt like hell. But aside from the worry of what he had done to himself, his main thought was to link up with others on his team and go forward in the plan of attack. And with his head throbbing wildly, this is what he did, either ignoring the question "What happened to your head," or trying to make a joke of it. And after driving out the opposing forces, Andrew's unit moved out into the woods, to work toward the second point of attack. And the journalists would report, they once again overpowered a determined "enemy" force.

By nightfall he was dug in with his compatriots, ready for the next day's orders, making sure to stay very alert to prevent a sudden counterattack, or even a clandestine kidnapping, by a Red Army patrol. His foxhole was uncomfortably wet, and when not on guard duty, he decided to eat some of his assault rations—sausages in little tins, hard biscuits, jam, dark chocolate, four cigarettes, and smokeless tablets with which he could heat the sausages. The tablets burned with a small blue light and no smoke. The tin was dated 1942.

Seeing the date in the faint blue light caused his mind to flash back briefly to that year. Everything was going wrong in 1942. The Germans and the Japanese seemed to be making tremendous strides toward world domination. Sinking ships ruined armies, whole nations held captive, the future of humankind looked bleak.

And then humankind mustered an indomitable will to fight back, to resist oppression, to set the world in order again. And did its best.

It was an especially long night, even with breaks for guard duty. The mosquitoes seemed larger and more rapacious than ever. His neck was extremely uncomfortable. The throbbing sharp pain would not go away, nor would the dull pain in his ear. Try as he might, there was no way he could lift his head from its position on his shoulder. It did not enter his mind to seek medical help. Remembering his experience of feeling near-paralysis years ago in the Cameron haymow, Andrew thought if he could just keep working at it, he could get his head straight again.

Usually, attacks would be scheduled for dawn, or near dawn. However, this morning there was a shift of plans and Andrew's unit was being assembled for forced march. He felt cold and wet and shivering and extremely uncomfortable when the early fingers of sun poked their way through the pines. The salmon-colored rays were comforting and warm. Somewhere nearby an aroma of coffee penetrated the forest. It seemed one of the sweetest smells that had ever entered Andrews's nostrils.

The battalion commander (a Major), happened to be walking through, checking on his troops, as Andrew was assembling gear and weapons for the march. The commander came over to Andrew. "Soldier, what happened to your neck?"

"Nothing that can't be straightened out, sir," Andrew joked.

"What happened?"

"Groundwind caught my chute. Turned me upside down.

Landed on my head."

The major surveyed him. "Why aren't you back with the medics?"

"Soon as we run this problem I'm planning to go, sir."

"The hell you are! Soldier, you get your ass over to that jeep and tell the driver to get you to a medic."

"Yes, sir," was all he could say. The bouncing of the jeep punctuated his injury to the point of aggravated sharp pain. The medic sent him back to an Aid Station, and from there he was transported to the base hospital.

A woman Lieutenant told him to sit in a chair, and within minutes returned with someone who appeared to be a doctor. He was wearing the bars of Captain. Andrew had to repeat his story all over again.

The Captain listened, had Andrew pull out the chair so he could walk around it, and then proceeded to do so. He circled three times, closely inspecting his subject. Then he came up and stood behind him. Andrew felt the Captain's hands around both sides of his head.

Then suddenly, without warning or conversation, the Captain snapped Andrew's head back into place. It was all done in a second. But Andrew was grateful to be an erect human being again. The sharp pain had diminished, but his neck was still terribly stiff. His head was straight.

The Captain asked him how he felt. Andrew said he felt fine, except for some stiffness and the remaining pain in his ear.

The Captain had a nurse give him a packet of aspirins and released him to go back to his unit, which he did.

[Twenty years later, in the first chiropractic examination he ever had, Andrew learned that the C-2 vertebrae in his neck—the one you can see clearly only by shooting X-Rays through a wide open mouth—had at some point experienced an 85% fracture. The chiropractor showed him the "scar" line and the puffy healing ridges along the vertebrae, and told him, "You were very lucky. That's the vertebrae that creates quadriplegics."]

Back with his unit, he had missed the forced march and rejoined them in a dense pine woodland as they positioned for another attack. It was a very dark night and Andrew's teammates were somewhat scattered among the pines, waiting for orders. Someone approached but he could not see who it was in the blackness.

"What are we supposed to be doing?" the figure asked.

"Beats the shit out of me," Andrew said, and the figure disappeared into the dark with no further word.

The evening before the next jump, scheduled to take a large pocket of the Red Army by surprise and cut off supply lines to the main force, the regimental commander assembled the men of his command. There was something he wanted to say.

"I went among you, to test our performance level. I made observations. And after a while I spoke to a young soldier standing by a tree. He did not know who I was.

"'What's going on?' I asked him. And the young soldier replied"—the Colonel paused— "'beats the shit out of me!'" The colonel pronounced the phrase emphasizing every one of the six words and spacing them out so there was a studied pause between every one or two words. He repeated it again for further emphasis: "Beats-the-shit-out-of-me!" He surveyed the group with a cool gaze.

"Now let's get something straight once and for all," he continued. "Tomorrow morning we're going to jump out of these goddam planes again, and we are going to <u>know</u> what we're doing. I don't want to hear any more of this beats-the-shit-out-of-me stuff. And I mean every manjacking one of you."

"What did he say?" someone asked later.

"I think he said we're jackoffs," someone responded.

Andrew was surprised his casual remark had created such an impact. He was now disappointed that his name strip had been invisible in the darkness. The Colonel might have gotten rid of him on the spot.

*

By the time maneuvers were finished, Andrew felt almost whole again. The stiffness in his neck was mostly gone, as was the pain in his ear. But he was still caught in the hard-edged reality of a system in which he felt trapped, betrayed by false promises.

He continued to haunt the Orderly Room, trying to get his name on orders for Korea. He thought if he made a nuisance of himself they would be glad to let him go. The war had now entered a phase some were beginning to call a stalemate. The impression was the United States and its allies had lost the will to win, only to hold ground, make sure there were strong lines of defense that could not be breached. He began to feel a need to escalate. He made up his mind. He would attempt to become the opposite of what he had always tried to be. He decided to become an 8-Ball.

Sergeant Benton was on to him right away, as soon as a number of intentional screw-ups became evident.

"Are you deliberately trying to piss me off, Cameron?"

"To be truthful, Sarge, I think I'm becoming an 8-Ball."

"Cameron, you don't have the guts to be an 8-Ball. Some guys just aren't cut out to be 8-Balls. You're one of them."

"I can do anything I set my mind to, Sarge."

Benton squinted, his famous squint. "Cameron, I've seen you run that gun. I've watched you in action. I got my eye on you to go places. So just don't get yourself in trouble. I mean big trouble. 'Cause if you do, I'll have your ass so deep in the stockade they'll need a lantern to find you for chow."

"One way or another I'm going to Korea." Andrew said.

Benton reached into his desk drawer, pulled out a number of medals, flung them across the desk. "What do you want? A handful of these?"

"Sarge, I say most respectfully, if my country is at war, then I am at war. I have to go where the fighting is. I come from a warrior race."

"Don't hand me that patriotic bullshit. Now, get out of my Orderly Room."

Andrew told McNabb of his plan.

"How do you become an 8-Ball overnight?" McNabb asked. "Seems to me you have to study for it. You have to make your mind think like an 8-Ball. Christ, that's too hard to do, unless you're gifted."

"I'll figure it out."

"How? Give me one example."

"First thing, I won't run the gun so hard. I'll leave the changers dirty when I clean it. Leave some sand in the gun. Maybe I'll leave some lint and grime on my brass. Maybe I'll keep my foot locker messy. Maybe I'll mess up on my PLFs. Maybe I'll goof up on the plane—That's an idea, the plane."

"Gonna freeze?" McNabb asked.

"Don't know if I have the guts to freeze."

"How else you gonna goof up in the plane?"

"Maybe I'll freeze," Andrew said.

As a general motive, he planned to put less thought and care into the day's routine, to slow down and quit hustling. Don't falter, he told himself.

Chapter 10

He ate leisurely that morning in the mess hall. He even went back for seconds of some stringy eggs. He drank his coffee slowly as the mess hall emptied. He tried to daydream and feel calm, but he was only mildly successful.

The face across the table briefly startled him. It looked like a badly scrambled egg. He dragged slowly on his cigarette, tense inside, as he regarded the puffed and swollen face of Jimsun. Jimsun ate absently, his face almost in his tray. Andrew had not at first noticed him coming in and sitting down, in from another bad night. He quickened his body for action. Jimsun glanced up from his tray from time to time but accorded Andrew no special recognition. McNabb had been right. Jimsun didn't seem to know him. Andrew let his body relax.

He drank his coffee in sips until the cup grew pale, warm against his hand. Slowly, he walked out of the mess hall, the last one out. He sauntered down to his barracks. He had not yet made up his bunk and cleaned up his area. That suited him. The men were strapping on their equipment, ready to fall out on the company street. Andrew's bunk alone in the room lay unmade. No one said anything to him yet, but their glances conveyed their thoughts in crescendos.

He could not go through with it, at least not now. He dashed to his bunk, made it up in swift movements. He cleaned up his area in record time. But it was ready, and he was, and fell out with the rest of them, on time. He cursed himself silently for his weakness. But inwardly he felt momentarily relieved. There must be a better way to be an 8-Ball he thought, some way that does not tear out my heart and conscience. Maybe McNabb was right. If you're not a natural born fuckup, you have to study their ways.

Ace Benton stood in front of the formation, chewing ass in general. He was dissatisfied. All first sergeants are dissatisfied. They are all, or almost all, hard-nosed perfectionists. Ace wore his six stripes with the diamond in the center, with easy authority. No one would think for moment of challenging him. He called the formation to order.

"Compan-ayyp! Tensh-Hutt!" he commanded. "Right-Face!" He paused. "Sharp! Sharp! Sharp!" He swore. "Right-shouldah-Hamhs!... Foh-wuhd-Haach!... Hut-fwhor, hut-fwhor, hut-hehp-hrep-fwhor... Hut-hehp-hrep-fwhor... Hut-fwhor..." He gave the company two column movements when they were on the road. "Hut-fwhor, hut-fwhor... Double time-haach!"

Ace counted the accelerated cadence as the company ran. "I'm gonna run this company for an hour!" he yelled. And he did. Out into the boondocks. Up hills. Down hills. At port arms. "This company is getting too damn soft!" And finally he ran them back to the Division area, where he led them for the next hour in physical training and bayonet practice.

Through it all, Andrew looked for a time when he could commit some action that would bring disfavor upon himself. He thought of falling out on the road run. His arms were gruesomely heavy, running with the M-1 rifle at port arms. But so were everybody else's. He could not bring himself to fall out. He would wait for another time. In the sharp, sweaty fog that inhabits an exhausted brain, the thought drifted again and again through his mind—Benton's words: "Some guys just aren't cut out to be 8-Balls."

Later that afternoon, he mustered the courage to try again. The company had assembled around some small platforms built for training in PLFs (parachute landing falls). Half a dozen at a time the men climbed the platforms and waited on the edge for the command to jump. They practiced hitting the pit in such a way—toes, calf, thigh, buttocks, pushup muscle—that the shock of landing would be cushioned over a larger area of the body. When it came to Andrew's turn, he somersaulted into the pit, landing on his feet.

Benton eyed him coolly, told him to go again. "You got one more chance to straighten up."

Andrew's second somersault was done with all the passion of an aerial performed. "That's it, Cameron. Fall out! Stand at attention! Snap to! I think we got some straightening up to do here!"

Andrew assumed Benton meant with his fists, and he was mentally prepared for that, felt he could hold his own against him. Staring straight ahead at the position of attention, he heard Benton mutter the word "somersaults" as though it had the stench of a dead and putrefied vulture. But instead of fists, Benton decided on a different course. He called the Platoon Sergeant.

"Smitty," he said, "I think this individual needs some extra training. At 1800 hours, fall him out and march him at attention back to these platforms. There you will instruct him in the proper performance of PLFs after which you will supervise his repeated performance of same—there will be no break—until 2030 hours."

Andrew felt a small moment of elation. Benton was wrong! He <u>had</u> become an 8-Ball. Just a matter of putting the mind to it. A few more episodes, he thought, and he would head the transfer list. Andrew liked Smitty and was sorry he would suffer to some extent while administering the punishment. Nor was Smitty a happy warrior. "Cameron," he said at one point during the punishment. "Get yourself straightened up. Don't get other people involved in your personal problems. You're already interfering with my love life."

As the days passed, Andrew made repeated screw-ups. All that happened was that he spent a lot of extra duty time peeling potatoes on KP, or "G.I. parties"—scrubbing latrine floors with a bristle brush—and in other activities designed to instill new and higher attitudes in him.

Andrew made one last attempt with Benton. "I demand a court-martial, Sarge."

"Cameron, you aren't getting a court-martial. And furthermore, all you're getting out of this fiasco is a lot of extra duty. I don't feel like doing the paperwork to send you to the stockade. Furthermore, if you think pulling this stuff is going to get you to Korea, you better learn right now you aren't only not going, but you're going to straighten up and soldier again. Shit, the Korean war is mostly a dead issue. Nobody wants to do anything big. But here—we're on constant standby, to be ready to climb into the planes ready to go if something breaks in Europe. Now, get out of my Orderly Room."

And as Benton had said and as more weeks passed, Andrew headed no list, and furthermore he was beginning to draw some angry comments from his buddies in arms. At the same time, he learned he was manifestly incapable of attempting to perform in an inferior manner. Unless he was attempting to do his best, he felt guilty and miserable. There was no single time when he decided to abandon the quest to become an 8-Ball. Rather, it simply wore itself out.

"Every man carries a curse," McNabb said over a beer. "That's yours. Admit it. You're a perfectionist."

Chapter 11

Andrew did not want the furlough. He thought it would break his rhythm. Every day counted. Life was moving forward without him. But orders are orders and he had to take his turn. He decided to take his furlough in Detroit. He drank a lot of gin with McNabb, then boarded a train and fell asleep. The swaying and rhythmic sounds of the train were almost comforting. He tried to sink into a temporary oblivion as he listened to their hypnotic urgency, mingled with a conversation in the seats behind him, the wheels rumbling, swaying, slipping North through the wood.

> I can do things for you, baby
> I can chugga for you, baby
> Chugga, chugga for you, baby
> Chugga, chugga, baby
> Chugga, chugga, chugga

He awakened slowly, sensing the train had become more crowded, that someone had taken the seat next to him. Through the window he could see a distant unshielded, glaring, single light across the fields of a remote farm. He glanced at his watch, then at her.

She seemed lonely in khaki.

He had never seen a woman in military uniform before, or if he had, he hadn't noticed. There is something about a woman in uniform that creates new dimensional relationships, a whole different way of seeing another person, a strange mixture of curiosity and excitement. And because he was also dressed in uniform, with pants bloused sharply just above the ankle position, he felt something kindred, as though without saying a word, some invisible unspoken bond was already forming between them.

She must have boarded some time earlier because she was already asleep, her head curled down, her face only inches from him. Out of the corner of his eye he regarded her with interest. He felt pleasant being near her. There was something almost tranquil in her bearing, and in the serene composure of her face. And she seemed so very young. And she smelled so nice.

Maybe when you waken, you will talk to me about God and loneliness, he thought. Maybe when you waken... He took a cigarette from his pocket and lit it, smoking slowly, careful not to wake her. And in time she stirred, stretching her sleeping muscles with feline grace. Andrew felt a quickening throughout his body. She took a cigarette from her purse and searched for a match. But Andrew flicked open his Zippo lighter and held it for her as she lit. She held both his hands as she inhaled, and her eyes were on him with interest rather than alarm.

"Where are we?" she asked, still somewhat sleepily.

"Somewhere between earth and Paradise," was all he could think to say. "That light across the field tells me we are probably closer to earth."

"You're a funny guy," she laughed. Her voice and laughter were pleasant, almost smoky and casual. Her whole bearing seemed to have an unstudied casualness that gave her a relaxed appearance and made Andrew feel comfortable to be with her.

"Andrew Cameron," he said.

"Hilda Cunning," she said. They shook.

He liked the warmth of her hand and the strength of her grip. There was also a way her lips were shaped that kindled something long and dry and flammable in him. He almost blurted out, "What's a girl like you doing in uniform?" But he thought better of it. Probably everybody asked her that. She was pretty, with dark straight hair and quietly beautiful eyes, but most of all it was something warm and bonding in her casual serenity that drew Andrew near. He enjoyed her presence.

And as they began to talk, Andrew found she was also going to Detroit, also on furlough. Both parents had died years before, and she was on her way to visit her sister on the East side of the city. And after a time, Andrew asked the blundering question.

"What's a girl like you doing in uniform?"

"Why do you ask?"

He blundered on, "You don't belong in it."

"Who does?" she said. "Who does? And what about you?"

"I'm trying to get to Korea."

"Why?"

"This is going to sound corny, but I feel I should be in the thick of the fighting."

"Are you so very patriotic?"

"I guess I am. I feel an obligation."

"I think I've got it," she teased. "The real reason—your girl said no, and you wanted to fling yourself into the sea. But it was too cold, so you came out shivering and went down to enlist. You said gimme a uniform and a shiny gun…"

"And a pair of shiny wings."

"So now you go flinging yourself out of airplanes."

"I only do it for the extra money."

"Was she beautiful?" Hilda asked, without missing a beat.

The question caught Andrew by surprise. His mind raced to find a quick answer, but the thought pathways ran into roadblocks and checkpoints. First was the word "she." The girls and women who had been especially meaningful for him since the end of childhood flashed through his mind.

Eileen Riddle—no. Too far long gone and by now she had probably forgotten him.

Glendeen O'Deneman—no. Deannie was gone forever.

Laura Boutin—now married and out of his life.

Cynthia Downing—off to strange new loves.

There was no one. And "beautiful?" Yes, he thought, every one of them was beautiful in her own unique way.

"You're taking too long to answer," Hilda teased.

"I loved them all," he said at last. "But all of them are gone."

"You must be very lonely," she said.

"And you…" he began.

"You never get used to loneliness," she said softly. "You keep searching… for something. I don't know the way to paradise," she smiled. "I haven't had any experience." She said it in a way that sounded ambiguous, mysterious. Inviting?

He didn't want to talk with her about God any more, or about loneliness. Only about afterwards. Maybe they could spend some time together. She agreed.

Andrew had no particular plans for the furlough. He just wanted to get it over with, get back to his fight with the army. Nor did Hilda. She had broken up with her boyfriend before joining the WAACs. She told Andrew "I joined up mostly to get away from him."

In Detroit, she would just hang around with her sister for a while until it was time to return to base. Andrew and Hilda agreed to spend their furlough time mostly together, with Andrew taking the lead on where they would go, what they would do. Only three things came to mind immediately—Joe and Jessica, Brundi and Charlene, and Zeedie, wherever she was. Maybe a few shows in town.

*

His old car was still in good condition, and Joe helped him move it off the cinder blocks and get it running again. They visited for a while, and both Joe and Jessica noticed his restlessness. "I've never seen you like this," Joe said. "What's going on?"

"Nothing I want to talk about."

"You having woman trouble?" Jessica asked.

Andrew laughed. "No," he said. "As a matter of fact, I met someone on the way north. She's in the service too. On furlough. We're going to hang out together. I'll bring her over. I've told her about your stuffed cabbage."

Hilda was easy to be with. She seemed to have no sharp edges. First, Andrew visited her for dinner at her sister's, an evening of warmth and laughter. Then he brought her to meet Joe and Jessica. He was surprised she was still in uniform. He had immediately changed into blue jeans and a flannel shirt, but Hilda preferred the military bearing. "You're more anonymous in uniform," she explained. "Sort of invisible." He felt it was odd, their difference in dress code, but said nothing about it. "I really like your folks," she said. "They seem very real." And dinner was everything he had hinted, and another relaxing evening.

On the street near her sister's house, they talked for a long time in the parked car, and as their closeness grew, Andrew pulled her to him and kissed her waiting lips. He could tell she was still rather inexperienced, and so he began to teach her what he knew. "You're a good kisser," she breathed.

"I'm out of practice. You can help me get back in shape."

"We'll help each other," she said with enthusiasm.

The next day he drove with her to Ann Arbor, to visit Brundi and Charlene. Ann Arbor in this season of the year flooded his mind with poignant memories. Fallen leaves everywhere, some raked into fluffy piles and smoldering with thick white smoke. And the smell of burning leaves lingered through the town. Andrew parked near campus so they could get out and walk. It was Saturday, and there was a football game in the stadium, and many groups of students were dressed in splendid autumn colors as they headed for the game.

The remains of late flowers still bloomed in some of the yards. The wide lawns were scattered with brown and yellow leaves. The old stone houses, covered with ivy and the charm of age, were set back deeply from the streets. It was a generally gracious atmosphere.

"You would never know that our nation is at war," Andrew said. "Then again, war was never declared. We just plunged in."

"I hate war. I want life to be like this," she said. "I never went to college, but this town could get me in the mood."

"Seeing this makes me think I should have stayed put for a while, finish up here and <u>then</u> go off to see the world."

"You still can," she said.

"I'm committed now. After it's all done—whatever it is that awaits me, I think I will."

They walked for a while under the billowing trees, shedding their autumn bloom, like great arched cathedrals beneath the dazzling blue sky. "In a way, the streets of Ann Arbor are lonelier than the streets of Detroit," he said.

"Why?"

"It seems like here there is a greater distance between reality and dream."

"Shouldn't it be the other way around?" she asked.

"You have a quick intelligence. It's very attractive. To answer your question, I think most of the dreamers in Detroit dream only little dreams... You come out here, and your mind begins to expand. Your dreams expand. You develop a more complex form of restlessness. In Detroit, where I grew up, I was mostly surrounded by small dreams. I developed what you might call a form of metaphysical claustrophobia."

"I think I like you, Mr. Cameron," she smiled.

"Maybe we can dream together, Miss Cunning," he said with a gentle kiss.

"I think I would like that," she said with murmuring lips. He drove her to the arboretum, always one of his favorite places, where they could see a rich variety of different trees. And they walked along the trails until the October evening darkness began to fall, stopping from time to time for lingering, affectionate kisses and gentle touching. And then they drove back to the Law Quad to see Brundi. Little rows of lampposts lined the street, hung with moons. "Very romantic," Hilda said.

They found Brundi putting away his books for the evening. He had been studying all day. And then Charlene came over and they walked into the downtown of the village for a beer and hamburger.

"Andrew," Brundi began with his usual intensity, "It looks like the war is practically over. Why don't you come home, get your degree, make some money?"

Andrew laughed. "The great philosopher Yogi Berra once said 'It ain't over til it's over...' I'm still planning to do what I can. Maybe I can help break the stalemate."

Charlene surveyed Hilda with interest and asked in her whispering voice, what it was like being a woman in the military.

"It's easier if you're a manly woman," Hilda laughed.

"Well, you're definitely not," Charlene said. She turned to Andrew, looked him square in the eye and asked provocatively, "Which type do you prefer?"

Andrew laughed. "Charlene, you have always been my type and you know it." The others joined him in laughter, but he noticed Charlene holding his gaze longer than he had expected. He wanted to ask about Laura, but it could not fit easily into the flow of conversation, so he let it go. Charlene did not volunteer any news.

Andrew found a small motel set back among a grove of trees and checked them into a little cabin. Hilda said nothing, as though all along this was the expected thing to do. And he proceeded to undress her piece by piece until he felt her shivering. He wrapped a blanket around her, but she continued to shiver.

"I can't seem to get you warm," he said as he undressed himself. "You're still shivering. I'll wrap you tighter."

"It's not from the cold. I'm not cold…"

"What is it then?" he asked.

"I've never done this before," she said. "Forgive me. I'm nervous as hell… but I can tell you're not."

He removed the blanket and held her close to him. "Hilda, sweet Hilda… I didn't know."

"Be… gentle."

"I'll be gentle as the evening sun." He turned off the overhead light and switched on the small shaded lamp beside the bed.

"Is there anything you want to tell me first?" she asked.

"I love the way you smell," he said. "You have a beautiful aroma. Like an expensive perfume."

"I don't use perfume," she said

"Not at all?"

"Never."

"Is that beautiful aroma all you?"

"It's all me," she smiled. "How does it make you feel?"

"Like I want to be very close to you. So much so that it can't be put into words."

"Is it all right if I tell you I love you?" she whispered.

"Open your heart. Let it all pour out," he whispered.

And he did proceed slowly. And he could feel she was trying to relax, but still tense. He caressed her for a long time, over her whole body, until the tension went away, all the while teaching her everything he knew about kissing, and where to kiss.

She was a good student and a quick learner.

And after they had rested for a while, she became casual again, now glowing, her leg thrown randomly across him. They smoked together, the thin gray streamers blue along their edges. "Well, what do you think of that," she giggled in his ear. "First time at bat and I hit a home run... The good pitching really helped." And now she moved her whole body over his, and as her hair hung down beside her cheeks, she looked lovelier than he had even imagined.

Her lips were slightly swollen, but there was something new in her eyes and in the serene composure of her face. Somehow, she looked more woman, as though her heart breathed through the pores of her cheeks. Looking up at her was like looking into a deep mountain pool filled with vivid mysteries.

"You are amazingly beautiful," he said at last.

"Let's snuggle for a long time and dream together," she signed.

"Right now, you seem the perfect antidote for all that's been bothering me," he said.

"There's more where that came from," she smiled.

They waited more than a week before they visited Zeedie.

Andrew and Hilda had a lot of exploring to do and neither wanted to be rushed. Andrew first tried Sarah's place where he found Zeedie still lived, but Zeedie was at work, Sarah explained. "She still works at Trees studios. She dances a lot, she comes home late. Maybe you should look her up there."

"Well, sakes alive," Zeedie said when Andrew and Hilda came into the studio late one evening, "We can't go to war, so the war has come here."

The large ballroom was filled with dancing couples. It was no longer dime a dance. The price was now twenty-five cents. Many of the taxi dancers ("hostesses") were ballerina-slender and exotically beautiful in the carefully tailored lighting. Zeedie had now entered her forties, and though still quite attractive and almost slender, she was now using too much makeup. Andrew wanted to hug her, kiss her on the forehead, but she held him back. "Don't ruin my face," she tried to laugh. "Takes me too long to get it on."

"How have you been?" Andrew asked.

"Same as ever," Zeedie said. "A dollar here. A dollar there... except what I share with the bouncers.

"Anyone exciting in your life?" he asked casually.

"Nobody you would know.... Now who's this?" She looked at Hilda, almost like a surveyor. "Looks like you got some excitement in your life. This your new girlfriend?"

"We are very good friends."

"Well," she said to Hilda, "get him while he's hot. Your good looks won't last forever."

Andrew tried to divert the conversational line. "My mother

was a welder during the last war. She helped build tanks."

But Zeedie would not be diverted. Still looking at Hilda, she said, "You look real snappy in that uniform. That's what I think I should get for myself, a uniform. Men go crazy for a woman in uniform."

And when they finally disengaged, and were on the way home to Hilda's sister, she said, "Forgive me if I'm being rude, but I think your mother is a little strange."

And in the days and nights before their furloughs ended, Andrew and Hilda joined together in love numerous times, in small motels. And when the time came, they held each other with deep affection and said their goodbyes, knowing they would never see each other again.

Chapter 12

Back to Ft. Bragg, and the stark reality that his private war was with the army. Andrew knew it was coming time to make a hard decision, to force the issue, to attempt to bend the army to his will.

His time with Hilda had been a most pleasant and relaxing interlude, but it was no more than that. He had never hinted it would go further, nor did she press. She had been a comfortable and comforting lover, but they did not promise any continuing communication. There had been a curious difference, making love with a WAAC, in uniform. It was like making love not only to a woman, but somehow almost to an institution. It had added a small tingle of extra excitement.

Andrew did convince her that with all her intelligence, she should go on to get a college degree, and she said she would. It would be a lot easier to do while in the army. From time to time when he thought of her, he remembered mostly the casual serenity of her face, and her girlish happiness at having hit a home run the first time at bat.

Andrew did not want to involve McNabb, but as a friend, he took McNabb into his confidence about his plan. There would be a training jump on January 4 and Andrew had decided he would freeze. "They'll have to kick me out then," he said. "It will be direct disobedience of an order."

"I'll go with you, man," McNabb said. "I never left a buddy in my life."

"Don't do it on my account. I've got my own demons to struggle with."

McNabb squinted. "I'm doing it on my own account."

"I think the only way I can find peace again is war."

"Fuckin' A, man."

With McNabb determined to join him, a new danger lurked. The refusal of both to jump could be regarded as mutiny, and if the intention to refuse could be shown to have existed in advance of the act, they might risk general court-martial, with much more serious consequences. Secrecy about the plan would be of paramount importance.

From then on, they discussed the plan only when they would take long walks in the boondocks after duty. In the November-December evenings the roads and fields and pine forests were chilled. As winter hovered near, there would sometimes be a scattering of snow in the woods, and the moon would fall in patches over the crunchy ground, hidden then emerging behind dark racing clouds.

McNabb was struggling with second thoughts. His identity was at stake. "The only way we're going to get off with six months is to convince them fear is the reason. If they think it's pure defiance, if they can make their case for mutiny, then we'll have general courts, and the penalty will be years, not months."

"If they can prove it," Andrew said. "Jack, don't do this on account of me. I'm going to plead with you. I'm fully prepared to go it alone, take my chances. I don't want to feel I'm juggling your destiny too."

"I'll juggle my own fucking destiny."

"The reason has to be pure and simple refusal," Andrew said.

McNabb was thoughtful. "I can just see Pickering—he's going to take this as a personal insult. He'll say, 'You mean to tell me that a man with a good name like Jack McNabb is afraid to jump out of an airplane?' That's gonna be the rough part, when he says that. Shit, maybe I'll just join the French Foreign Legion when my enlistment is up."

From time to time, Andrew quietly contemplated the grim prospect of prison. He did not wish it upon himself, rather he simply accepted it as the price he had to pay to go into the war. He also considered that this would be a way to enlarge his understanding of the human condition. Somehow, this thought made the whole prospect more bearable to think about.

When not with McNabb, Andrew spent a lot of time reading. He had brought back form furlough a copy of Herbert Spencer's First Principles, a book of plays by Christopher Fry, Fitzgerald's fifth translation of The Rubaiyat by Omar Khayyam, and The Prophet by Kahlil Gibran. When off duty he would go to the Combat Club but leave after a couple of beers. Through Christmas and New Year's holidays he spent most of his off-duty time reading.

The evening before the jump was splendid early January weather. The evening sun hung low and orange, frozen in the winter treetops, and in the broad sky beyond, long streamers of frozen clouds were molten around their edges with its rays, wild orchid and pale amber within. Mike Company had been in the field all day, practicing firing and studying offensive tactics, running exercises across the scalps of small hills out of which the pine forest grew. And when darkness fell and they were all dismissed for the night, they cleaned their weapons in preparation for the jump. Andrew made sure his rifle and machine gun were spotless, then sat with McNabb for a while on the edge of McNabb's bunk, smoking and saying little.

Big Ed stopped by to ask, "Why ain't you guys at the Combat Club?"

"Ain't no pussy there," McNabb joked.

"Ain't no pussy anywhere around here," Big Ed said.

"Maybe we'll be down a little later," Andrew said.

"You guys have been so quiet, sounds like you're cooking up something," Big Ed said.

"Since when does the army allow you to have time for secrets?" McNabb said. And as the three of them joined in mild laughter, Big Ed left.

*

January 4, 1952. Until the final moments in the plane, Andrew did not know for sure whether McNabb would join him in mutiny. He continued to hope McNabb would not, but he was prepared in his mind for whatever McNabb would do.

It was a cool, crisp January morning. A thin slab of light in the Eastern sky heralded this day of Andrew's decision. He had slept only fitfully. He was tired but intensely awake. He strapped on his GP (general purpose) bag with his machine gun. He had emptied his bladder in preparation for what he expected would be a long day.

The plane was in flight for more than an hour as it flew a large circle then approached the drop zone. It had run into a long twisting pocket of choppy air. Several men were sick and vomiting into paper bags. The bags held the vomit, but it made the sides of the bags wet, and the fingers clutching the bags were wet and sticky with it. None of this was unusual, except in degree. If anyone became airsick on a jump, usually it would be only one or two. This morning it was four.

The plane lurched into the approach then slowed down, alternately gaining then losing altitude. The pilot seemed inexperienced carrying paratroops into a jump.

On board, at the head of one of the sticks, Lieutenant Bakke was jumping. Bakke was in charge of the mess hall and the cooks, and for him this was just another routine jump to continue his eligibility for hazardous duty pay. Bakke was a rather nondescript Lieutenant, one whom you would hardly notice in a crowd. His years in mess hall kitchens had given his complexion too much of a white sweaty color, as though he needed to spend more time in the sun. But he was the officer in charge right now.

"Stand up and look up!" Bakke commanded.

All stood, except for Andrew. And then, a few seconds later, Andrew noticed McNabb had also remained on the bench seat, from the stick across from him. McNabb was going to do it.

When it became evident two men remained seated, Bakke shouted back, "Get them up!" And when it was apparent no one would interfere, Bakke unhooked and shouldered his way back through the parallel sticks. He stood before Andrew. "Stand up and look up!" he shouted.

"I'm not going to jump!" Andrew shouted back with a smile, shaking his head No.

"I'm giving you a direct order. Stand up and look up!"

"Not today!" Andrew shouted. "Not any day!"

Bakke then turned to McNabb and repeated the exercise. "Fuck you!" McNabb shouted.

By now they were nearing the drop zone. Bakke hurried back to the front of his stick, hooked up, and moments later when the green light flashed, led the troopers out the doors. Two men, still vomiting, crawled to the doors on hands and knees and left the plane that way, rolling out one late second after the green light had change to red.

It was done.

After they landed with the plane, Captain Pickering, accompanied by his driver and a corporal from Military Police, drove to where they waited on the airstrip. He was angry, shouting even before the jeep had halted. He jumped out of it as it skidded to a stop in front of them.

"A couple of gutless washouts!" he shouted.

Andrew and McNabb stood at attention in front of him. He paced back and forth a few times, collecting his words. "This is no coincidence, and nobody's going to tell me it's a coincidence—This is mutiny!" he shouted in their faces. He repeated the word slowly with loathing, deep disgust, deep disappointment.

He looked at Andrew. "I had big hopes for you in this Company, Cameron, and frankly, I'm ashamed." Then he looked at them both, one to another. "I don't know what you men have

187.

on your minds, but you've committed a serious offense. This could mean years in jail for both of you. I hate to see a man wreck his life, but this could mean dishonorable discharge, forfeiture of all pay and rights. Forfeiture of honor… I'm going to give you both another chance."

He addressed Andrew first. "Cameron, put on your chute and get back in the plane."

Andrew remained at attention, eyes straight ahead. "I refuse to jump, sir."

"Don't give me that bullshit! You've got a good record. Don't ruin it now. I know goddam well you're not afraid to jump. Now, put on that chute!" he repeated. Andrew did not move.

Pickering turned to McNabb. "Are you willing to spend the next few years in jail?"

"No, sir"

"Then put on that chute and get back in the plane."

"I refuse to jump, sir," McNabb said, eyes straight ahead.

"You're not going to stand here and tell me you're afraid."

"Yes, sir. I am."

"This is conspiracy. The odds of this happening by sheer coincidence are astronomical." Pickering pondered the issue for a few moments more. "This is your final chance," he said to both of them, then stood in front of McNabb. "You say you're afraid to jump out of an airplane." He eyed him coolly. "You know, I've got a hunch that I'll bet you are."

Andrew could sense McNabb suddenly stiffening even more than the rigid posture of attention. He thought Pickering was aiming for McNabb's weak spot. But McNabb did not move.

Pickering stepped back, contemplated them for several moments further. "I'll have you both hanged if I can." And as he turned back toward his jeep he said, "Corporal, I want you to put these two men under barracks arrest until I return."

Andrew heard the engines of the plane roar as it taxied across the strip away from them. It suddenly felt unusually cold and quiet on the airstrip when the plane was gone. The Corporal unstrapped his holster. Andrew could hear the thin sound of metal being pulled through a brass grommet. He wanted to say something to McNabb but dared not. Disobedience of a direct order was one thing. Conspiracy or worse, mutiny, was a whole different matter. He did not want to say anything that could be overheard, anything to give evidence to confirm their suspicion.

Back in Mike Company, they were allowed to eat lunch under guard, with a corporal standing watch, complete with a holstered .45 automatic. Back in the barracks, they were ordered to pack all their clothing and personal belongings and stand by, still under guard. Pickering sent an order for them to fall out to the company street in full dress uniform, with all their gear. And as they were halfway dressed, Pickering changed the order.

"Have them fall out in their fatigues instead." Then he had Mike Company fall out in full dress uniform. Andrew and McNabb stood in front of their comrades, in fatigues, under guard. They were made to face the company. And before the entire company, Pickering addressed them.

"You have made a black mark against my record, against the record of this company, against the tradition of honor, and against yourselves... I learned this morning that you suffer from an illusion. You think if you fuck up bad enough it will get you an assignment to the Far East... Well, you've another thing coming. And you'll have a long time in jail to let it sink into your minds."

Then before the entire company, standing at attention, they were stripped of their wings. They were each wearing the customary fatigue jackets with cloth wings sewn above the left breast pocket. Pickering moved first to Andrew. He took a single-edge razor blade, cut a corner of the thread, then ripped the emblem off the chest. He did the same to McNabb. Then he made his final remarks. "The next sonofabitch who pulls a coward stunt like this, I won't even let him into the barracks to get his goddam gear. I'll have the sonofabitch standing at attention outside the door, and I'll throw his goddam gear out the door at him myself personally."

Andrew could not entirely ignore the humiliation of facing his entire company, his comrades in arms, having his wings stripped from his chest, the stripe torn from his sleeve. But he knew it was even worse for McNabb.

And afterwards, Andrew and McNabb marched before the guarding Corporal across the large field, to the Replacement Company, the "Leg" (Straightleg) Company where they were to wait under barracks arrest for their court-martial. From their new temporary quarters, Andrew could see the Combat Club barracks in the distance across the field. He glanced down at the spot where his hard-won wings had been. It was naked. A little piece of thread hung down from that empty spot on his chest. He ripped it off.

In a momentary lull, when he could whisper to McNabb so

that the Corporal couldn't hear, Andrew said "We're on our way."

"Fuckin' A, man, but it was harder that I thought."

*

The court-martial process moved swiftly. They were tried and convicted in two weeks. Captain Pickering and some army lawyers tried their best to proceed with a mutiny or conspiracy charge, but there was not enough hard evidence.

All the army could charge, for certain, was disobedience of a direct order. Major "Bulldog" Gayney was the chief trial judge. The penalty was six months in the stockade, demotion to recruit (Private E-1), and forfeiture of two-thirds of their meager monthly pay. In shorthand lingo, the sentence is called "six and two-thirds."

Chapter 13

Until you actually experience it you will never know, and can never completely imagine, the profound wave of panic that sweeps through you once you are behind prison bars and hear the lock click shut behind you. You feel trapped, with no room to maneuver, in a dangerous place, without weapons or resources. A feeling of unbearable loneliness comes over you. Your first impulse is to break free, but you cannot do it and you know you can't. The weight of world institutions holds you down.

The rush of these feelings through Andrew was quite unsettling, even with McNabb at his side. He thought to himself: If I just keep putting one foot in front of the other, I'm going to walk right out of this place, into the sunlight again. I've got to keep my head down, keep a low profile. He shared this thought with McNabb. McNabb agreed.

"We've got to keep a low profile."

After three days behind bars, they were transferred to the stockade, frequently referred to as "The Yard," or sometimes as "The Hotel."

*

On the morning of their transfer a cold January mist swirled across the broad fields surrounding the compound. The Stockade is ringed with a sturdy high chain-link fence double crowned with thorny barbed wire. At each corner of the large square stands a guard tower. As the towers rise out of the mist, they look like gray-windowed ghosts. Guards are leaning against the railing of each tower shivering and nervous with M-1 rifles in hand, one clip of ammunition each. And down below, a guard patrol walks forever along the double fences, from tower to tower, rifles on shoulders, one clip of ammunition each.

The Stockade compound is square, on open ground, divided into two parts by a single chain-link fence. The rear of the compound is empty, used for dismounted drill, for work formations, and to sleep prisoners on the ground ("Tent City") when they break minor rules. The front half of the compound holds the buildings where prisoners are quartered—four military wooden barracks, two stories tall, in an even row. Behind the prisoner barracks are two smaller one-story buildings. One is used for showers and latrines. The shower is 20 showerheads in the ceiling, for 20 men at a time, over a concrete floor with a drain. The toilets are all in a line, with only inches of space between them, even worse than the regular army barracks.

The other building is used for a dayroom where prisoners are assembled for periodic lectures, once-a-week fight films, and for religious services on Sunday.

The headcount averages two hundred men. They are in for a whole variety of reasons, mostly for some form of rebellion against established order. Some are in for gruesome crimes. The worst cases are held here, or in the main jail, pending shipment to a federal prison. Some are dangerous individuals.

You are allowed only two pieces of reading material: The Bible and The Uniform Code of Military Justice. Nothing else.

You are allowed three names and addresses with whom correspondence (censored) is allowed. Both Andrew and McNabb declined. There is no one either of them wanted to write to while in prison. Neither of them owned or wanted a Bible.

Contraband includes Benzedrine inhalers, books, pencils, pens, paper, magazines, cards, dice, games, cigarette lighters, food, jewelry, watches, valuables, knives, straight-edge razors, liquids of any kind with alcohol content, lye and caustic powers, medicines, mirrors, money, stamps, narcotics, sedatives, pin-up pictures, portraits, presents and gifts, pulp magazines, radios, shoe polish, tools, Vaseline and other lubricants, and weapons of any kind. Although not mentioned specifically, human dignity is also contraband.

Rules would be enforced by means of sweeping shakedowns—sudden, aggressive, and sometimes violent inspections especially for drugs and the worst forms of contraband.

The hard labor written into each man's sentence specifies he will have to exert himself in physical labor in excess of that normally required under regular duty conditions and not complain about reduced rations.

The rules prohibit particular offenses—alteration or destruction of clothing, assault, communication by sign, complaints, possession of contraband, destruction or defacement of property, disorderly conduct, disrespect and insolence, disturbance or fighting, escapes and attempts to escape, failure to repair, failure to police quarters, wastage of food, gambling, insubordination, malingering, malicious mischief, obscene drawings or pictures, profanity, refusal to work or inattention to work, sex perversion, smuggling, stealing, talking in ranks or loud talking in compound, trading, willful agitation… And for each of these things a punishment is specified, ranging from Tent City to confinement in solitary ("the black box," or the "Black Hole" or simply "the Hole") or to additional time added to the prison sentence. The informal punishments are not listed.

As Andrew and McNabb contemplated the list, they shook their heads slowly. "It's not going to be easy to get out of here," they decided. "They can nail you if you piss upwind."

"Let's just remember—very low profile," Andrew said.

"Fuckin' A, man," McNabb said.

*

The test of determination to lie low would encounter a harsh reality, and very quickly. The Captain in charge of the Stockade (the Confinement Officer) was a drunkard and a sadist. Andrew and McNabb were both assigned to the second floor of the fourth platoon and were sound asleep on their cots when the incident occurred. Since they were not allowed to carry watches, Andrew guessed the time was between two and three o'clock in the morning. The lights flashed on in the barracks and Captain Witkins, the Confinement Officer, came into the fourth platoon and up the stairwell with the frenzy of a crazed bull moose.

Witkins was a troubled man. You could see it in his eyes. He had a rather square and puffy face, wavy dark hair, and a stocky build that suggested physical strength. He had somehow gained the rank of Captain but could not make it to Major. He was getting too old to be a Captain. His wife had long ago left him and taken the children. For a long time it had become his habit to drink heavily at night, brood over his solitary drinks, then sometimes come into the compound to vent his rage. This was one of those nights.

The Captain reeled against the wall. The Corporal who accompanied him grabbed him before he fell and steadied him. His voice was guttural, the words slurred. His face was the mottled gray color of city snow. His eyes blazed like two Russian pissholes in the snow. He charged for the nearest bed, grabbed the suddenly-awake prisoner and slammed his fist into the side of the prisoner's head, knocking him to the floor.

"Get outta that goddam bed, you goddam sonofabitch!"

The Captain then addressed the room in general. "Get outta them goddam beds, you goddam sonsabitches! Straighten up your displays."

The prisoners were not sure what to do. Some got up and stood cowering next to their beds. Some came in front of their beds and stood at attention. Andrew was one of these. Several men had not awakened in the commotion. The Captain staggered over to the nearest one and smashed his fist into the sleeping face. As the prisoner careened, bleeding, from his bed, the Captain tried to hit him again, but stumbled and fell over him. "I said get outta that goddam bed, you goddam sonofabitch! Straighten up your display!" And the prisoner cringed under the powerful weight of the double bars, and hastily re-arranged the few things he was permitted to have, as clothing, at the end of his bunk. The Corporal quietly attended the Captain.

Prisoners who were slow to waken, or had not yet wakened,

196.

received the same treatment. The Captain hit them all. He then staggered into a buttcan hanging from a post, and accidentally knocked it to the floor, spilling its contents of foul water and very small cigarette butts across the clothes of the prisoner he had just hit. "Get back to the latrine and clean this shit up," he yelled. And the prisoner dashed toward the stairs with his befouled clothes.

Again and again the Captain shouted that he was making a "goddam bed-check," and that "the displays look like shit," and that "everybody better get their asses off their bunks and fix 'em."

All this was happening swiftly, and although Andrew was fully awake, as was McNabb, and standing at attention at the foot of his bed, he was not sure how he would react if the Captain struck him. Based on what he had already learned in jail, if he struck the Captain, he could get ten or more years added to his sentence, without appeal. Since he was not yet really a praying man, certainly not for himself, all he could do was hope he could control himself if the worst were to occur. At one point the Captain almost lurched into him, his fist ready to strike, but the Corporal maneuvered the Captain in a different direction. For a moment, their eyes were locked into each other, but the Captain looked away and moved on, without saying anything to him. Andrew would never forget those eyes. Two bunks later the Captain kicked another prisoner out of bed and hit him in the back of his head as he scrounged around his display on the floor.

"This place looks like a Chinese whorehouse!" he bellowed. "Corporal, fall them out on the compound and give then an hour of drill!" And as the prisoners hurriedly dressed, Andrew could see the captain blundering across the compound on his way to bed. It was said by the old-timers that Captain Witkins would make a bed-check this way every few weeks. In the months to come, Andrew would learn the chilly truth.

*

The non-commissioned officer in charge of day-to-day operations of the Stockade was Sergeant Kubla, a Master Sergeant. He liked to refer to himself as "the Terrifier." He referred to himself also as the "chief attitude adjuster." He called the prisoners "bad actors." "They're all bad actors," he frequently said.

Kubla was physically large, powerful, black and dazzling in appearance. His skin was like ebony. He had a very outgoing disposition and a hearty laugh. No one would question his authority. He looked like a young judge, or a boxer or both.

The prisoners represented a broad array of colors and class, with darker shades predominating.

The overwhelming majority were from regular army units, but many were paratroopers. Almost all had a chip-on-the-shoulder bristling response to authority figures, and chickenshit rules and regulations were chickenshit.

Tradition was that a Yard Boss would be selected from among the prisoners to run the day to day operations of the compound and to maintain order and discipline, something like a Chief Operating Officer of a business corporation. Sergeant Kubla made the Yard Boss selection and personally oversaw his work.

The current holder of the title was a heavily built muscular man with brown skin and a nickname meant to intimidate. He was called Crocodile or Croc for short. Part of what made him feared was his habit, in a fight, of biting off some piece of his opponent's anatomy, whatever he could sink his teeth into. Croc ran the compound pretty much on a survival-of-the-fittest philosophy. On Andrew's first day in the Stockade rumors about Croc were whispered. "He beats up on somebody once a week just to remind everybody he's in charge. That's what Yard Bosses do. They have to make sure they keep your respect." Andrew decided to steer clear of him.

Work details went out every morning, except Sunday, after a reduced-rations breakfast of soggy eggs or thin oatmeal gruel, and an hour of dismounted drill. Andrew would never forget the shock of his first morning under the gun. All prisoners, except for a handful performing work details inside, were assembled in the rear of the compound. Guards were lined up outside the gate to escort them to trucks which would take them to places of work.

Sergeant Blacktower stood outside the gate, his guards lined up behind him. He stood on a small platform to address them. Blacktower was a tall slender, rangy, rather nervous man whose dark skin tones had a rather greenish hue. His fatigues were crisply creased and his boots spit-shined to a glistening splendor. He spoke with a studied crispness. He conveyed the immediate impression that he would put up with no nonsense. Every morning he delivered the same lecture to the guards, because the guards were pulled in from different line companies each day and had not heard the speech. The prisoners could repeat it verbatim.

"These aren't soldiers," he would say, "they're prisoners. They got no rights. You don't take nothing from them. If they turn up the peaks of their fatigue caps, hit 'em with your rifle butts. If they won't work, bring 'em back to me. They ain't allowed to have cigarettes and they ain't allowed to smoke. If they run, shoot 'em. That's what I gave you ammunition for."

It was mostly a lie. Only Blacktower seemed to believe in its reality. In practice, things were more relaxed. The guards usually tolerated all but the largest infractions of the rules. They knew some of these men would be back in their same companies after their sentences were served. They would be living together as comrades again. Occasionally, someone would escape from a work detail. Seldom would a shot be fired. The escapees typically would show up at the gate of the Stockade after several days, hungry, and asking to be let back in, knowing their sentences would now be extended.

Andrew decided he would have to be especially alert for an immature guard with a reckless trigger finger who would try to enforce the rules too literally, too rigidly. "Low rifle" was becoming his mantra.

Both Andrew and McNabb were assigned primarily to the garbage detail. Both regarded this as one of the better jobs. The garbage cans behind the Officers' Quarters, especially, were ripe pickings. There would frequently be a half-eaten sandwich, dry crusts of bread, a half-eaten apple, sometimes meat. These were great supplements to the reduced rations.

There were also many cigarette butts, which Andrew carefully picked through, avoiding butts too heavy with lipstick or dried lip saliva. The smoking habit which he had begun almost casually was now gripping him with the beginnings of an addiction. He did not feel the tug of the addiction until he decided to quit and found he could not. At least not yet. He cursed himself and vowed to try again.

One morning McNabb found a whole side of pork someone had thrown out. No one knew how old it was, but McNabb kept it aside. In the dump, over a black-tar smoke fire, and with guards looking on, McNabb roasted the pork on the end of a dirty wooden broom handle. The heavy fat coating of the pork dripped rapidly into the fire and flared up in crackling bright flames. After a while, when the fat ceased to drip, McNabb continued to cook the thing until it was only a crisp, black mass of something they knew contained pork somewhere inside.

"You have to cook the shit out of pork," McNabb explained. Andrew and McNabb ate as much of it as they could in the time remaining, tearing off hot portions of the meat with their bare hands. McNabb offered a few choice pieces to the guards, and several prisoners working nearby, but all declined.

On alternate days, when not on garbage detail, their work assignment was a partially sunken stadium which had to be excavated to a deeper level, mostly by hand, in preparation for an eventual outdoor sports arena. Shovels, pickaxes, wheelbarrows —it was the classic definition of hard labor, especially working into the cold almost frozen ground. It was after one of these days when Andrew saw a picture of his new reality that would long remain in the back of his mind.

It was a late January afternoon. The sky was clear and crystal blue, the sun deep golden orange, magnificently beautiful as it ventured toward evening. And from down below, in the sunken bowl of the stadium under construction, Andrew could see his captors. The guards were ringed in a perimeter around the lip of the higher ground, silhouetted in the last shimmering rays of the setting sun. And sergeant Blacktower, who had just come out on a work inspection tour, was standing among them, bristling with hostility. The crisp late January air carried his words with succinct clarity:

"One false move—just shoot 'em!"

Coming in from a day's hard labor brought forth further assaults on dignity. Some prisoners would push a shank up their rectum to hide it. Knowing this, all prisoners were required to squat several times at the gate. Those who refused were assumed to be fearful of the shank rupturing their intestines. The old timers knew there were other ways to hide a weapon.

*

Working with McNabb in this new environment unearthed new mysteries about him that Andrew had not yet sensed. He thought he knew his friend very well, but now he was discovering deeper layers of his personality. He began to notice subtle changes in him. It was as though McNabb took a certain pleasure in throwing dirt on himself, real and symbolic. He seemed to want you to be aware of the dirt ("See how dirty I am?"), to be loved in spite of it, to be loved even more because of it—a strange insecurity that McNabb's tough-guy exterior masked with great effectiveness. And the more Andrew came to understand these hidden elements of his personality, the deeper his feelings of friendship grew.

He also came to see more clearly that McNabb accepted no

authority for anything at all. For him, everything was relative. There were no fixed moral grounds.

"Who's to say?" McNabb would repeat.

Andrew found it especially surprising to see how quickly and with what zest McNabb entered into the game of "Dozens," played by prisoners both while at work and when they had nothing else to do.

The Dozens, as played by men trying to break the agony and monotony of confinement, is entirely different from Eskimo song duels to which the game is sometimes compared. Eskimos settle their hostilities "like other civilized men," by use of physical force, but when they want to inflict real psychic damage they duel it out in song. They go at each other with highly stylized songs centered in a barrage of contemptuous, disparaging, and even slanderous verses. By custom and tradition the epithets must be thrown at the opponent in a rigid rhythmic form. The winner is decided by the community according to skill and creativity.

The game of The Dozens played in American prisons comes at you with more edge and lesser creative skill, full of gut and gristle.

The Dozens is a game about mothers (mostly) and sisters (sometimes). It was originally invented in some long-ago forgotten prison as a series of twelve metrical rhymes, each cataloguing a mother's (or sister's) sin in morally reprehensible and extremely graphic detail. The mother in question is always the mother of the man you play it with. The object of the game is to defile your opponent's mother worse than he defiles yours. If you can do it in slick staccato rhymes, all the better for winning points. Cheers of onlookers translate into the points awarded.

Because of the depth of filth inherent in the game, there is an unwritten rule: You only play it with a willing opponent. The rule is: "If you signify, you qualify."

When someone makes an unkind reference to the mother of a non-player a rejoinder is expected only if the game is on. If the non-player wants out, this is accepted. ("I laugh and joke, but I don't play that game.")

But there is another unwritten rule—once you signify, you qualify forever. You can never back out again. Your mother is fair game, forever. You can't duck in and out of the game.

Curiously men would call each other motherfuckers without reference to the game. It was as if there were a parallel reality without connection. "Motherfucker" was not regarded, in itself, as a sign of signification. The term was so common in their speech, it had lost the harsh bite of its meaning. Men said it without even a moment's visualization of the vile and repulsive act itself. "Eat it raw, motherfucker," was almost like saying "don't bother me."

Andrew was sick of the game the first time he became an involuntary witness. Through the ages the game had lost the disciplines of its origin. Rhyme and strict metrical rhythm had largely disappeared. Only the degenerate images remained. Your opponent's mother was always a two-bit slut full of warts, dried cum, and syphilis marks. ("Wasn't much left of her cunt, so she liked to blow me off, then suck my ass. She had this special way of doing it. She liked to tongue it first, to lick the nice squishy stuff.")

For Andrew, already hardened by a year and a half of military barracks talk, this new level of emotional warfare was almost like venturing into a strange, alien world. It was so unreal in its depravity it did not even summon any reserves of emotional discipline and restraint. He thought of Zeedie, but quickly put the thought out of his mind. He did not want his remembered vision of her associated with these impoverished depths of human despair.

One night the game got out of hand. There was a new arrival named Blanch. He was rather short, half bald, pasty-faced, always sweating, and troubled by something he would not talk about. He was in for thirty days for being AWOL. There was an immediate bad mixture of human chemistry between him and Two Blow, a tawny paratrooper in for aggravated assault.

"I said I didn't want to play," Blanch said.

"Called me motherfucker, motherfucker," Two Blow said.

"That doesn't count. Motherfucker doesn't count."

"The <u>way</u> you said it counts. If you signify, you qualify."

"Your ass signifies. You're stretching the rules. I'm not a player. Back off, motherfucker," Blanch repeated.

But Two Blow would not cease. He aimed insult after insult at Blanch's mother, even following him around to ensure no barb fell wasted.

"She's dead, cocksucker," Blanch cried out one time in anguish. "God rest her soul, you motherfucker," Two Blow continued. And he would not let up.

The next day, Blanch was able to smuggle in a trenching tool from a work detail. He had shoved it under his shirt and down into the back of his pants. The guards missed it in the pat down. That night, long after dark, Blanch crept up to Two Blow's bunk and pulverized his face with the heavy steel blades of the shovel. Two Blow was still alive, but barely. His face was unrecognizable. His brain injuries were permanent. His head was only a pulpy deformity.

*

The fight with Crocodile came near the end of Andrew's fourth week of confinement, in mid-February, completely unexpectedly. Both Andrew and McNabb were trying to be extra careful to maintain a low profile. They worked hard, kept their few possessions in proper order, avoided talking in ranks or during dismounted drill, and otherwise tried to stay within the general boundaries of the rules.

Andrew had done nothing to provoke Croc. Croc simply came up to him one night in the barracks, just before lights out, as though it were now Andrew's turn.

"You the big dog," Croc said. His Florida hillbilly accent was rather pronounced. In other circumstances it might have been charming.

"Whatever you say," Andrew said.

"Got bit by a big dog once," Croc said.

"Sorry to hear that."

"Always wanted to make that big dog pay."

Croc was speaking in a tight-lipped menacing tone. At first, Andrew tried to avoid a confrontational eye contact. He wanted nothing to interfere with his quest to remain low profile. But Croc was coming closer and closer, almost an inch or two at a time. It was clear that Croc wanted to fight him, and this angered Andrew because he had done nothing to invite Croc's displeasure.

It was also clear that Croc liked to play with his victim first, like some animals do. Croc preferred to argue for a while before a fight, to strut and puff, to seek psychological advantage, to whip himself into an emotional frenzy. Croc seemed to take pleasure in the preliminary torment, as if basking in remembered glory.

"I think I wanna have big dog suck my cock, right here, where everybody can see." Croc moved within a foot.

Andrew now knew the fight was certain. The terror of six additional months in jail flashed through his mind, but he could not think of any way to disengage. At least, no honorable way. So now as Croc inched closer, Andrew locked his eyes into Croc. The stare-down would begin.

"Didn't know there were hillbilly queers," Andrew said.

Croc came directly up into his face, eyes locked, only a few inches away. Andrew continued the stare-down.

"You called me a fucking queer," Croc said.

"I bet your mother doesn't even know," Andrew said, taunting him.

"Big dog gonna die for that," Croc hissed. "Nobody calls me a fucking queer and lives."

Now that it was inevitable, Andrew quickly hardened his body for the showdown, Croc's face now almost nose against nose. With great suddenness, Andrew brought his right hand up from his side and caught Croc with a savage blow just under Croc's left jaw. He focused all the power within his body into the punch. He was standing flat-footed and had the extra leverage from the floor. And as he moved his hand straight upward, concentrating his entire force into the strike, he simultaneously let out a quick, violent explosion of air from deep within his lungs, as if to punctuate the assault.

He felt that Cameron fierceness within him, like an attacking wolverine.

He had hit Croc with the heel of his hand, rather than his fist. And the impact of the blow, its power and swiftness snapped Croc's head in a sideways spiraling rotating motion that dislodged the spinal nerves along the vertebrae on his neck.

Croc was down, sputtering air in short, quick gasps, across his open tongue. But he could not rise again. He was out, unconscious. The large crowd of prisoners, from both floors, who had gathered to see the fight, just stood where they were stunned.

Croc was in a coma. He went to the hospital. Andrew was sent back to the main post prison, and into the "hole," wondering why he had put himself in this precarious position.

*

The Black Box wasn't as hard as he thought it would be. At first, Andrew was comfortable in solitude. His active mind now would have extra time to think things through. His main immediate concern was when he would get out. Croc had not regained consciousness even in the hospital. He had entered a coma state. No one knew when he would recover. As Andrew was led to the solitary confinement of the Box, a sadistic guard passed on the rumor— "If he dies, they'll get you for manslaughter. You could get at least 12 years. In jail everything doubles. If he recovers, they'll get you for fighting. Either way, you better make yourself comfortable. You may be here for a long time."

He closed his eyes against the blackness. They felt funny closed. He had to hold them shut for a while to get used to the sensation. Then it didn't seem to matter. He felt he could sleep with them open in the darkness of the Box. But after a time his mind was becoming dull and quiet and peacefully depressed. He would sink into sleep, then wake without any definite knowledge of the passage of time. And when he woke, he was not entirely sure he was awake until he blinked his eyelids. He knew he had to exercise his mind like a running machine.

In the blackness of the Hole he strained his ears to attempt to hear any small noise that would help him stay anchored. The few noises that penetrated his solitary state were low and muffled, but he listened with great earnestness to identify their source and character. He knew he had to keep his anchors, to maintain his sense of self. He tried to maintain a consciousness of time, but it was difficult. The sense of time becomes much different in the Hole, more dreamlike. He began to recite to himself many of the poems he had once memorized and felt a warm glow when he found he could still recall them all.

Somewhere between poetry and madness, he said to himself, forming the words as though in a composition, I will linger with unbridled hope in the darkness of this dungeon, however long it takes. I will somehow bend the army to my will, make them deliver on their promise.

In three days he was released from the Hole. Croc had recovered and was on his way back to the Stockade. Andrew blinked a number of times to accustom his eyes to the light again. But his anxiety was relieved. He would not face manslaughter charges.

Chapter 14

Under guard, he was moved again to the Stockade. It was mid-afternoon and McNabb and the others were out on a work detail.

Sergeant Kubla summoned both Andrew and Croc to the Orderly Room. They stood before him. Kubla was in a taunting mood.

"Croc," he said, "I gave you this job because I thought you could handle it. Now look at you."

"Sarge, I ain't finished with him yet. It was a lucky punch."

"You don't even know what hit you," Kubla laughed.

"Just give me one more lick at him, Sarge."

"You had your licks. You ain't gonna lick nobody. You ain't got the job no more. Tomorrow you go out under the gun," Kubla said with firmness.

"Just one more lick, Sarge."

"You gonna lick the back end of a shovel from now on. I can't have a Yard Boss who's not up to the job. Your job was to keep order inside. All you've done is bring me problems. I need a Yard Boss who brings me solutions."

Then Kubla turned to Andrew: "What are you in for?"

"Mutiny," Andrew said, then reconsidered. "To be specific, I refused a direct order to jump out of an airplane."

"You know, of course, you can get six more months for

211.

fighting… I have the power to waive that."

Andrew wondered if Croc were to suffer the same punishment, but Kubla answered the unasked question right away. "Croc, of course, is exempt this time. Yard Bosses are expected to fight …" He looked directly at Croc. "And win."

Andrew addressed Kubla. "As far as I'm concerned, I would be happy to put things back the way they were."

Kubla gave an explosive laugh. "Where are your brains? Things can never be put back the way they were. Every day is a new day. Yesterday is history. Every day, you stand on the shoulders of yesterday."

Kubla continued. "Well what do you have to say for yourself for messing up my Yard Boss?"

Andrew tried to gauge his answer according to the expression on Kubla's face. He could not be sure. "It was a lucky punch," he said.

"I need that kind of luck here," Kubla said. "When's your time up?"

"Twentieth of June if they count good behavior."

"I'm the one who makes the count," Kubla said. "Cameron, you are now the new Yard Boss."

"Sarge," Andrew protested, "I just want to do my time and get out of here, keep a low profile."

Kubla smiled. "Anybody who puts the Crocodile into a coma with one punch has no chance of a low profile in here. Your reputation went around the Yard like a bolt of lightning."

"Am I allowed to say no?"

"You could … then again, Captain Witkins wants me to

process charges against you for fighting …of course in a couple of days he' forget he asked me, if I let him."

"You've got me by the nuts," Andrew said.

"Do you want the job?"

Andrew hesitated. "Sure, I'll take the job."

Kubla smiled. "We already emptied Croc's things out of the Yard Boss room. He's now in the fourth platoon. You can move in immediately. You've seen how the place runs. First thing in the morning, fall everybody out. Headcount. Drill. They're your babies now. They're all bad actors. Don't ever let them smell your blood."

*

Andrew found McNabb as soon as he was back in the compound. McNabb grinned. "Low profile, eh, Big Dog?"

"I tried my damnedest."

"Rumor is you're hot shit now," McNabb said, still grinning.

"Jack, I'm the new Yard Boss."

McNabb's grin slowly disappeared. His face became serious. He began to rub his chin.

"After we finish drill tonight, come over to my room. I have Croc's old room in the second platoon. We got lots to talk about."

McNabb continued stroking his chin, squinting. "I don't know, man," he began. He pulled out the small butt of a cigarette, lit it, and let it hang dangerously close to his lips. "I hate to say it, but you're gonna have to be on your own for a while. I can't talk to you, at least not privately."

"What's the matter, man?" Andrew asked. "I fought Croc fair and square."

"I know that. I was watching. This has nothing to do with the fight."

"Tell me what's bothering you."

McNabb was slow to answer, as though the words were straining against his throat. "You ain't with us anymore."

"What do you mean?" Andrew asked, still puzzled.

"What did you say your new title is?"

"Ah."

"Know what I mean?" McNabb asked.

"I didn't want the job, Jack. I tried to refuse it. I still don't want it, but I had to take it. Witkins wants to press charges for fighting. Kubla has the power to make it go away. He had me by the nuts."

"So you joined their side. Why did you do it, man? Why?" McNabb spoke almost in anguish.

"Jack, I thought you would understand."

"All I know is I'm here and you're there," McNabb said. "Jack, I'm not any different from what I was a few days ago. I didn't join anybody. I have no intention of being a flunky for the Guardhouse."

"Don't you remember why we came here?"

"I haven't forgotten for a second," Andrew said.

"You're gonna get involved," McNabb said.

"Jack, you're the only buddy I've got."

"As I said, I've got to keep some distance. I don't want anybody to think I'm eating cheese for the Guardhouse."

"Jack, in a million years, nobody would ever peg you for a cheese eater."

McNabb put a friendly hand on Andrew's shoulder. "I'll leave you with one piece of friendly advice."

"What's that?"

"Never close your eyes in the shower."

After lights out, Andrew sat for a long time on the single bunk of his six-by-nine new quarters, smoking the dry ends of somebody's old cigarette butts.

*

Kubla's last instruction to Andrew was: "I expect you to solve problems any way you can. Whatever you have to do," he said with a winking grin.

With McNabb keeping his distance, Andrew felt lonelier than ever, but he put his loneliness aside and began to think about the hundreds of new decisions now required. First, how to create order and the <u>appearance</u> of order. That seemed to be the primary mission.

The next morning, after the bitch box had summoned the compound from sleep, in the still-dark North Carolina chilly pre-dawn, Andrew stood before his new charges on the small platform in front of the guard house, his fatigue cap slanted a bit forward on his head so he could squint more effectively from under its protective bill.

The whistle blew from the Guard House. The prisoners fell out. Most of them seemed sleepy and sullen. Most were restless, rebellious, underfed. They formed a loose series of four ranks of about fifty each, their faces strangely illuminated by the two single unshaded electric light bulbs on each side of the Guard House door, and by the shadowed waves of light from the searchlights still burning from the guard towers.

He knew the success or failure of his administration would be in those first few moments before them. They would quickly take his measure. They would note <u>everything</u>—the sense of command he would project, the way he would stand, the way he would hold his roster, the look in his eye, the timbre of his voice, what he would say. A hundred things would interplay in those first few moments that would set two hundred complex decision processes in motion and would make the initial determination of whether he would be master or they.

He had already decided not to copy anything Croc had done, except in one respect. Croc had made it a point to demonstrate his personal exemption from certain rules and restrictions, even to the point of flaunting the status of his position. Though extra shoelaces were contraband, prisoners were allowed primary boot laces so they could go out on work details. Croc made it a point of wearing his boots with no laces at all, the tops flapping open, his pants tucked loosely inside. He was the only prisoner so attired and with indelible black ink, he had sketched a clenched fist on the back of his fatigue jacket, against the rules. Croc also wore a police whistle dangling from a heavy gold chain about his neck, confiscated after the fight. All the guards wore police whistles.

Andrew decided he would do none of these. He would run the compound according to the ordinary rules of military discipline, and in his own attire, habits and bearing attempt to reflect the same discipline. He would not flaunt anything. He especially would not wear a police whistle.

The one thing he would try to emulate was Croc's sense of rhythm. His lilting style of calling cadence and maneuvering the platoons through dismounted drill was almost musical. Andrew liked that. It was so much better than the flat, sterile drill commands he had experienced in military life up to now. Croc had done it in such a way you almost wanted to <u>dance</u> to his commands. Every command was almost a musical note, with a brief lilting back-tone.

Andrew briefly contemplated asking Croc to continue to lead the dismounted drill formations, one hour before breakfast, two hours after dinner, sometime more. But he quickly decided against it. To place Croc in that position would almost be like throwing in the towel, admitting he did not have the stuff within him to be Yard Boss. He would have to tough it out.

Because of the nature of Andrew's vocal structure, leading the dismounted drill formations would be extraordinarily difficult to do. All that made his voice what it was worked against the projection of harsh commands. Ordering the massed movements was simple. The routines were not complex. The hard part would be to project his voice in such a way that two hundred prisoners would snap to every command. Croc had a booming voice that easily mastered the lilting rhythms of exact cadence. Andrew had a different voice, often described as husky, but in any case, difficult to project. But he <u>did</u> have rhythm. As he stood before them, he deliberately paused for half a minute, as a projection of power. Then somehow, in his very first command to the assembled formation, Andrew found a way. He would project his voice from somewhere deep within his diaphragm and <u>will it</u> to carry crisply through the chilly air. He tightened his vocal structure.

"Company!" he commanded. Pause. "Ten-Hut!" He cut the word sharp and crisp as though it had been chiseled off his tongue.

They came to attention but they did not snap to. Rather, they sort of pulled themselves into that position. Andrew felt a small shiver of panic in his stomach, but quickly conquered it. He surveyed the ranks, taking his time. Noting the reluctant, the rebellious. He wanted them to understand he was taking note, that he had <u>time</u> to survey them. He paused again.

"Dress right!" he commanded, sharp and clean again. "Dress!" He cut the word in two and hit them in both ears with it.

"Straighten up!" he admonished them. They shuffled into an approximately straight series of ranks, each standing an arm's length apart.

"Readayp!" Pause. "Hrunt!" He felt the precision of his voice. "Hat ease!" he ordered and two hundred pairs of eyes were upon him.

First, he called the roll, according to military procedure—last name answered by first name. The headcount matched the records. Then he addressed them briefly.

"Good morning," he began. "My name is Andrew Cameron. I'm in this place or the same reason you are—I fucked up. They gave me this job of Yard Boss. I didn't want it, but here I am. And for as long as I have this job, I plan to do it to the best of my ability... There are only two things I want to say right away.

First, being in jail doesn't give any of us the right to be sloppy. Things are going to be run in an orderly way... Second, many of you think you got fucked by the system. Well, maybe you did. But as long as I'm in this job, and in whatever ways I have any power to control, nobody's going to fuck with you unfairly. Follow the rules and we'll get along just fine. We all want to get out of here in one piece. Let's work together and do it."

Then he formed them into platoons and led them to the rear of the compound for drill. In every way possible, Andrew tried to copy Croc's drilling style. Knowing Croc was now among the prisoners, Andrew wondered for a moment how Croc would assess his imitation, but he dismissed the thought. Andrew thought he was coming very close. He had quickly captured the rhythm and some of the lilt, but he could not get every nuance. In a way, it was almost as if he were an actor on stage, sensing the moment-to-moment reaction of the audience. He could, after a while, <u>sense</u> their willing obedience to his commands. He could sense that all two hundred of them, himself included, were sweeping along in almost mesmerizing rhythms akin to the exact cadence of a dance. And over time this new thing in his experience became so infused within his being, he would never entirely lose the sense of it.

*

In the beginning no one gave him any grief. Kubla was right. Andrew's reputation deserved or not, had swept like wildfire through the compound. And in these early stages of his reign, no one wanted to take him on.

There were certain ongoing work details inside the gate and

he decided to keep these in place for the time being. One of the inside work assignments was to rake the entire dirt compound every morning and ensure the grounds were clean of all debris. A number of men worked at raking. Each would typically select a patch of earth and rake without regard to anyone else's patch.

The result was that, viewing the compound as a whole, the rake strokes formed a crazy-quilt pattern of lines in the dirt, going every which way. Even though the yard was raked, it looked untidy, unkempt.

Andrew went out to the various yard work details and gave them an amended instruction: All rake strokes were to run in continuous parallel lines from front to rear of the compound, each crew to coordinate to make it happen. And as he observed the beginning results of his new instruction, he overheard one prisoner confiding to another:

"Do you know what that white stuff is on top of chickenshit?"

"No, what?"

"That's chickenshit too."

But by the end of morning the compound had a very orderly appearance. Kubla looked at it and was pleased. "I got the right man for the job," he said.

Andrew knew he had to make immediate plans, strategies, and to organize effectively for mission accomplishment, order, and security. He had either to retain, or appoint, platoon sergeants for each platoon. Then there were the inside jobs of barber, medic, fireman, cooks and others. As casually as he could, he made it a point to talk to a large number of prisoners individually, to find out more about them, to register their concerns and problems, to attempt to learn which men were the natural leaders, which men bonded together in cliques, and to assess where the hidden trouble spots were that might spring up by surprise.

There were several dangerous or unhealthy cliques he had to break up, as much as possible, right away. He dispersed them among the four platoons by changing bed assignments and work details. By the end of his first week he had appointed platoon sergeants (two of whom he retained from Croc's administration), being thoughtful about balancing color and ethnic lines. He tried within the boundaries of his perception to find tough natural leaders with a sense of compassion and respect for human dignity.

Throughout this process, McNabb maintained a respectful distance. They seldom spoke, and if they did, only a few words.

The suckups crawled out of the woodwork very quickly, and Andrew almost always sent them back into the woodwork as soon as they emerged. He did not want to feed into the loss of personal integrity spying requires. Some offered to serve as his intelligence system, or to do personal things for him.

The only offer he seriously considered before turning it down after several minutes, came from a man who offered to be his "bodyguard." The man who made the offer was "Smack" Jackson. Smack told him "Near as I can figure, they put me in jail 'cause I'm 23 years old and from West Virginia... Some guy attacked me and I put him away fast..."

Smack was a tall bull of a man with a shaved head and friendly disposition. He was not too bright, but he seemed to be thoroughly sincere and without guile, a very likeable man. He would have made a perfect bodyguard but Andrew decided he didn't need a bodyguard.

In the stockade the term "snitch" was never used. The chosen term was "cheese eater," and there were at least a half dozen of these. The most interesting was Dick Suchier.

Suchier approached him stealthily long after dark, in the fifth night of the Yard Boss job. He rapped so quietly on Andrew's door it took more than a moment to identify the sound.

"What do you want?" Andrew asked quietly.

"I came to tell you something," Suchier whispered. Suchier was a mousy, nervous, rather thin and small high-strung prisoner who was convicted of selling military equipment that he stole from a Straightleg unit supply room where he had clerked. He had a pinched face and unkempt straight brownish hair that sometimes fell into his eyes.

Andrew let him in the room and shut the door. "What's up?"

"Bed-check," Suchier whispered.

"Who's gonna get bed-checked?"

"You, maybe. I ain't sure. I think it's you. It's probably you. It's definitely you."

"Who's gonna try it?"

"That's all I can tell you. I just came to warn you." Suchier was not speaking in a low tone of voice.

"Why?" Andrew asked. "When?"

"You're breaking up the cliques. I don't know when. I brought you something. It's outside the door."

Andrew opened the door for him and Suchier reached down

222.

to retrieve what he had brought—a heavy iron bunk leg. He handed it to Andrew.

"Why are you doing this?" Andrew asked.

"Nobody likes me," the little one said.

"You're not alone in the world. Now go back to bed."

"…There's something else."

"What?"

"You can do me a small favor," Suchier said.

"Tell me what …" Andrew said guardedly, unsure of how he would respond.

"You know Sexy Jansen?"

"I've seen him."

"He's queer."

"Every queer seems to get the name of Sexy Somebody," Andrew said, remembering Phipps.

"He's after my ass. He's got huge testicles. He fills his scrotum with water in the shower. Then he splashes it all over me. He wants to fuck me up the ass. He wants to play Drop the Soap in the shower. He says he wants to ram some Lifebuoy soap up my ass first. He says Lifebuoy soap has mystical powers."

"Lifebuoy soap is contraband." Andrew said. "I don't know where he got it. I'm not gonna let that happen if I can help it. That's not a favor. That's simple good manners," Andrew said.

"Sexy keeps mocking me… You know how they call the names at Roster—you don't do it, but Croc always did—he used to pronounce it 'Suckyar.' I told him three times its pronounced 'Sook-e-ay.' It's French. But every time Croc would say 'Suckyar' I would have to say 'Dick.' That's my real name…

Why the hell didn't my parents just name me Fucking Richard? But they liked Dick. And Sexy mocks me with that all the time. He wants to suck me and fuck me blind."

"Did you ever think about changing your name?"

"I never thought of that."

"Make your own definition of yourself. Whenever I call your name, just answer Richard. Get used to it."

"Thanks."

"I'll do what I can. It's not a favor."

"Please get him away from me. I'll kill him if I have to."

"Let's not have it come to that."

"There's one more thing," Suchier said. "Rumor is if they can't bed-check you, they'll get you another way … They'll get you someplace else. In the shower or when you're on the toilet. They'll get you when it's easy."

"Thanks." Andrew sent Suchier back to bed. The little one seemed reluctant to leave. But then he tip-toes slowly and quietly through the barracks in his olive drab G.I. shorts. Andrew closed the door, propped the iron bunk leg where it was in easy reach. It reminded him of his old friend Guardo. And for a little while he smoked the slender butts of old cigarettes.

And when he closed his eyes again, he realized that he would have to sleep half-awake from now on, alert to the slightest sound.

From then on, Andrew placed an empty butt can along the top edge of his slightly opened door, in such a way it could not be removed from outside but would fall to the floor if his door were opened. Just in case he should become tired beyond endurance and actually fall asleep.

The next morning Andrew reassigned Jansen's bed and work details to keep as much space as possible between him and Suchier. Then he spoke to Jansen privately.

"But sir," Jansen protested, "I'm in love with him. Haven't you ever been in love?"

"Jansen, this is your first and final warning."

However, Jansen proved to be incorrigible. In less than a week Andrew walked into the shower to find Jansen with his arms around a protesting Suchier, trying to maneuver a big erection in place. A fellow prisoner, shaved head, was laughing and using the basin of his own scrota to fill with water and throw it on Jansen to cool him down. Andrew stopped it immediately and, with Kubla's approval, transferred Jansen to the main Post prison.

*

Several prisoners began to place themselves within the orbit of Andrew's personal gravity. They did not seem to be suck-ups in the sense they brought no initial offer of personal favors. They did not offer to become cheese eaters. They did not ask for favors. Rather they came one by one to inhabit the space around him, drawn by their sense of the puny "power" of his position. All were draftees from straightleg companies. All were former small–time hoodlums who would continue their nefarious careers after release from prison and the tours of enforced military duty were ended.

Andrew was aware of what they were doing, but he did not shun them or force them away, in part because he felt a profound loneliness, in part because—aside from the ways they had chosen to live their lives—all were colorful and interesting characters. He had not known men like these before, and they wanted to be near him. The new companions had not known each other before military service, but they quickly found each other, and bonded in a sense, in prison.

- <u>Larry Cummings</u> ("Monk") was in for suspicion of murder. The military could not yet prove its case, but in the certainty proof could be found, they were holding him secure.

  Monk was only five-foot eight, but of a stocky build that bordered on pudginess. He had short dark brown curly hair, and gray-green eyes shaded in mystery. If you were alone with him you knew your life was not necessarily secure. In fact, he sometimes bragged about this. ("I know how to make people disappear. No remains. That's my specialty.") He was a beast of prey in human form. He had a price list—how much it would cost you to terrify someone, or to break someone's finger, hand, arm, jaw, legs, kneecaps, or to throw acid in the face, etc., or to extinguish him (or her) forever. Women cost more than men. They were easier, he explained, but he had a sentimental streak, and the extra charges were to assuage his guilt.

  His favorite attack position was the drop kick—jumping up high and quickly smashing his feet into his opponent's stomach, chest, or face. He taught Andrew the technique. Monk was also a black belt karate expert, highly skilled in the use of hands and feet, and for his bulkiness, amazingly fast.

Monk had begun life with a religious devotion that bordered on zealotry. His passion was so intense he had entered a monastery at the age of 18 and thought he would remain there to the end of his days. For three years, according to the rules, he did not speak a word. Until one dreadful night when the Abbott crawled in bed with him with the smell of liquor on his breath.

Monk's first three words, after three years of silence, were: "Holy fucking Jesus!" He fled the monastery and decided to go the polar opposite way. He would go against God with a vengeance. And he did. He took sadistic pleasure in his maimings. And he began to talk again. So much so it seemed sometimes he would never shut up.

- Al Pisky ("Alibi Al") was in for assault. He was six feet tall with a rangy muscular build and shoulders always a little bit hunched forward as though symbolizing his characteristic aggressiveness. He had unusually large fists and enjoyed using them.

  Al had straight blond hair smoothed (when not in jail) with Brilliantine, and his eyes were cold blue steel. He did not so much look at you as shoot visual bullets into you. One look at him, and you would know instantly that nothing in the world mattered to him but his own desires. Like Monk, he too had a price list for his deeds of darkness, and the two of them spent as much time as they could debating the merits of each list.

  He did not know karate, but he tried to make up for what he did not know by brute force. Frequently, he made sure

227.

you knew it. ("I know how to take care of business.") He was good at covering his tracks and twisting his way out of bad situations with a glib tongue. He relished his reputation as a smooth talker.

Al often talked about his grand dream, the symbol of worldly success. "I plan to drive into the parking lot of Scott's Restaurant. I will be in a black Cadillac convertible with the top down. And I'll have two beauty queens beside me... Everybody will know I made it big."

- Johnny Carbo (Carbo) was finishing a sentence for armed robbery. He was of average height, more rounded than stocky. He had straight brown hair and a rough, mottled face and large lips. His eyes had a curiously flat look, and even when laid upon you, seemed to be wanting to look somewhere else. Of all of the new hangers-on Carbo used the most colorful array of language expressions. He would invent terms such as "mindshit" to described "the crappy thought residue that oozes out of an unbalanced mind." He had read what he described as "most of the second-rate works."

He was particularly devoted to the author Phillip Wylie (Generation of Vipers and Opus 21) and Wylie's steady avalanche of attacks on "momism." Carbo often referred to "the great god Wylie," and would bow down low with both arms extended in momentary supplication. ("He tells the truth about the way things are.")

Carbo was married but didn't spend much time at home. He said he made no secret of his unfaithfulness, but his wife was very understanding of his need to "fulfill" himself. ("Karen doesn't make a big congressional act out of everything.") And he took a powerful pride in his protective instinct. ("Karen knows I will lie, cheat, steal, and even kill if I have to—She knows she will never go hungry or without a home. She knows I'll take care of her.") Carbo also had a fatalistic streak that would allow him to plunge into danger without any real assessment of potential consequences. His grand dream was "to die with a ritzy smitzy hard on—real top hat"—either with Karen or whomever else was handy.

- <u>Winkie Malone</u> (Winkie), so called because of a permanently twitching eye, was the oldest and the shortest member of the new quadrille. Winkie was in for thievery. He never used a weapon. His cunning mind and slender, wiry build allowed him to get what he wanted by stealth. His sphere of operation before military service was New Orleans. ("I know every hidden doorway and every secret passage in New Orleans. Mardi Gras is like my big payday. After Mardi Gras I can knock off for a few months.")

    Winkie had been a submariner in World War II. Assigned to the Pacific, and on a bombed out boat that was sinking rapidly, Winkie did a heroic thing. Although he was out of the vessel, he heard his commander was still inside and wounded. Winkie clambered back into the sinking submarine and rescued him with enormous effort just as the dangerous waters of the Pacific were taking their final swallow. After the war Winkie reenlisted, but in the infantry. He wanted nothing more to do with submarines.

Carbo once tried to describe Winkie. "He's got the heart of a saint, and the mind of a criminal. You always have to stay at arms-length from him."

Monk and Alibi Al had come over right away to tell him they liked his fighting style. "Do you know what Croc's in for?" Monk asked.

"No."

"He beat up two M.P.'s. Beat the shit out of them. He's a mean sonofabitch."

"I'll watch my step."

And so, for a short time, these were Andrew's new companions. Monk was their acknowledged leader, to the extent they would recognize anyone as such. But each of the four seemed to have an unusual fascination with Andrew. He was, they said, unlike anyone they had ever known. And mixed in with this was a tinge of awe, the awe of the unknown. They couldn't figure him out, especially his patriotism.

*

After he had more or less completed the reorganization and administrative procedures of the Yard, and found his leadership was winning favorable impressions during the weekly inspections, Andrew found he had a lot of empty time on his hands.

During the first few weeks of his reign, no one challenged him to fight or made fighting necessary, but this would soon change. McNabb was still keeping his distance, but the four new companions would gather around him whenever there was opportunity.

Because he had been a voracious reader, Andrew missed the company of books with lingering sorrow. He gave thought to reading the Bible but could not bring himself to do it. He regarded it as mostly mythology. All that his grandfather Cameron had tried to teach him had by now faded, imprisoned somewhere in the remote recesses of his mind.

He thought if he could create a real Day Room, with books, magazines, chess, checkers—this would be a great improvement in his own life and in the lives of the restless prisoners. In the meantime, he would continue to count the days to his release, each one more agonizing as the uncertain date came closer.

He felt the restlessness especially when work details went out the gate in the morning and wished he could be among them. The surrounding double chain link fence and ever-present patrolling guards seemed more oppressive than ever. There wasn't really a great deal of work to do inside.

He took his concerns to Sergeant Kubla. "Sarge, I'll give you three reasons why we need a Day Room."

Kubla laughed. "Save your reasons. Ain't gonna happen."

"All of us need something to occupy our minds while we're inside, something to keep our minds alive, something to pass the time."

Kubla interrupted with another laugh. "The workday here is fifteen hours. You're worried about passing time?"

"Sunday, everybody goes crazy just waiting."

"The Chaplain comes down…"

"I don't see why a man's mind has to wither away just because he's in jail."

"We have movies once a week."

"Joe Louis fights. That's the only film you've got. I think I know his style by now... I'm thinking we should have a small library at least."

"Ninety percent of these guys can't do better than comic books."

"It doesn't have to be John Stuart Mill. Something that gives some nourishment to the soul—other than the Bible."

"What's your beef with the Bible?"

"It's okay for people who need a crutch."

At that word Kubla seemed to stiffen, lose some of the joviality of his mood. Andrew sensed he had inadvertently tossed an exploding moral grenade. Kubla was not happy.

"Cameron," Kubla said, "if anything like that is ever done here it ain't gonna be quick. Now I would suggest you spend your time running the compound. That's all your job is. You ain't a social director. You ain't been put in here to be a reformer or a crusader. We gotta work slow here. Everything's gotta be improved slow. Talk to me about it some other time. But not soon."

"What did it mean to be Yard Boss?" Andrew wondered all over again, trying to define his role. Could everything in the universe be reduced to this one small jot of earth, or was it all as simple as it appeared to the naked eye? He reminded himself for the thousandth time that he must keep as low a profile as possible, get out of here, get to Korea to fight and either live or die, and if he lived then get on with his real life. He wanted to keep his mind clearly focused, brush aside all that was extraneous to his personal mission. He swore to himself not to lose sight of the reason he had come here.

Sitting on the edge of his bunk late that afternoon, he tried once again to formulate in his mind what role he could play within the defining boundaries of his mission. And it occurred to him that he would not serve simply as a connecting link between the Guardhouse and the prisoners, but rather he would serve as a solid plane—like a governor—between the two. On one hand, he would be a shield, as much as was within his power, protecting the men from the full brunt of harassment from Captain Witkins and a few of the more sadistic guards. On the other hand, he would attempt to create a work culture and sense of order that would somewhat minimize the potentials for Guardhouse pressure. It would be in this way he could see himself as a balancing force.

And he would do everything in his power to stay alive. He would listen to the hum of the compound and waken swiftly if any note of it were out of place. He would be especially careful in the shower or the latrine, ready to rise instantly into action. And he would sleep on the nervous edge of sleep. He could rest his mind again once he got out of here. Or so he thought.

It was almost a month into his administration when the aura of the mystery from the fight with Croc wore off and he had his first challenging encounter. In fact, it had now begun to work in reverse. He had become the man to take down, the symbolic pathway to someone's sense of small personal glory.

The first of these challenges was, in a way, one of the worst. A tough and blocky paratrooper named Spacek decided to take him on one night after drill. Everything about Spacek seemed rectangular—head, body, hands, even his abundant muscles.

"I'm gonna take you out," Spacek said.

"Let's do it and quit all the small talk," Andrew said, and invited him to join him in his room, where they could fight in private, out of the purview of the guards.

And without further conversation, as soon as Andrew shut the door to his room, they went at it. Spacek seemed unusually strong, and like Jimsun months before, almost immediately began to wrestle rather than punch. But Andrew quickly got the better grip and had Spacek against the bed, maneuvering for a knock-out punch. Spacek quickly brought his thumbs up to the base of Andrew's eyelids and tried to dig in deep.

"You sonofabitch," Andrew shouted. "You're trying to claw my eyes out!" Now in a flurry of anger as Spacek pushed his thumbnails hard against the base of Andrew's eyes, Andrew dislodged his hands and knocked him to a semi-conscious state with a flurry of punches. Spacek was now in a sitting position, bleeding and dazed, against the corner walls of the small room.

Andrew picked up Spacek's hands and looked at his thumbs. Spacek had grown his thumbnails long enough and hard enough to sharpen to deadly instruments. They were like small triangular spades (this explained why Andrew was dripping blood from beneath both eyes). Spacek had attempted to gauge his eyes out.

Andrew pulled Spacek to his feet and wanted to strike him again, but he quickly remembered the Black Box and the prospect of a longer prison term. He restrained himself.

"Spacek, tomorrow I'm going to order the barber to cut your

nails… And if you want to take me down, do it like a man. I'm ashamed we once wore the same wings."

And Spacek stumbled back to his bed among the cadre of assembled onlookers.

Monk, Al, Carbo, and Winkie all tried to give Andrew advice for future reference. "What you do," Monk began, "is, as soon as you get them inside the door—you walk in behind them—you twist them around fast and give them a hard shove onto your bed. Then as soon as they're sitting there a little bit stunned, you slap their face hard two times. Forehand. Backhand. Whack! Whack! Then you tell them what's what. And if they try to go for your eyes, you slam your fist, or the back edge of your hand, straight up against their nose. If you do it right, and fast enough, you drive the cartilage from the nose straight up into their brain, like a spear."

"But that would kill someone," Andrew said.

"Maybe," Monk said. "Or maybe some brain damage. Either way, you win. I'm gonna teach you karate."

"That's too fancy," Al said. "I say just beat the shit out of them and make them clean it up."

"I can get you a weapon if you've got a place to hide it," Carbo offered.

"Just tell me who," Winkie volunteered, "and I'll put some drugs under his pillow. One word in the right ear, and wham! He'll be out of here and no more worry."

Of all the advice, Andrew decided he would accept one offer. He would learn karate from Monk. Monk taught him to leap into the air and propel both feet in midair into an opponent's chest or head with explosive force. He taught him how to momentarily stun an opponent simply by making a sharp, explosive "Huh!" from deep within the diaphragm. If done right, it would stun someone just long enough to provide a small advantage while your fists were traveling to their destination. And Monk taught him how to swiftly and sharply "box" someone's ears with the flats of both hands, either to cause severe pain or deafness. And he taught him more than he already knew about how to concentrate the force of mind power, how to focus the whole being in every blow. But Andrew knew as he was learning, he would probably never use most of this knowledge. He could not contemplate personally killing anyone.

Andrew had a chance to try out one or two of his new moves right away. "Stonehead," a new arrival to the yard, would stare aggressively into your eyes without blinking, until you looked away. This was his way of establishing dominance. When he tried it on Andrew, he ended up with two black eyes and a revised attitude.

After a time Andrew became sick of the continuing need to fight, but he knew he could never show it. ("Don't ever let them smell your blood," Kubla had said.) In the end, he knew, no matter how well you do it, there would always be someone who could do it better or harder. It would just be a matter of numbers. If he fought enough men, one of them would beat him soon. He could not muster the passion and the moral agony and the torment that drove his fists forever. Someday he would get tired, or drop his guard, or simply meet a man, bigger or smaller, in whom these things burned with a hotter flame. He felt weary and prematurely old. Less than three months to go.

Croc did not make any further attack. He was still not sure what hit him. Nor had any pressure come from the Guardhouse. Kubla never asked Andrew to "straighten out" any specific prisoner. Had he ever pointed anyone out for discipline, Andrew would have immediately rejected the proposal. The one thing he would not do was to become a Guardhouse stooge. He would die first.

*

A ray of sunshine came into his life in April, in the form of a guard they called the Big Swede. Swede was a college graduate (University of Michigan) who got drafted and placed in the Military Police shortly before he planned to begin a job in sales and marketing. He was a large and friendly, intelligent man with an easygoing disposition, always with a smile half-formed on his lips.

Swede and Andrew connected right away, and Swede would join with Andrew in conversation whenever possible. They talked about the University of Michigan—the campus, the professors, the buildings, the magnificent foliage of the autumn falling leaves. Andrew told Swede about the large system of tunnels beneath the campus, and his discovery of the "Phantom of the Opera" room below the original old English building. But he did not mention Laura, or what they had done there.

And they talked about books and ideas, about God and the universe. And Swede confided in him his grand dream. "I would give everything—everything—just to spend one moment in eternity."

And Swede smuggled in a book for Andrew, <u>Moulin Rouge</u> by Pierre LaMure, a paperback. And Andrew held it like a precious jewel, something to read at last. Because it was contraband, Andrew carefully dislodged a board from the wall structure of his barracks room and hid the book within the wall. He would tear out one or two pages at a time, read them furtively, and either swallow them or flush them down a toilet when he had read and savored every word. Until he had opened the book, he had not fully realized how passionately he had longed for something unattainable, something to read. It was almost like a narcotic.

And Andrew learned from him. It was not so much that Big Swede loved. It was that he approached this whole business of mankind from a viewpoint of love, and it was not abstract. Swede looked like a longshoreman after a hard week on the docks, except his eyes were not those of a dock worker. They were searching, wondrously inquiring eyes, and there did not seem in them the ability to inflict harm, no matter how profound the reason.

Swede was a gentle man, but he had the kind of gentleness that rests on real internal strength. And his temporary presence in Andrew's life was like filling up a vacuum of loneliness his life had become. Sometimes in the late evenings Andrew and Swede would walk together within the confines of the compound, and Andrew was astonished as he gradually learned that Swede was not especially conscious of the aroma of love he projected. He seemed to have no self-consciousness of his goodness. But whatever the Swede radiated was so visible to others, the prisoners did not regard him as some alien. Andrew could walk with him freely, and talk with him, without risk of being thought of as having "gone over to the other side." Swede generated a warmth that filled the compound whenever he was in it.

*

The same rotation of guards that brought in the Big Swede, brought in Andrew's new nemesis—Nelson A. Gumpster, who began right away to polarize the compound. Gumpster was a sergeant and was placed in charge when Kubla was off duty. And he projected an atmosphere of moral hostility that quickly infected the Yard, an unending stream of harsh judgments that seemed to issue out of a tortured mind.

Gumpster was a little man with a pallid countenance—wiry, erect, with beady eyes and a thin brown mustache. He wore a very visible hearing aid and was quickly given the name "Radar" by the prisoners under his supervision. And the name seemed to fit. Radar seemed to enjoy the wispy power of his position. He would hover over the prisoners, sneak up on them, threaten them, punish them for the most trivial infraction of the rules. He created a climate of fear. Not only the fear of drawing more time, but rather the greater fear that some of the prisoners expressed. Someday, or night, they might just cut loose and kill him, and that would be "the end of his whole goddam campaign of harassment."

Radar seemed to hate everybody who did not look exactly like myself, which was the human race. With great regularity he would refer to individuals, (or call them to their face) as Wops, Jews, Kikes, Spics, niggers, Dagos, Polacks, or whatever other epithet came to mind. He created an especially inflammatory atmosphere when he openly referred to people as Niggers.

Andrew's determination to be a shield from Guardhouse harassment did not contemplate the likes of Radar. Radar was a malevolent force he could not effectively contain. And so he decided to be extremely careful in his presence, following even the most chickenshit rules and doing everything "by the book."

As April winds blew into the compound it was hard enough to maintain order among the restless and rebellious prisoners. The coming of Spring had got all their juices flowing. And now, with the poisonous tirades from Radar, tensions were beginning to mount. The polarization was becoming more intense. Word began to spread of a possible race riot. Everybody was quoting Radar and choosing sides among the cliques.

Andrew sought out the leaders who seemed to be fomenting the riot atmosphere and talked to them individually and in small groups to attempt to subdue the riotous passions. But he was only mildly successful. Tensions continued to build. Again and again Radar's agitation was mentioned, but Andrew said he could do little about it.

"Fuck Radar," he would say. "Let's not let him control our futures. Let's stay cool. Let's keep our focus on getting out of here in one piece."

"We're not gonna take it anymore."

"Bite the bullet," Andrew would say.

"Shit on bullets," they would say.

Andrew tightened up control of the chow line, which is where some of the more visible tensions originated. He assigned several of the toughest men in the compound to prevent line bucking. But this only helped for short time before the plan began to unravel in the face of human inertia.

*

Kubla spoke one evening to the assembled prisoners, trying to reduce the hostile atmosphere. He told them he was born color blind and made them laugh about it. "I have seen riots in confinement," he said. "Just remember, there's no place to hide once it's started. Weapons come out of nowhere. You get ganged, cut up, shanked up, killed in a bad way. Just don't start. Keep your cool. Stay alive."

As the tensions were mounting in the compound, Andrew had sought advice from someone he had befriended a short time earlier, Willie Sloane. Willie was serving only a short sentence 1-30 days for AWOL. He had left the Post without authorization to visit his dying sister. Andrew and Willie quickly formed a connection. In addition to Willie being a thoroughly likable person, filled with humor and intelligence, Andrew felt he had been too harshly judged. He enjoyed Willie's company. Several times in the last few weeks they had engaged in extended conversation.

Because Willie had skin tones the color of milk chocolate, Andrew had turned to his friend for advice as the passions mounted in the Yard.

"Willie, what do you think I should say?"

"Andrew, whatever you say tell the truth."

Andrew followed Kubla on the platform. He wasn't sure what he would say, only that he had to say <u>something</u>. He would make it up as he went along. And some of the thoughts that came out his mouth surprised him.

"I'm not colorblind," he began, wondering even as he said it why he had begun this way. "I won't pretend I'm colorblind. I have 20-20 vision. We can all see that we're the same in some ways, but different in other ways. We're not equal in our endowments of abilities. But we <u>are</u> equal in our spirit. I don't know if there is a God, but if there is, I know he likes variety. We are all part of the same human brotherhood. We all have something deep within us that <u>commands</u> respect for our individual dignity... I don't care whether you're white or black. Our blood runs the same color. There's going to be one law for everybody. There's not going to a white law and a black law.

There's going to be one law for everybody. And I will pledge my life to uphold it in every way I can... Skin color means nothing to me. I don't look at color. I look at character. Trash is trash, and it comes in all colors. I look at what's in a man's heart. And our hearts are all the same color ... Let's get over this problem. Let's not allow <u>anybody</u> to get his grip on us, to instigate us to make our troubles worse. Let's put our troubles aside and work together... This is what our mothers would want us to do... I will do everything I can to make teamwork possible. And I've been in this job long enough for you to know, <u>by my actions</u>, that I'm not feeding you a line of bullshit. I'm telling you the truth. And you know I'll keep my word."

Fortunately, Radar was off duty that night, so his presence among them would not have an incendiary effect. Whatever foul thoughts emanated from his tortured mind would not pollute the atmosphere or dampen whatever spirit of progress might have been aroused.

Andrew observed the body language of the prisoners but he could not sense immediately whether a turning point had been reached. There were no overt signs one way or another, but by the following morning he could see some evidence the sputtering fuse was dying. It was not as though someone or some group had called off the riot. It was more that it had not fully gathered force. There was no single moment when it was over, but Andrew sensed the waning passion, and with deep gratitude.

Chapter 15

May began with a gentle morning mist that filled the early dawn. Its sleepy arms stretched across the fields and grasses of the other world and into the restless compound. And then soon it was washed away by a quiet spring rain that left glistening memories in the sheen of distant pines and along the hard twisted chains of the double fence. Fresh droplets sparkled in the rays of the newly risen sun.

And then came a warm and balmy breeze, lingering with the cradled smell of pines, hinting of how beautiful the world was outside. And for a little while in the quiet morning light there was a palpable sense that the beauty of the world was formed in holiness. It was a Sunday morning that made you want to bare your chest and express your soul. And huddled in their little acre of gravity, the prisoners beheld these things that touched their inner depths with stirring poignancy. Spring: Billowing, flowing unreachable. And the breeze brought forth a single petal from some old forgotten rose and pressed it against the outside fence. Andrew watched it for a while before it fell to oblivion.

The anthill incident came later that afternoon, after the ground had dried and a colony of ants was busy at work gathering food and tending to their queen. They were so industrious they aroused Andrew's curiosity. He stood above their little home and watched them work. There was only a single slightly mounded entrance from which they hurriedly ran forth and returned with fresh food, not stopping for a second. He admired their steadfastness. It was only a small nest of ants, the kind that grow small wings to carry out their single mating flight. Once mated, the wings are lost, and the remaining destiny of the ant becomes earthbound. Some of the ants were taking wing, in preparation for this golden moment.

Because it was Sunday, and warm, and because Radar was off duty and could not harass them, the prisoners milled about the compound in small groups, talking and passing time.

As the ants scurried in and out of their home, another prisoner, one they called Rondo, took the short butt of a cigarette and plugged their hole with its burning end. And the ants that were outside the hole got word of it and ran back to the entrance. But the entrance was closed off by the fiery end of the still-burning cigarette.

The ants ran around the hot butt and passed in close trying to drag it away. But it was too big for them. They could not move it with all their effort. Then, one by one they drew back in a single line and began to run up on the burning butt. They flung their small bodies across it. They would sprawl across it, writhing painfully as they burned to a little ash upon it. And each one followed the other, followed by another, until at length they succeeded in extinguishing it.

And the ants that were left carried off their dead brothers, and tugged and tugged at the dead butt, finally pulling it from the hole. And a little baby ant emerged from the hole and was greeted by a tumult of his brothers. And then the thronging antdom followed him out and they all began to rebuild the entrance to their home. And as they labored, Rondo, suddenly raised up his boot and crushed them all and caused great ruin to their home.

Andrew stepped over to him, and without conversation punched him hard in the chest, knocking him down. And Rondo lay on the ground, resting on his elbows. Not ready to get up, but not badly hurt.

"Christ, what d'ja do that for?" Rondo said in an almost tearful voice.

And Andrew did not answer him. He only looked at him for a few moments and then began to walk away.

"They were only fucking ants!" Rondo said to Andrew's back. "Who the fuck do you think you are?"

But Andrew decided not to answer that question either. He wasn't sure he would know how to answer.

*

May was especially painful for Andrew because the June 20th release date was now so near and yet so far. Anything could screw it up, extend his time. He was on edge. He tried to avoid fighting and mostly succeeded. Out of sheer necessity, he began to use a greater part of his brain instead of his fists. He became better at anticipating trouble and taking skillful steps to prevent it or outmaneuver it. He became better at using humor to diffuse tense situations. He became better at keeping his main priorities in focus as trouble brewed in its endless cauldron. Knowing he was so close and knowing the potential treacheries, his mind was on red alert all the time.

Fortunately, none of the rumored "bed-checks" had been

attempted. He had gained a reputation for fairness that went a long way to dispelling feelings of revenge among the prisoners. Even so, he continued to sleep on the razor's edge of sleep, to be especially careful in the shower and latrine. And he longed for the time when he could close his eyes and sink into a deep sleep once again, without the anxiety of knowing that at any moment an attack could come out of nowhere and he would have to respond with all his being against a creeping, armed antagonist.

In this warped sense of time that is the handmaiden of prison life he sometimes felt as if he had been confined forever. Thoughts would pass through his mind that he was losing his identity, that he was degenerating, becoming evil. Sometimes he felt haunted by the chain-link fence and wondered if his eyes looked haunted. He could not tell for sure in the vague reflections from the tin sheet mirrors of the latrines. He longed to get out the gate again. The outside world was becoming dreamlike.

Some nights when the moon was like a golden apple in the sky, his memories were harder to control. Sometimes when he thought of the women he had loved, or tried to love, he had to get a firm grip on his emotions to keep from punching out a wall. Just the thought of a female body in his arms would almost drive him crazy with desire. Sometimes he cherished freedom with an intensity that approached madness. But you would never know this to look at him. He had become quite good at hiding his feelings behind a mask of matter-of-factness.

It was on one of these evenings—full moon and empty arms—when the incident with Radar occurred.

It was an evening in late May and he was sitting on the floor at one end of the Dayroom where old sports films from the 1930's were shown. Prisoner attendance was compulsory. And on this particular night Andrew was sitting quietly with his head leaned down upon his knees. He had seen the film twice already and knew every punch Joe Louis was going to throw. The room was quite crowded with men sitting on the floor and around all the walls, their legs doubled up and sweating. There were no chairs. The room was dark as the projector spun with a ratchety noise.

Andrew was not physically tired. He was depressed. And he closed his eyes and put the room and its sounds far away until there was a long steady quietness in his mind. He was almost in a meditative state when it happened.

Radar swung his boot swift and hard against the side of Andrew's head, snapping it sideways with a painful jolt. "I'll teach you to sleep in here!" Radar yelled.

Andrew was on his feet in an instant. Not yet thinking straight, he quickly had his hands around Radar's neck, but not before Radar followed with another curse: "You're a prisoner too. Just like these other shitpiles. So don't get smartass with me."

Every man in the room rose at once. Andrew was still not clearheaded. He knew enough not to squeeze or attempt to throttle Radar, but his anger was so strong he could not immediately pull his hands away.

He was not even fully conscious of being physically lifted. Only that two pairs of strong arms had pulled him away from Radar and were now quickly hustling him out the door into the compound, walking him swiftly away from the Dayroom.

"Take it easy, buddy," McNabb said.

He saw his two saviors, one at each arm, walking him hurriedly to the large open rear field of the compound, McNabb and Alibi Al.

"Thanks. I'm all right now," he said. They let him go but continued to walk with him among what had now become a throng of milling prisoners.

"If you killed him, it would be another 32 years," McNabb explained, "ten years at least."

"I was in such a faraway place in my mind when he kicked me, it took a while to get back," Andrew said.

"Thirty-two years ain't worth it," Al said.

And presently a squadron of guards came through the gates to restore order. Radar was ordering them around with an aroused fury. All prisoners were told to return to their barracks for lockdown and inspection. And Radar busied himself looking through rules and regulations, trying to find the exact way to charge Andrew with a general court-martial.

The next morning, as all of this came to Kubla's attention, and after the morning roll call and drill, Kubla summoned Andrew to the Guardhouse.

"I got some papers here, "Kubla began. "Radar wants to send you away."

"Maybe it's a case of mistaken identity," Andrew said tentatively, hoping to avoid the worst. "It was very dark and there was a lot of confusion."

"That seems to be Radar's problem. According to the papers here, he can't produce a single witness."

"Not one?" Andrew asked with some relief.

"Not one."

Andrew reflected briefly on all the snitches he knew who inhabited the ranks of prisoners. If even the snitches were on his side, he felt a brief comforting warmth. But he knew he still stood on dangerous ground. Hearing Kubla call Radar by that name was reassuring. He felt he was in friendly hands.

"Now exactly what happened?"

"Do you want the truth?"

"I want the whole truth."

"We were watching a fight movie in the Dayroom. It was dark. I had seen this same film twice before. I leaned my head down on my knees to do some thinking. And Radar came up and without warning kicked me hard against my head… The kind of job I've got here doesn't take a lot of brains, but it does take reflexes. If I waited to find out who's clobbering me, I might have been dead a month ago… I grabbed Radar around the neck but I didn't squeeze. That's all there was to it. Two of my buddies hustled me out of there immediately… Officially, Sarge, I didn't do anything."

"Cameron," Kubla said, "you run a tight, smooth compound here. Every other Yard Boss I had was always grieving me with troubles. You've been keeping the troubles away. And you've been pulling good reports from the brass about the condition of the Yard. When the brass walks away happy, they don't come to grieve me with many things… You've got a lot of support behind you."

"Sarge," Andrew said, "what if you put me back in the ranks? Send me out under the gun?"

"You really want to go out the gate again?"

"I'll swing a sledge. I'll do anything…"

Kubla thought for a moment, looked through some more papers. "I guess you've put in your time as Yard Boss. You lasted a long time…" Kubla continued. "In the meantime, as I look through your papers. I think I have a better idea. An improved idea," he grinned. "As of next week, you're eligible to become a Parolee, assuming you've served your time with good behavior."

"Can you get past Radar?"

"As I said, Radar can't find a single witness. He said you tried to kill him. But no one saw it. Not a single witness. Not one. I can't process the paperwork without a witness."

"I'm immensely relieved, and hopeful," Andrew said. "I guarantee there will be no further incidents."

"Now's the time to keep your low profile," Kubla grinned.

That evening, after drill, McNabb, for the first time, came over to Andrew's room, and they talked for a long time, until lights out. "We're fucking close to getting out of here. You had me worried for a minute you might screw it up," McNabb said.

"I was on the verge of losing self-control," Andrew confessed. "I will be forever grateful that you and Al came to my rescue. I'm not sure what would have happened if you hadn't been there."

"Fuckin' A, man," McNabb said.

*

Some things seem to come in bunches—good times, hard times, Mack trucks, temptations—in this case, Andrew's continuing experience with Radar. And it happened only three nights after the Dayroom incident. Andrew had occasion to save Radar's life, in a manner of speaking.

It was during the regular two-hour period of dismounted drill, following the meager dinner meal. Andrew was putting all the approximately 200 prisoners through their routines in the large empty section in the rear of the compound. Radar had come out of watch time, and after a while, when Andrew had halted the formation, Radar went into action.

He called out to Willy Balducini by name and asked him to step forward. Balducini was in for only 30 days, having gone AWOL to visit a pregnant girlfriend. Radar, for reasons mysterious to everyone, had decided to single him out for a barrage of sadistic verbal torment.

Some men are born with the kind of complexion that never looks completely washed. And Radar chose to dwell for some time on the fact that Balducini looked unclean. "You don't need a shower," Radar said, "you need a hose."

"And one more thing," Radar continued. "You can't soldier, Balducini. You have no coordination. You can't drill. I don't know how they learn you in the Wop army, but you're in the G.I. army now and you better shape up… you better clean up too. I don't know whether they learn you to wash yourself in the Wop army, but you gotta clean up over here." There was real personal malevolence in Radar's voice.

It was not only that Radar degraded him. It was also the <u>way</u> in which he expressed the humiliation—the sneering tone of voice. And as Andrew watched the assault continue past the point of insult, he noticed that Balducini had taken a farther step forward. And then another swaying step forward.

Very quietly—Balducini was a quiet man—he walked slowly forward toward Radar. Radar ordered him back into ranks, but he continued forward without a word. Balducini was a rather large man, with shoulders like a bull. And as he proceeded slowly toward Radar he had a death look in his eye, a look of mesmerized utter determination. The quietness that came over the assembled prisoners verified that they knew. There was something of the presence of death in Balducini's entire bearing that seemed to say that Radar would die as surely as Balducini walked.

In the hush of what now seemed inevitable, Radar ceased his torment, turned, and swiftly walked away toward the Guardhouse. (In fairness, he did not run.) Balducini did not alter his speed or course, nor did the expression in his eyes change character.

Radar had almost closed the big iron chain link gate that separated the rear from the front compound. And as Balducini approached the gate, Andrew saw him hit it with his hand and it jarringly opened again. Radar had now reached the Guardhouse steps. Everything was happening in what seemed like a slow-motion movie.

Andrew quickly turned the formation over to his platoon sergeants and moved to intercept Balducini. He grabbed Balducini's two muscular arms, and Balducini offered no resistance. He stopped. And Andrew turned him gently around and led him back toward the formation. Balducini put his hand into Andrew's hand much as a little brother would do. And it moved Andrew strangely. It was all weird. No passion. Nothing quick. All slow motion.

"Why are you doing this for me?" Balducini asked.

"It seemed like the right thing to do. You've got a lot of life still to live."

Balducini stopped for a moment, looked at Andrew. "You know what?" he asked, almost as if he had just discovered a secret.

"What?"

"I'm not a Wop. I'm a Dago."

The next morning Radar had another sheaf of papers on Kubla's desk, trying to extend Balducini's prison sentence. But Kubla was becoming philosophical. "Seems like someone's always trying to murder you," he told Radar. And again there were no witnesses. Not one.

And later that evening Radar came up to Andrew to say, "Cameron, maybe I had you all wrong."

"How do you mean?"

"You stood up for me. I didn't think you would."

"Anybody would have done the same thing," Andrew lied.

"No. You don't know what I mean. These guys hate me in here. I didn't think anybody would stick up for me. Thanks."

"Think nothing of it," Andrew said.

But Radar did not drop the charges against Andrew or cease in his effort to have him prosecuted.

"He's one to figure," McNabb said.

*

Two days before Andrew's and McNabb's eligibility for

Parolee status would begin Andrew wanted to be especially careful that nothing would go wrong at the last minute. A big inspection was scheduled for this day, and the inspectors were late. Andrew had the whole compound raked clean, all rake strokes running in close continuous parallels from front to rear.

He did not want 200 pairs of boots marching over it before inspection. The parallel rake strokes had gained him favor as a symbol of orderly administration. Normally, he would march the prisoners through the wide separation between the second and third platoon. But since this was the most immediately visible aspect of the compound, he wanted to keep the grounds intact until inspection was over.

So instead, he marched the formation over to the side and along the strip of ground separating the first platoon from the double fence. And as they proceeded across this area, Andrew heard shouts from the rear of the Column. And he halted the formation, told them to be at ease, and turned to see several men floundering in a ditch that had suddenly appeared beneath them. A tunnel had just collapsed as the last men of the formation were passing over it. A group of prisoners, unbeknownst to Andrew, were digging a tunnel from under the first platoon and had now got as far as the first fence before its shallow roof gave way in the sandy soil. No one was in the tunnel at the time.

Andrew felt immediate sorrow that he had inadvertently foiled the diggers plan. But he also felt a small wrinkle of fear that this episode would result in adding more time to his sentence. To make matters worse, he almost bumped into the inspectors. They had come up behind him and were now peering interestedly over his shoulder, down into the crumbling earth. And then they did a terrible thing to him.

"Good job, soldier," a Major said. "That's one way to flush them out."

Andrew was mortified. On one hand the approval of the brass would work in his personal favor. On the other hand, the Major's comments might mark him as a rat, a Guardhouse flunky. He was hoping his reputation for straight talk would help him past this new hurdle. Which it seemed to do in part. There was a mixed reaction among the prisoners, some accepting his explanation that he didn't know about the tunnel, some believing he had deliberately exposed it.

*

Nevertheless, Andrew and McNabb went out the gate as Parolees on schedule. Now it was early June. Kubla released him from his duties as Yard Boss and buried the paperwork of Radar's complaint. A close friend of the Crocodile became the new Yard Boss.

"Good job, Cameron," Kubla said. Andrew's reign was ended. He was retired. And now that he was retired, he vowed he would never raise his fists to anyone again, except in self-defense, or to save someone from attack.

Now he could go out the gate as Parolee, no longer under constant guard. He could carry cigarettes. He could drive a truck. Both he and McNabb took a driving test right away, were given army licenses, and assigned to drive garbage trucks. No more fighting. He could do the rest of his time standing on his head, he thought.

In the meantime, three of his former companions had been released or were in process of release. Monk got out because no one could find convincing evidence he had murdered anyone. No dead body. No tracks. No smoking gun. He was boastful on his way out. "I told them they would never find anything. What I didn't tell them was that's my specialty."

Carbo had been released in April and Alibi Al would finish his sentence in mid-June. Both had won time off for good behavior. Carbo had sent word to Andrew that he was in Miami, working on something big, asking him if he wanted in on it when he got out. Andrew sent back word immediately. No thanks.

Driving the garbage truck gave Andrew a renewed connection to reality. The wind blowing in his face, the sun warm and streaming across his arms, the simple joy of doing something mechanical—all of it filled him with satisfaction and gave him a measure of freedom, however small, that satisfied the beginnings of his longings. At the dump he would see McNabb and they would gather stray books and magazines to fill their glove compartments.

Within a week he also came upon a recent newspaper, with a poignant headline: <u>Korean Peace Settlement Soon</u>. And Andrew asked some of the guards what they had heard, and they said rather casually, "The war's almost over. Didn't you get the rumor? They should have a peace agreement within a week or two."

Both Andrew and McNabb had volunteered for Saturday details washing trucks in the motor pool. Better than being inside the gate. And as Parolees they had more discretion about how they would spend their time. It was like an honor system.

Andrew churned the headline and the rumor through his mind again and again. He wanted the war to end. He wanted no more killing and violence. But up to now, since the armies had reached stalemate positions, he simply had assumed the war would go on until there was a specific resolution, a definite end. Now he pondered the situation and began to think his assumption was wrong. He could not imagine a deadlock going on forever. This is not the way of the universe, he thought. Surely there would be a breakthrough. Surely there would have to be a winner and a loser. In the meantime, he wanted to break not a single rule so he and McNabb could get out on schedule.

"What do you think of the rumor?" Andrew asked.

"Doesn't matter to me," McNabb said. If this one's over, I'll just go over and join the French Foreign Legion. Those bastards are fighting somewhere all the time."

McNabb's answer astonished Andrew. McNabb was losing his resolve. Up to now he thought they had identical motivations. Now, it seemed McNabb was moving somewhere else.

Andrew had experienced loneliness and depression, from time to time, but never, until now, had the thought of taking his own life even entered his mind.

It was on a Saturday afternoon, the second Saturday of his partial freedom. Andrew had finished washing a truck in the Motor Pool and was waiting for McNabb to return from somewhere.

The Motor Pool was quiet as was the entire surrounding atmosphere. It was a lazy, peaceful quiet. Andrew was sitting on the tailgate of the truck he had washed, smoking an actual full-length fresh cigarette. And he felt the quietness of the atmosphere almost bathing his body with peace and contentment. His legs dangled off the tailgate and he looked straight out into the golden beauty of the afternoon sun, feeling the treasured warmth of its rays. Few afternoons in his entire life had ever seemed so mellow.

He began to contemplate. First, the beauty of this moment. He tried to absorb it fully so that no part of it would be lost. And then he began to think back upon his life and purpose, and of the driving force of will that had brought him to this place. He contemplated the serenity and beauty of the sun. He contemplated his loneliness in that sun. He wondered if all his struggles had been for no real purpose at all, if all were now lost.

The end-of-the-war rumor had shaken him. He wondered if he had lost his worth to the human race. And his mind roamed back to the quiet times he had so much treasured on the Cameron farm. He remembered the stillness of the morning, the faraway cry of the mourning dove. He remembered the rustling of the afternoon breeze through the maple leaves above, and the stillness, the utter stillness of the pine Bush.

And he pictured Zeedie in his mind. Maybe she had been right all along. Maybe she could not love him because he was not worth loving.

An aura of utter defeat swept through him. And as he contemplated it, he realized it was not an aura, not a phantom-like mist. Rather, the sense of defeat was really a mirror in which he could now see for certain who he really was.

He imagined himself dying, here and now, in this vast quietness, in the warm rays of that gentle sun. And he contemplated putting himself to death. He thought it would be a perfect time to die, amidst such beauty, so mystically quiet and warm.

Is my life my own to take? He thought. Or do I hold it as a precious gift from somewhere higher than my mind can reach? Is my life my own, or is it borrowed in trust? And he imagined himself again dying by his own hand.

And that thought—that dreadful thought—danced around with its twirling, seductive beckoning for a full minute in his mind before he gathered his sense and threw it to the winds.

He felt life flowing back into him from the ragged edges of despair. He felt that perhaps, just perhaps, his life was not his own possession, but rather lent to him in trust from a power beyond himself.

These thoughts lingered for a while in his mind. And then he heard a bugle sounding faraway across the Post. The sun was at the horizon and the bugle was sounding Retreat.

Then he heard the bitch box from the Stockade, calling the prisoners out into formation. And as though he were waking from a dream, Andrew eased himself off the tailgate as McNabb returned. As the rush of life flowed back into him, for a few moments he felt this whole force and beauty of the universe filling him with an unimaginable peace and reassurance.

*

Both Andrew and McNabb were released on the sixteenth of June, four days earlier than planned.

"One hundred and forty-six days," McNabb said.

"How do you know?" Andrew asked.

"I counted," McNabb said.

The charges brought against him by Radar were still pending, but quickly gathering dust in Kubla's desk drawer.

The two of them were sent to the Replacement Company (Repl Depl), where they could look out again for a few days across the large field to the barracks of their old comrades … the 504th. They were certain now they would be transferred to the Far East Command.

A West-Point-looking straightleg Lieutenant interviewed both of them. He reviewed the paperwork but said little. "I have your transfer orders," the Lieutenant said.

"Where to?" Andrew said, trying to control his excitement. "Korea?" he asked.

"My orders are to transfer you to anyplace except Korea," the Lieutenant said matter-of-factly.

"Where are we going to go?" McNabb asked.

The Lieutenant grinned as though to a private joke. "You're not going anyplace. Your orders are for Camp Rucker, Alabama. And that's no place. You must have pissed somebody off big time. You'll have a 10-day Delay-in-Route."

"That's where old paratroopers go to die," McNabb said with a cynical smile.

Andrew was stunned. He thought Korea would have been a logical decision. Now, everything was uncertain again. They might as well have shipped him to a graveyard.

*

On the second evening of their assignment to Repl Depl, Monk and Alibi Al came over in Monk's big Cadillac, with a friend they called Hugo, Monk said he wanted Andrew to join them to celebrate Al's release this day. He had a special place to go. Andrew was reluctant. He had no plans to socialize with any of them in the outside world. But they were insistent, and Andrew thought to himself "what the hell," and said he would join them. And besides, he felt a debt of gratitude to Al for helping to save him from killing Radar. Al and Hugo took the back seat. The passenger seat was the only one left, so Andrew got in thinking nothing about it. He noted that Hugo sat behind him. There seemed nothing unusual about the ride until Monk pulled off onto a dirt sideroad that led back into the pine forest.

The moment Monk pulled off Andrew realized he might have inadvertently put himself in a bad place. He could not think of a reason why, but the dirt road they had now entered certainly did not lead to a "special place" to eat. He wanted out, but he was not in a good position. Thoughts were racing through his mind— what was this all about? He could think of nothing that might have put him in the cross hairs of their gunsights. He thought of Monk's frequent boasting that he knew how to make people disappear. He thought of Monk's karate expertise and Alibi Al's brute strength and aggressiveness. He wondered who Hugo was, who had said no more than hello to him and was now sitting behind him. He thought that, for reasons he could not fathom, he was now being taken on a "Mafia Ride."

He took a cigarette from his shirt pocket and lit it, casually holding it in front of and close to his face so that he could make it difficult for Hugo to throw a thick piano wire about is neck and pull it tight. And he didn't think he could take all three of them at once. What to do? He pondered, keeping the cigarette poised close to his face.

"Where're we going?"

"We wanted to talk to you a little bit," Monk said.

"About what?"

Monk pulled over into a grove of pines. The area seemed remote. Monk stopped the car and they all got out. Andrew felt measurably better. At least he was now out and in the open. He was sure all three of his fellow travelers were armed. Monk and Al had made it a point to let people know they seldom went anyplace "undressed." But facing them, at least he would have a fighting chance.

The three of them gathered around him, Monk in front and Al and Hugo on each side. "What's this all about?" Andrew asked.

Monk took the lead. "We think you ratted out Carbo."

"Where? How? When?"

"You remember when Kubla told you Carbo's dead?"

"Sure."

"Well, you said 'Carbo's not dead. He's in Miami. I just heard from him.'"

Monk went on. "We had a big thing planned. It was intricate and complex. It depended on people thinking Carbo's dead. We spread the rumor to the right people. We even had a fake newspaper article printed. It depended on Carbo being dead. You blew the whistle."

Andrew remembered the casual conversation he had had with

Kubla, when Kubla told him he knew for sure Carbo had come to a bad end. His response to Kubla had been innocent and natural. No one had bothered to bring him in on the deception.

As he quickly contemplated what to do, he made an immediate assessment of his chances. If he said or did anything that sounded like pleading, <u>anything</u> that would suggest weakness, he knew they would go for the kill. Fair or not, that was the way they lived. So he decided to take the opposing path. It was his only hope.

"Listen here, you fucks!" he said angrily. "If you plan a job and need cover, you've got to get word to the right people! If you wanted me to cover your ass you should tell me! You left me out of the loop! So don't come crying to me because of your own failures! If you want me to cover you, keep me in the loop!"

The thought that was flitting through the back of his mind as he said these angry words was this: Monk and Al had first become his acquaintances in what amounted to a superior-subordinate relationship. And once initially established, the essential <u>form</u> of this relationship never entirely disappears from future situations. There is a tendency to treat someone formerly in a superior status, to some extent, as though that relationship still existed.

Andrew was hoping this, plus his outrage and anger, the absence of any show of fear, would keep him in a position of psychological strength among them.

There was a pause as Andrew's words and strong attitude sank in. Andrew pulled all his muscles, and his will, into position to fight for his life. But Monk broke the spell. "We knew you were okay," he said. "We were sure it was just an innocent mistake. We just wanted to talk to you a little bit."

Andrew knew the highest point of danger had passed, and he quickly tried to reinforce the change in atmosphere. "Where the fuck are we going to eat? You guys sure know how to work up an appetite."

And they laughed with him, all except Hugo, who appeared rather stupid, waiting for further instructions.

Chapter 16

Back in Detroit, after hitchhiking there on his 10-day Delay-in-Route, Andrew encountered a mixture of feelings from Joe and Jessica—surprise, consternation, curiosity, all the rest. "Where you been?" they asked.

"In jail," he said casually as he registered their astonishment.

He told them the basic story but left out all the gory parts.

"What the hell was going through your mind?" Jessica asked. "Why did you mess up your life?"

"Don't ever tell anybody—anybody—you spent six months in prison," Joe cautioned.

*

Unopened mail was waiting for him, including a letter from Clara's brother, wondering why he had not come to Clara's funeral. Andrew read that one first.

"I forgot to tell you," Joe said. "Your great uncle called to tell us. We told him we didn't know where you were. She died in April. There was no way we could reach you."

Andrew took a long walk through the city streets to think about it, to remember Clara at some length. The two of them had never bonded in the way Andrew had bonded with Kenneth. But he loved her. He loved her simplicity and her goodness. There had always been a spirit of goodwill in her heart, and he was sorry he had not been there to pay his final respects.

There were two other letters, the first from Cynthia.

"Dear love of my life, I know you are getting my letters because I put return addresses on them and they don't come back. It seems like the earth just swallowed you up… Don't do this to me! I spend hellish hours…

You told me I had eyes like warm chestnuts. Oh, love, how that sustains me through your ruthlessness. Write to me and I will come running into your arms…

Wondrously waiting,

Cynthia.

Her letter was dated May 1. He decided he would write to her, but not immediately. By now she would be rapturously in love with her latest discovery.

The next letter he opened almost holding his breath. It was from Mienda, dated May 15.

Dear Andrew,

I bet you're surprised to hear from me. You probably forgot me a long time ago. But I never forgot you. The violin you bought me with your hard earned money changed my life, and I have never forgotten your kindness. You are a caring person, and I have begun to care for you and wondered if you feel the same. Sometimes I cannot think of you and breathe at the same time. I think [crossed out] I know I'm old enough for you now. Please let me know. I don't want to waste my dreams.

Sincerely, Mienda

PS: Kuki is married and has 3 kids. Mother is fine and my career is stimulating. I was wrong when I said I will be on my third concert tour by the age of 21. I'm only beginning my first—I leave for Vienna in 2 weeks. So at the ripe old age of 17, I am already a year or two behind...

PPS: Somehow I know your spirit will be with me - I remember the kindness of your eyes, the sound of your voice. Forgive me for getting mystical, but I <u>really</u> need to know how you feel.

Sincerely (<u>Again</u>) Mienda

The letter aroused his heart. He remembered Mienda with the greatest desire. He remembered her freshness, her innocence the peace and harmony of her soul. If there were any human being he would want to be with right now, maybe forever it would be Mienda. But aroused as he was, he reflected that at age 17 she was still jailbait and he could not come near her with sexual desires. It was probably a good thing her letter had missed him. It would be many months before she returned, and by that time, he would surely be in Korea.

He decided to write back. She was using her mother's address.

Dear Mienda,

Sorry to be so slow in getting back to you. I was away. And to make things worse, by the time this letter reaches you, I expect to be overseas (Korea) and out of touch again.

I just want you to know how much your letter means to me. I share your feelings, all of them, but know that in any event it will be at least a year before I can reciprocate. If your feelings continue that long—I know mine will—it would be the most wonderful gift in my life to hold you in my arms, to treasure you for all that you are, and are becoming.

Sincerely, Andrew

*

Andrew decided to drive out to Ann Arbor to see Brundi. There had been no attempted communication between them during the time Andrew was in jail, but that was not unusual. Neither one was given to writing letters. Charlene was working all day, so Andrew drove Brundi over to the arboretum for a long walk.

"I need to stretch my legs. Too much sitting. Too much studying. Too much small print. My brain feels like mashed potatoes," Brundi told him. The arboretum was still one of their favorite places to take a long walk, even circling around the same paths.

Andrew told him only the bare outlines of some of his military experiences. He did not tell him he had refused to jump. He did not tell him he had spent almost six months in jail. He only mentioned he was still trying to get to Korea but had hit some snags. But even as he was talking, he sensed a dark shadow falling over his words. He was not telling Brundi the whole truth. Was that a form of lying? He was sorting through his mind trying to decide how much more to tell Brundi, wondering if he would understand.

Then Brundi broke into his train of thought. "Give it up, man. That war is history."

"It's not over yet. Nobody has won yet. There has to be a winner and a loser. The universe doesn't tolerate stalemates. Balance, yes. Stalemates, no. There has to be a tipping point."

"Nobody cares. From the sketchy things I've read, the only paratroopers in Korea are back guarding prisoners in Koje Do."

Andrew did not mention that his precious wings were gone. "I'm transferring to a regular ground combat infantry unit. Korea is still my destination. I have to get into what's left of the war. I have to do everything I can to bring it to conclusion."

"A strange passion if you ask me," Brundi said, direct as he always was.

And through the afternoon, as they proceeded on their long walk, hardly looking at the beautiful trees, their talk began to turn to larger issues.

Andrew began. "Do you ever think about the human condition?"

Brundi gave out a hearty laugh. "Only when I get past the condition of my finances, and that's never."

"Wouldn't it be like restful play, to turn your mind for a while away from the minutiae of your law books? Once you get a little altitude, you can roam the universe."

Brundi laughed again. "I hardly have time to roam Charlene. Sometimes I think her needs are greater than mine."

Now Andrew laughed. "Let me know if you need any help."

They both laughed. Brundi spoke first. "Why do you want to roam the universe? It's empty space."

"Whenever I hear a phrase like 'the human condition,' I always feel drawn to it with a magnetic fascination. I can't think of a single article or book that I have passed by, that attempts to portray the general state of mankind, not one. I have to explore it in my mind."

"You must be a busy guy," Brundi said.

"Not really. There aren't all that many of them."

"What are you searching for?"

"Understanding... And yet I've always finished these encounters vaguely dissatisfied, as though I were seeing the glint, only a single facet, of the whole diamond, as though someone had discovered a dismembered fragment of truth without having the unifying vision to place it in relation to other truths, or to all truth. I always hunger for more. The appetite for comprehension is insatiable."

"Andrew, that's quite a mouthful."

Andrew continued as though his friend had not spoken. "And yet, what is the human condition? Are we not as diverse as life itself? Why do we all hunger so to know one or two things for sure? One or two things which apply to every human being? I'm trying to discover a few things—maybe there are a hundred things! I don't know—the few things you can say that portray truths so central that every human being is simply one more variation of one great idea that unifies us as a planetary race and brotherhood..."

Brundi broke in with his succinct logic. "Andrew, my friend, Alfred North Whitehead once said, 'seek simplicity, and distrust it.'"

"Thanks."

"My bill will be in the mail"

"I thought lawyers bill by the word."

"I'm learning value billing." They both laughed.

Andrew continued. "But don't you spend some time wondering why we're here, what is the purpose of human life?"

"You're assuming there is a purpose," Brundi said.

"When I see life take form, whether it's from the seed of a flower or a tree, whether it's a hatching egg, whether it's a newborn baby, whether it's someone just at the point of a new discovery—I see an amazing power of purpose. I don't need philosophical or religious proof. I can see the power with my own eyes."

"The power is easy enough to see. But how does power translate into purpose?"

"How can there be power without purpose?" Andrew asked.

"You're just making an assumption," Brundi said dismissively.

"I've wondered and wondered about human purpose. We are such a small speck in the face of creation, I have no doubt we have brothers and sisters throughout the universe. We can't be alone. That would be such a colossal waste."

"You're piling assumption upon assumption," Brundi said.

But Andrew continued, taking note of Brundi's comment, but not trying to rebut it yet. "It occurred to me that whatever is the purpose of human life, it must be something that affects everyone. However different each person becomes, there must be at least <u>one thing</u> every person must achieve in human life. Everything else is individual."

"What one thing have you decided?"

"I'm still working on it. But whatever the one thing is, it must be something common to every member of the human race."

"Nobody can answer that."

"Consider this. It seems to me the one thing common to every human being is that, once created, we continue to grow. Even if there is only a mind at work in a stunted body, growth occurs. If there is a functioning mind, there is growth. It's inevitable."

"That part I can agree with."

"What I don't know yet is whether we just grow large and more complex, or whether we grow <u>toward</u> something in some open-ended way. And if we grow toward <u>something</u>, what is the something? Because that's where purpose must originate… it's a two-way street. Human beings are <u>given</u> purpose, and yet each person must <u>create</u> a purpose. And life is designed that they should meet. It's a wonderful equation. Almost mathematical… or musical. I'm wondering."

Brundi laughed. "When you invited me to take a walk, I thought we were just going to look at some interesting trees. I didn't know we were going to walk through the outermost layers of the universe."

"Brundi, one of the things I've always liked about you is you're so grounded. Your lawyer's mind is always so matter of fact. Aren't you curious?"

"I let Charlene figure these things out. She tells me what I need to know."

That evening Andrew had dinner with Brundi and Charlene, a warm and pleasant evening with no discussion of philosophy or religion.

Charlene still wore bangs and was beautifully attractive in her white peasant blouse, which showed her treasures with sparkling effect. It was hard not to look at her too closely or too long. From time to time as she came near, Andrew smelled the tantalizing fragrance of a very inviting perfume. He tried to put Brundi's casual comment out of his mind, but it kept coming back, teasing his conscience… "Sometimes I think her needs are greater than mine."

Andrew asked about Laura.

"She's extremely happy," Charlene said in that whispering voice that always made him want to come near her. "She and Nicky are getting married in late September or early October. They plan to time it for the height of fall foliage in New England. What a romantic way to begin. I envy her."

From time to time throughout the meal, Andrew noticed that Charlene would look at him with lingering eyes, but always when Brundi was not looking. He worried about Brundi, but there was nothing he could say. But as he regarded her slender, graceful beauty, he knew, too, that his own thoughts were becoming impure. He thought his mind and soul needed a thorough cleansing.

Chapter 17

As the bus pulled into the gates of Camp Rucker, the sign told Andrew right away he had been transferred to a National Guard unit. That's what the Lieutenant must have meant.

On his first morning of duty he could see it was all they said it was. Compared with the intense training and gusto of the paratroopers in Ft. Bragg, Rucker seemed like a sleepy backwater town. The level of discipline, the cadre, the troops, the work culture were sloppy in comparison with the 504th. It seemed unbuckled.

But there were a number of men who stood out. First Sergeant Cramer, an old soldier. He had the bearing of authority all First Sergeants wear, but he was essentially a gentle man, serving his time until retirement. Whatever drive he once had had no longer showed.

Captain Garvey, the Company commander, was probably too kind to be an effective officer. And it seemed by deed and rumor he was possessed by other interests outside the Company, and merely provided the surface overlay of administration rather than drive it. For all practical purposes the Company Clerk ran things from the office.

Umberholtz, the Company Clerk, was a rather tall man with a friendly disposition, large glasses, and a shock of unruly reddish hair. He seemed to project a sense of personal discipline and administrative order. Andrew sought him out right away, to see if he could persuade him to cut orders for Korea.

"You're a little bit late," Umberholtz said. "Five hundred men were sent to the Far East last month, 30 from this company alone."

"I will deeply appreciate anything you can do."

Umberholtz told him he would help him if he could. Whatever flags had been put on his records in Ft. Bragg seemed to have disappeared. Umberholtz gave no hint there would be any impediments. They would just have to wait for the next shipment.

Andrew told McNabb about his conversation and curiously, McNabb did not express any particular interest. He tried to persuade McNabb to see Umberholtz, and McNabb said he would do it, but not now. And this was the way it would continue. At Andrew's persuasion, McNabb made occasional trips to see Umberholtz, but his attempts were rather offhand, lackluster.

In the meantime, Andrew was sometimes appalled by the quality of training. In one case, he saw a Sergeant First-Class trying to drill a company of troops, carrying an army field manual with him, looking up the sequence of commands.

The troops complained about running around the block. They complained if they had to do 20 pushups. They did not take pride in either their weapon or their military bearing. Andrew was constantly fighting back the inner urge to shout, "Shape up!" He told McNabb about his displeasure.

McNabb cautioned him "Don't start thinking you have to shape up the whole company before you leave. Know what I mean?"

In late July Andrew was given a 3-day pass. He decided to venture south, a bus ride to Panama City Beach on the Gulf of Mexico. McNabb decided not to join him, rather to hang around the camp and read adventure novels.

Andrew rented a one room cabin for the three days, one block from the beach. He did not have a specific plan, only to swim a lot in the salty waters, and to read. On the first morning he put on his bathing suit, took a towel from the cabin, and walked to the beach. He did not use a sunscreen. Growing up, he had never used a sunscreen, and hardly was aware there was such a product. Nor had he ever spent time on such a beach. Panama City Beach is made of eroded quartz crystals. They make the shoreline sparkling to look at. And the fine, thin crystals go way out into the water, creating a bright green emerald appearance to the surrounding sea. The beach is dazzling white, highly reflective of the southern sun.

What Andrew did not know was how deadly was the combination of brilliant sun, glistening white sand, and salty water. Nor did he know he would meet someone like Elfie Whitaker.

Elfie was small and slender, hardly five feet two, and possessed of a boundless energy. She was also a talkative little creature with a glorious figure and dancing eyes. She had an engaging personality, a rich Southern accent, and was easy to talk to. She was a local girl. She said she was 19.

Andrew was attracted to her buoyant personality and swam over to her as she played a version of volleyball with her girlfriends. He said hello, and that was all it took to begin an engaging conversation and move her away from her girlfriends. They alternately talked and played with each other and swam together for a long time. Then they took a long walk on the white-hot sand of the beach staying near the rippling shoreline where the sand was cooler. She told him she had never been more than fifty miles from home but planned to go to college in the fall. Now she was working as a waitress and living at home to save money.

As they talked for hours, Andrew lost all track of time. In a way, after his long absence from female companionship, she fascinated him. He wanted to learn more about her, to be with her through the night, or whatever part of it he could negotiate.

He told Elfie he would go back to his cabin, take a shower, change clothes, and pick her up at home for an early dinner at five o'clock. They kissed briefly and tenderly, Elfie with twinkling eyes, and Andrew left her on the beach as she rejoined her girlfriends.

He walked back to his cabin and was hardly inside the door when he began to realize how much damage sun and white sand and salty water had done to his skin. He was barely out of his bathing suit when he began to vomit. He felt terrible inside and could not stop vomiting. The flesh of his entire body—except for where his bathing suit had been, the top of his head and bottoms of his feet—erupted with large liquid-filled blisters, puffy and swollen. His entire body felt like a raging fire.

He knew he could not keep his date with Elfie. He could not even get dressed to go tell her. He hoped she would forgive him.

There was nothing he could do.

And so he spent the rest of his 3-day pass in a condition of deep pain and major sickness in his stomach. He vomited constantly, way past the point of having anything in his stomach. It was only green bile, and even that was finally hard to produce. The blisters so totally covered him he could not lie down or sleep. He could only sit on the single chair in the room, or on the toilet and try to stay alive. His main thought was to stay alive.

The thought of seeking medical help never entered his mind. He thought he would have to tough it out. He stayed naked through this time. Clothing was too painful to come near his skin.

And when it came time to find a bus to return to camp, he worked himself slowly and painfully into his clothing and his boots and found the bus and stood, holding on to the upper railing, for the whole trip back. Every bump in the road, thousands of them, sent shock waves of pain through his entire body. But the worst was yet to come.

*

The next morning his unit had to fall out early for an hour of physical training. Even getting into his fatigues and boots was such a painful process he had to clench his jaws and make short gasps of breath, which he would not let go out of his throat. And the exercises aggravated the pain sometimes to unbearable levels. He silently cursed his stupidity. The blisters still covered almost his entire body.

Sometimes at the height of pain, the thought would come into his mind that he should drop out of the exercises until his body healed. But he quickly rejected these thoughts. The military rule is that anyone who cannot perform his duties because of sunburn receives a Summary Court Martial and 30 days in jail. Automatic.

If I go back in, Andrew thought to himself, I may never get out again. Thirty days might find a way of translating into 30 years. He remembered Radar, and how close Radar had brought him to brushing up against 30 years. Or was it 10 or 32? As McNabb had said, "I won't tempt fate twice," he muttered to himself. So he decided to simply work through the pain. He would not drop out.

McNabb was no help. He only laughed.

Within three days the blisters were subsiding and the intense pain was mostly gone. He was grateful that it was over, not knowing yet how difficult the rest of the healing process would be.

The very worst of it came a week or so later when Saturday morning inspection required everyone to fall out in full dress uniform and stand at attention for a long time under the hot Alabama late morning sun.

All the sunburned flesh of Andrew's body was beginning to peel and had now begun to itch with unbearable intensity. His whole body was peeling and agitated by a monstrous itching. And as he stood at attention in the hot, glaring sun, he knew he could not move a muscle to relieve it. If he could not perform, he would go to jail again, simple as that. This thought fairly screamed across his mind.

As the long inspection continued with a maddening casualness, the intensity of unrelieved itching and the burning rays of the July sun had begun to make him feel faint. He remembered not to lock his knees. Men who did that would sometimes faint and fall straight forward from the ranks. As faint as he felt, he tried to very slightly move his knees up and down so they would not lock. <u>Very</u> slightly. He vowed he would not faint. But the itching was so widespread and intensely asking for relief, his mind was driven to the edge of madness.

And in the severe state of his encroaching madness, he cried out within himself.

All he could think about was to just hold on. For one second more. And for one second after that and for one second after that, until finally it was done and the troops were released.

It was another close call. His mind had never been driven to the sheer edge of madness before. He did not venture back to Panama City Beach through the rest of the summer, and soon forgot Elfie altogether.

The news from Korea was, there was no news. The armies had drifted back into stalemate positions again as the seemingly endless peace talks were on.

*

Throughout the summer Andrew had tried to blend in, to keep a low profile, get through this temporary impasse and he would be on his way. But in late August he forgot his resolve and it almost blew out a tire on his drive forward.

Inspection day was upon them and Andrew prepared for it the way he would have done in Ft. Bragg. Caption Garvey checked him closely, wrote down his name and told his assembled troops, "I want to see every man in my company looking like this man."

Garvey called him to his office to ask him further questions. From Andrew's answers, from his knowledge of military tradition and procedures, and from his knowledge of weapons and tactics, and for his keen manner of providing direct, specific answers to each of Garvey's questions, Garvey told him he was marked for better things.

"I'll give you a platoon immediately," Garvey said.

"Captain, I'm only a Private E-1."

"How the hell did that happen?"

Andrew didn't answer, in part because Garvey had no interest in the answer. He was moving rapidly.

"As soon as this rank freeze lifts," Garvey continued, "I'll give you enough rank to make a career out of this army. We'll be needing a new Field First Sergeant soon. Cramer is getting ready to retire, 30 years…"

Andrew took over the third platoon the next day. McNabb needled him about it. "Say, Mr. Low Profile, when are they going to turn the company over to you?"

Andrew did not enjoy the needling. He answered sarcastically. "Soon as they finish putting wall-to-wall carpeting in my room."

Given the assignment, he tried to do his best. He gave his troops more strenuous morning exercises, more toughening and coordination routines, and in general he tried to shape them up and form a disciplined and effective fighting force out of them. He worked hard at it. He wanted to keep himself in shape, too.

Several weeks later he was named Soldier of the Month. He was afraid his goose was cooked. He went to Umberholtz.

"You've got to get me out of here."

"There's a big shipment due in October."

"Please put me on it," He paused. And do me a favor. Let Captain Garvey sign it without looking at it a lot. He's got his eye on me to hang around here," Umberholtz smiled knowingly.

And in the middle of October the list of transferees was assembled and, true to his word, Umberholtz made sure Andrew's name was on it.

"We all admire your persistence," he said in a friendly way, "but between you and me, the CO thinks you're crazy."

It was done. He would be on his way. He would report to Ft. Lawton in Seattle to await shipment overseas. Andrew thanked Umberholtz several times, then rushed out to find McNabb.

"I've finally done it. They've cut orders for me. I'll be out of here in two days. You should see Umberholtz. He's a real friendly guy. He'll help you get on the list if he can. He can get you out of here, too."

"I don't know, man. Doesn't seem like there's enough left of the war to make it worth my time."

"But this is what we fought for."

"I'm not sure we were always fighting for the same thing. Korea, yes. But there are all kinds of wrinkles around the edges."

McNabb's response surprised Andrew, but not totally. Ever since they were released from jail, he had seen McNabb holding back. He could not fathom the reason. In any event, McNabb did not go see Umberholtz.

*

After he left Camp Rucker, Andrew never heard from

McNabb again. Neither one of them was a letter writer. But he learned several years later what had happened to him. Andrew, by chance, met a legionnaire named Hinto who was one of McNabb's former comrades. Hinto was of indeterminate origin. He talked with a peculiar accent Andrew had never heard before. He was of average height, swarthy, and carried a large scar across his cheekbone. They talked over several whiskeys.

Upon release from military service, McNabb went back to New Hampshire. He spent a year or more in a rather solitary existence, hiking and camping in the mountains and lakes and forest of New Hampshire, his favorite domain, much of the time living off the country. And then, as he had earlier predicted, he went overseas and joined the French Foreign Legion, "France's Colonial army."

He had been tremendously attracted to the military culture of the Legion—its codes of honor: "Never surrender your arms." "Don't ever leave anyone behind." "Commit yourself to unwavering solidarity with one another." McNabb was moved by the spirit of these things. Thousands of men, from more than 100 countries, including many Germans, were now his new companions.

"The hardest part for McNabb," Hinto said, "was learning absolute obedience to orders, to learn to act without thinking. It took him a long time, and a lot of hard discipline, for him to get used to that."

McNabb's unit went on from Algiers to what was then called French Indo China. And in the last battle of that Colonial War, 1954, McNabb died heroically at Dien Bien Phu, half an unlit cigar butt still clenched in his teeth. He died in the arms of Genevieve de Galard, the "Angel of Dien Bien Phu," a nurse who had stayed behind to care for the valiant wounded who had been sent into that futile battle.

McNabb was not alive to witness the final humiliation, surrounded by overwhelming numbers of Viet Cong—the surrender of what few Legionnaires were left, giving up the glory of old France forever.

Andrew was deeply curious about his old friend.

"How do you know about the cigar?" he asked Hinto.

"I was right beside him when he died," Hinto said, then stared into space.

#

March of the Cameron Men
by Mary Maxwell Campbell
1829

There's many a man of the Cameron Clan,
That has followed his chief to the field;
He has sworn to support him, or die by his side,
For a Cameron never can yield.

I hear the pibroach sounding, sounding,
Deep o'er the mountain and glen;
While light springing footsteps are trampling the heath,
'Tis the march of the Cameron Men.

Oh! proudly they walk, but each Cameron knows
He may tread on the heather no more;
But boldly he follows his Chief to the field,
Where his laurels were gathered before.

I hear the pibroach sounding, sounding,
Deep o'er the mountain and glen;
While light springing footsteps are trampling the heath,
'Tis the march of the Cameron Men.

The moon has arisen, it shines on the path
Now tread by the gallant and true;
High, high are their hopes, for their chieftain hath said
That whatever men dare they can do.

I hear the pibroach sounding, sounding,
Deep o'er the mountain and glen;
While light springing footsteps are trampling the heath,
'Tis the march of the Cameron Men.

About the Author

Paul Snider grew up in the back streets and alleyways of Detroit and, alternately, on an apple farm near Georgian Bay, Ontario. He moved fifteen times before he was twelve.

His religious life has often been checkered, with patches of light and shadow. During the Korean War he was what has been described as "an atheist in a foxhole." Nevertheless, he survived the war with two purple hearts.

Years later he learned he was not an atheist at all. What he had been denying all along was the clouded, inconsistent, man-made image of God.

Photo © 2017 Jonah Levy

As he continued the search for knowledge of God's higher ways, he met a woman with a shimmering spirit. She told him what she had been taught. "Everything you need to grow is already around you, and within you."

There seemed to be a deep truth in what she said. This was the beginning of his rebirth.

Paul is the father of seven, husband (to Mary) of 59 years, now retired from a business career, and living in Illinois.